SILENT RIDGE

BOOKS BY GREGG OLSEN

DETECTIVE MEGAN CARPENTER TAPES
Snow Creek
Water's Edge

Lying Next to Me
The Last Thing She Ever Did
The Sound of Rain (Nicola Foster Thriller Book 1)
The Weight of Silence (Nicola Foster Thriller Book 2)

GREGG OLSEN

SILENT RIDGE

bookouture

Published by Bookouture in 2020

An imprint of Storyfire Ltd.
Carmelite House
50 Victoria Embankment
London EC4Y 0DZ

www.bookouture.com

ISBN: 978-1-80019-312-3
eBook ISBN: 978-1-80019-311-6

For Darlene Dibley,
Whose strength after great loss, inspires all around her.

PROLOGUE

Boning knives spread across the top of the bathroom vanity, glint in the flat light. Blood on the razor-sharp blades contrasts starkly with the light-colored pattern in the tiled surface. A woman's body hangs from the steel shower head over the spacious garden tub. One master bath wall is a mural of a giant, brilliant-yellow sunflower. The theme carries over to the shower curtains, but the yellow vinyl is spattered with red blotches. Propped against the mirror, behind the knives, is a laminated South Kitsap High School photo of a teenaged girl.

The flayed skin of the woman slumps in the bathtub like a flesh suit. It had taken time. The intention was to cause as much fear as possible and to avoid killing the woman until every drop of humanity was bled from her.

Meddling bitch. I wish you could see the look I'm going to slice off of your daughter's face. I wish you could hear her screams.

The fun part is over. The butcher's apron is peeled off, rolled up and stuffed into a trash bag. The bag will be burned later.

The knives have to be cleaned of all the filth this pleading victim has left on them and are washed under the tap until the water turns from red to pink to clear.

My friend used to say: you take care of your tools and they will take care of you.

In the cabinet is a toothbrush, a bottle of peroxide and another of bleach. The blade is scrubbed until it gleams. The knives are wiped dry with a hand towel. The towel is put in the trash bag. The knives are slid into a cloth case, blades down. The case is rolled tight and secured with a string. The bleach and peroxide swirl down the sink. The containers and the toothbrush are dropped into the bag.

The knife case is carried into the bedroom, where clothes are set out. Some bloody smears are on the bathroom tiles but that's no worry. It just adds to the story.

Dressed now. One more look in the bathroom. The skinless body, like a snake shed of its skin. The eyes are still begging, even in death. It's more than she deserves.

One final step. The laminated photo of the girl, the one Monique knew as Rylee, is brought to the bedroom and left on the bed. Next to it is a recent snapshot. Rylee supposedly died years ago, but, like everything else about the girl, it was a lie. Monique helped her disappear. Rylee is alive. She is now Megan Carpenter. No matter who she pretends to be, she will be dead soon.

Back to the rental boat where the waiting begins. Two days pass. Maybe a mistake had been made? Maybe no one will find the body? Monique has no friends. Not here, at least. It may be weeks before someone finds the body. But a few hours later, an elderly woman walking a yapping dog down the street. The old woman keeps looking at the house. She walks the dog halfway up the yard and stops, sniffing the air like a dog sniffing another dog. Then she goes to the door, which was deliberately left unlocked. The old woman goes inside. She quickly comes back outside. Her face is white. Her hands shake.

She dials three digits on her cell phone.

CHAPTER ONE

"Jefferson County Sheriff's Office. Reserve Deputy Ronnie Marsh," the young, red-haired woman says into the phone. She listens and jots some things down in a leather-bound notebook. She hangs up and blows a strand of hair out of her eyes and comes over to my desk.

I'm Sheriff's Detective Megan Carpenter. Ronnie is a younger version of me, but my hair is shorter and blond where hers is red and down on her shoulders. Makeup covers a smattering of freckles high on her cheekbones. I only put on a touch of eye makeup.

Mascara when I need to look especially alert.

When I first met Ronnie a month ago, she had graduated from the law enforcement academy and was doing her rotation through the various sheriffs' office units. Over my objections, she was assigned to me by Sheriff Tony Gray, my boss, my friend and mentor. I didn't think she'd last two days working here.

She was injured during the last case we worked together and offered medical leave until her broken wrist healed. Instead, she had Sheriff Gray release her to desk duty. I talked him into extending Ronnie's rotation time here in the office, claiming my files were in bad need of some type of order and we needed someone to answer the phone and make coffee and food runs. Even when she was wearing the cast on her arm, she proved herself capable. The cast is a thing of the past and, best of all, she's dating Marley Yang, who is the supervisor at the crime lab. I finally had an in.

I wasn't above using people. And I was doing her a favor at the same time.

Ronnie comes to my desk holding her notebook so I can see what she's written. "Detective Carpenter, this just came in."

Her handwriting, like everything else about her, is stylish. I read the words she's written. My jaw drops and I feel a lump growing in my throat. I don't recognize the address but I sure know the name. For a moment I make myself hope she's written the name wrong, or it's someone else. But my gut tells me otherwise.

Monique Delmont is dead.

She's been murdered.

Sheriff Gray got the call an hour ago and is just now notifying me. Not that he would know to notify me. He has no way of knowing about my relationship with Monique. But he knows I work murder cases and get good results. He should have called me. Plus, I'm curious why Sheriff Gray is working this one himself. He doesn't usually act as lead investigator.

Ronnie stares at me like I'm a hair sample under a microscope. I haven't hidden my shock very well. I used to be good at it; back then I didn't have any attachment to anyone or any place and lied about who I was. One day I was a college student, the next with a newspaper, and so on.

I've been with the Sheriff's Office here a long time. At least, it seems like a long time when my life used to consist of living in one random place after another for short stints.

"Do you know her?" Ronnie asks.

Of course she would ask. I don't say anything and keep looking at the notebook page. Mrs. Delmont doesn't live in Jefferson County. She lives just south of Tacoma. I don't understand.

"You're sure about this?" I ask.

"That was Sheriff Gray on the phone. He said you should come."

I get up and close my laptop.

"Can I come along?" she asks. I knew she would.

"Not this time. You're on light duty. If something happens and you get injured, it will be the sheriff's ass on the line." *And mine for bringing you*, I don't say.

Her disappointment is as clear as the shock of the news was on my face. "I need you here," I say. "Maybe later if the sheriff agrees." She's not satisfied but I don't expect her to be. She has good instincts most of the time. But it still didn't stop her from opening her door to a stranger and getting kidnapped.

CHAPTER TWO

There are two marked Jefferson County Sheriff's Office vehicles parked in the yard, two white panel vans, and an unmarked Jeep when I arrive. One marked vehicle is Sheriff Gray's; the other belongs to Deputy Copsey, who is standing at the front door of a two-story pre-Victorian home. The Chevy panel vans and the Jeep Cherokee are parked closer to the house. One van has a flower shop logo and belongs to my friend and forensic consultant, Mindy Newsom. The other van is Jerry Larsen's; Jerry is our coroner. The back doors of the coroner's van are swung wide open. The Jeep belongs to the crime scene unit.

I don't remember coming to this particular part of town before. But this is in Port Townsend, my town, not two miles from my place. The house is nice, in a nice area, with a good view of the bay and the forest behind, but it's a step down from the last place I saw Monique.

I'm unsure if we were friends or what. What I know is that we were bound together by murder.

Her daughter, Leanne Delmont, was sixteen when, along with my mother, she became one of my biological dad's victims. My bio-dad is, or was, Alex Rader, policeman by trade, serial killer by choice. Leanne died helping my mom escape from that psychotic bastard.

When I first met Monique, I pretended to be a reporter writing an article about how murder affects families.

I lied to Monique about who I was and what I was doing, but she finally figured it out. When I really needed help, she was there for me. She helped me get into Portland State University even though I hadn't graduated high school. She helped me with money and paid for a place to stay. I trusted her. But in truth I put her in danger by doing so. Now the danger has come back with a vengeance.

She should be at home in Tacoma. Why did she come here? My stomach sinks. This is my fault. I can feel it.

Sheriff Gray sees me pull over and comes down the steps and across the yard. The look on his face is grave. This is going to be very bad.

"Megan," he says, putting his hand on my arm. I don't like to be touched, but I allow it from him. He's probably my best friend. He knows things about my past that no one else does. Not everything, but most.

"Did Ronnie give you the victim's name?"

He can't know I have a connection with the victim. If it is her. But he knows something because he's watching me closely for a reaction. I nod and wait for him to say more.

"You don't have to work this one," he says. "I can assign it to another detective. In fact, I probably should. But I think you should see something in either case." Sheriff Gray takes out his phone and pulls up a picture.

I brace myself, thinking there will be pictures of the body and it will be her. Stabbed or shot. Hanged or having died some other horrible death. But what he shows me is only a digital picture of a photograph. The image is not very good, so I know Tony has taken it. He still hasn't embraced tech. But it's good enough that I can see it's a snapshot of me coming out of the Jefferson County Sheriff's Office and walking toward my car. The picture looks like it was taken recently. That's a guess because I don't have a wide variety of clothes. But I do recognize the look. It isn't anger. It's pain. I was shot twice in the chest while wearing body armor. I'm still bruised and have some trouble breathing or moving at times. Right now is one of those movements. My breath catches in my throat.

"What's this about?" he asks.

Good question. And I don't have a clue. "How long has the victim been?…"

"Larsen thinks maybe two days."

"That would make it Saturday."

Tony puts the phone back in his pocket. "Hard to say for sure. The heat was cranked all the way up. It's like a furnace in there."

I see the sweat stains under his arms and around his collar. He looks like he needs to sit with an ice pack. He's waiting for an answer but I have the right to remain silent and I use it.

"Megan?" The look he gives me brooks no argument.

I don't mean to, but I do the one thing that shows I'm about to lie. I look away before I speak. "I really don't have a clue, Tony."

His mouth sets in that way it does when he is struggling with something.

"Sorry, Sheriff. I don't know what's going on." This sounds sincere. And this is partially true. I recover enough to think before I speak, but before I can tell another lie, he takes a small plastic evidence baggie from his back pocket. He holds it out but I don't take it. Inside is a laminated photo that I instantly recognize as my South Kitsap High School yearbook picture. I was sixteen when it was taken. It is the same photo that was in the Port Orchard paper when I was on the run. The headline was about my murdered stepfather, my missing mother, my missing brother and myself. I was wanted by the police as a suspect. There is no name under the picture. No caption of any kind. Not even where the photo is from. I breathe easier, but I'm still on edge.

"Look, Megan, I got here first and found this and the other picture in the bedroom. I took a photo of one and I bagged this one before anyone else got here. No one has seen it but the two of us."

I avoid his eyes and deflect. "How did you get the run here?"

He knows I'm stalling but he plays along. He can see that I'm upset. He knows me too well.

"A neighbor walking her dog smelled something bad. She called the police and I was close. I got out of the car and I knew that smell."

I knew that smell too. I haven't seen many rotted bodies but one is enough to lock the acrid odor in your memory.

"The front door was unlocked. I went in and found the body—and the pictures—and called for Crime Scene and Coroner. I called for Mindy Newsom too."

Mindy is a contract forensic scientist, and she's been my friend since I arrived in Port Townsend. She had just graduated from the University of Washington with a degree in forensic science and was new to the Sheriff's Department when I was new. Sheriff Gray even converted an old conference room into a lab for her. She was certified by the state as a criminalist and then the job became part time. Jefferson County didn't seem to need her skills on a regular basis. She left, got married and had a baby. While she was on family leave she opened a flower shop downtown.

"Where were the pictures?" I ask. I hope it sounds like I don't really care, but my voice is shaky.

"Before I tell you anything else, you have to be honest with me."

"I will be. I mean, I am."

I'm lying.

"Do you know Monique Delmont?"

"How do you know it's her? Did you find identification? Has someone identified her?"

Tony is the sheriff but he was once an excellent detective. I'm sure if he says it's Monique, it's her. The pictures speak for themselves. I know they connect me to her.

"Megan? Do you know her or not?"

I look him in the eye and tell part of the truth.

"I know *a* woman named Monique Delmont from over in the Seattle-Tacoma area. I met her a few times while I was in college. I was friends with a girl that was friends with her daughter." My story is complete bullshit because her daughter had been dead for many years before I tried to find out who killed her. That was how and why I met Monique.

"I don't know if this is the same person, but if it is, I have no idea why she would have a picture of me coming from the office." I don't say anything about the laminated one. I don't have to. "I could maybe identify her, but it's been a while."

"You won't be able to identify what's in there," he says, and hooks a thumb over his shoulder. "Crime scene has her purse and her driver's license. The address on the license is in Tacoma. Just like you said. Now tell me. Do you know this woman? Don't try me, Megan."

I don't speak.

Tony lets out a sigh and hands the evidence bag with my high school photo to me. I take it this time.

"The photo I showed you on my phone has been collected by Crime Scene." He starts to say something else and then stops.

I let out a breath. He doesn't say it but I know what he's thinking. He's going to say if the picture has any bearing on the case, he wants me to do the right thing with it. I plan to do the right thing. I'll burn the damn picture first chance I get.

I look around and there are no other houses close to this one.

"You said the woman who found the body is a neighbor?"

"She is," he says. "She said she hasn't seen anyone strange in the neighborhood. She didn't see anyone come or go. She said the woman, Monique Delmont, moved into the neighborhood about two weeks ago. Alone. They had tea together a few times but not at this house. She said she'd never been inside except when it was owned by the Donaldsons. They moved to Florida and rented the house out. I don't have their information yet."

"I can get it easy enough," I say. "Do you have the neighbor's address?"

Tony takes out a slip of paper but doesn't give it to me right away. "This is her name and address. You sure you want it?"

"I'll take it," I say with my mouth, but my heart wonders what I've just done.

"Do you want someone to work this with you?" Tony asks, and hands me the note.

I shake my head and then think better of it. I'm a loner. It seems the best way to do things because I don't trust anyone. But Ronnie has softened me a little. Not that we are best friends or anything. But I can stand her being around. Sometimes. When she's not yapping her stream-of-consciousness crap and won't shut up.

She's good with the Internet. Better than I am. And she can keep a secret. The last case we worked together cost her a broken wrist, stitches in her face, bruised ribs and black eyes. The creep came to her house while we were viewing a security camera recording. He shot me point-blank and kidnapped her. He thought he'd killed me. It was his mistake. I assassinated him for it. I'm pretty sure she saw the whole thing, but if she did, she didn't tell anyone. She claimed to be unconscious. The look she gives me sometimes says something different.

"Ronnie's on light duty," I say, "but I can use her help on the computer if it's okay?"

Of course, he agrees.

CHAPTER THREE

I didn't ask Tony *how* Monique was killed but instead I said I wanted to see it myself. The note Ronnie had given me just said murder, but my lack of questions told the sheriff that I was up to my neck in this case already. I'm a trained detective. I should have been asking about the victim and not defending my own connection. I lied to him. He knew it.

Monique was an advocate for victims of violent crimes. I didn't keep in touch with her, but that didn't mean I didn't keep track of her. She was in the news many times, lobbying some piece of legislation or another. She had become active with parole board hearings, keeping some of the more violent offenders off the streets. She had most likely made enemies because of that. My gut is telling me that's not the reason she's dead.

I haven't gone into the house yet but I already have a suspect. The way Monique died isn't as important as the fact that she's dead in Port Townsend. She didn't contact me but pictures of me are found at the scene. If she knew where I lived, why didn't she call? Maybe running from someone? None of this makes sense. I can be totally off base, but I know of only one person with a connection to me who has threatened her in the past.

Michael Rader.

Alex Rader's brother.

I killed Alex because he kidnapped my mother when she was a teenager. He raped, tortured and meant to kill her but she got away. Not entirely, though, because he'd gotten her pregnant with me. He was a serial killer. And a smart one. Alex killed three girls that I know of. All about the same age as my mother was when he kidnapped her. All blond cheerleaders. All three murders were attributed to different men. All of those murders he committed led to wrongful convictions because Alex Rader was a police detective. He made evidence disappear. He planted evidence. To make matters worse, I believe Alex's brother, Michael, who is a prison guard, later eliminated all those men in prison. None of their deaths were ever solved. Michael is as evil and dangerous as Alex.

I tried to erase my trail, my existence, and I believed I was successful. I should have been dead to the world. But Michael knows because Monique told him. She told me he had threatened to kill her family if she didn't. I didn't blame her for that, but I'd entrusted her with the evidence I'd found in Alex's house. The evidence that proved he had killed other girls. She'd promised to take the evidence to the authorities so those families could finally find closure for the loss of their daughters. She'd given it to Michael instead and it still hurt to have the only person I trusted betray me. I'd had to keep running to protect myself and my brother Hayden from Michael.

Only three other people, besides Michael and Monique, know I am still alive: Hayden, an ex-boyfriend, Caleb Hunter, and Dr. Karen Albright, my therapist.

Hayden hates me for the same reason I hated our mother. I betrayed and abandoned him. He has a right to hate me, but he would never do anything like this.

I haven't had contact with Caleb for years. I think he would like to keep it that way. I'd burnt my bridges with him. He knew what I'd done and it sickened him, but he isn't capable of murder.

I spoke to Dr. Albright last month. But she isn't capable of murder, either.

But someone else knows I am alive; someone who sends me emails: "Wallace," is how he signs off. It's someone who knows who I am and who I was. They know where I live. They knew about me and Monique.

So, for now, discounting Hayden, Caleb and Dr. Albright, I have at least two suspects for this murder: Wallace and Michael Rader.

The photograph taken of me leaving the office proves I'm being watched. And my high school photograph shows a connection to my past. Is Wallace the killer, is Michael Rader? Is Michael my stalker?

"Are you ready?" Tony asks as I take one more look around the outside. The house is surrounded by tall trees on both sides. I have a clear view of the harbor and nothing but trees to either side. There is little to no traffic. A woman is walking her dog. She stops to clean up after the dog and continues on. I look at Tony but he shakes his head. That's not the neighbor. Several boats are anchored with people on the decks. It's a nice day. In one sailboat two guys are drinking; a girl dives in the water. There's another with some fishermen and a sailboat with a woman sunning on the deck. Most of the boaters are curious about all the police activity. I'm surprised neighbors haven't gathered in the yard.

Deputy Copsey is standing beside the front door. He's hard to miss with his strawberry-blond hair and biceps that are barely contained by his uniform shirt.

The door is open to the unmistakable smell of decay. It burns my eyes and nose. Sheriff Gray offers me a tube of eucalyptus ointment. He's rubbed some under his nose. I decline. I've done this before. It's best to push through it. I know I'll have to take my clothes to a cleaners when I get off and the smell will take a while to get out of my nostrils.

"Ma'am," Deputy Copsey says with a nod and a grin as Sheriff Gray and I come up on the front stoop. He knows I hate being called "ma'am." It's his way of telling me I'm one of the crew. One of the guys. One of the troops. I don't care if I am. I have a job to do.

"Deputy," I say, and smile.

Copsey writes our names on the log. He will note everyone's comings and goings and record the times.

A crime scene deputy I don't recognize is laying a folded white sheet on the left side of the carpeted stairway. He's wearing white Tyvek coveralls with the hood pulled up, gloves, seafoam-green paper booties. He comes back down the stairs, careful to stand on the folded sheet. He hands us gloves and booties. Sheriff Gray has a little trouble with the latex gloves. His hands are sweaty and the gloves stick to his skin. The crime scene guy offers me a hair net. I decline by staring him down. I'm getting good at that.

He gets me back. "This way, ma'am. Sheriff. Stay on the sheet."

I don't correct him about the "ma'am" shit. I'm standing at the base of the stairs. My imagination is on crack. Sheriff Gray hasn't remarked on the condition of the body except that I won't recognize the victim. That speaks volumes.

I start up the stairs and the smell gets stronger with each step. I wonder if stink rises, like warm air. The carpeting is a deep-pile mix of gray and black and tan fibers. It's been a while since it was vacuumed. I always assumed Monique was a clean freak. She must have changed.

With each step I expect to see blood. Yet there isn't any. I get to the top of the landing and the tech leads us down a short hallway. Doors are open on the left and right. Straight ahead a door is partially open to what looks like a half bath. There are little decorative towels hanging beside the sink. Unused. The neighbor told the sheriff that Monique had moved in about two weeks ago.

She wouldn't have used this room.

The tech leads me to the door on the right. I know the room on the left will be facing into the woods, and so I suspect this room will have a view out over the water. The room comes into view in slices as I slowly move up to the doorway. A tallboy dresser is against the wall to my left. The top is bare. No photos or trinkets. I take another step and see a door just beyond the dresser. Probably the master bath. The door is open and another white-clad tech is bent at the waist, a camera clicking away.

On the far side of the room is a bay window with sheer curtains and room-darkening shades. The shades are halfway open and the sheers distort the light. A bed is to my right with a king-size mattress and an expensive-looking royal blue duvet. The carpeting is thick, cream colored. The tech in the bathroom doorway is straddling what looks like bloodstains.

The body is not on the bed or on the floor. It helps to think of her as "the body" and not Monique. I have distanced myself from her as a person.

There are faint smudges, pinkish smears, on the carpeting between the bathroom and the bed. Someone has stepped in the blood and tracked it across the room to the foot of the bed. It passes through my mind that there's something odd about the smudges. If a shoe had smeared the blood, the edges would be defined, sharp, rounded. Instead, it looks like a hand was dragged across the carpeting.

Then I see it.

Toes and a heel.

The killer had been barefoot.

There's no indication of a struggle in the bedroom. There was no sign of that downstairs unless it was in another room. A squat double dresser is set against the wall under the bay window. On top of this are several framed pictures. Monique and her daughter, Leanne. Another of just Leanne. Leanne with another older girl and a young boy. The boy is maybe six years old and is looking up at the girl with a smile that reaches from side to side. Leanne's older sister is Gabrielle. The boy is Gabrielle's son, Sebastian.

I dread notifying Gabrielle that her mother is dead. I know Sheriff Gray will offer, but I have to do it.

CHAPTER FOUR

Early Monday morning

From the boat she could see a truck with SHERIFF'S OFFICE markings arrive. She had binoculars with her but didn't use them yet. She wanted Rylee to come. The truck had parked in the yard and an older, heavyset man got out. She focused the binoculars on his face. It was Sheriff Anthony Gray. He was approached by the old woman with the dog. The woman was pointing at the house and then holding her nose. The dog was straining against the leash. The smell of rotting meat must be intoxicating to an animal. It had been two full days since the killing. Before she'd left the house, she'd turned the thermostat all the way up.

The sheriff was telling the woman something. Probably to stay there. Then he went up the yard and inside. He came out within minutes and went to his car without speaking to the woman, who was trailing along behind him, nearly dragging the dog behind her.

It would be a while before Rylee was called. She went below deck, made a strong drink, got the camera with the zoom lens, put on a wide-brimmed beach hat and went back out. She turned her deck chair to face the shore. She was wearing a black one-piece with a cover-up and sandals. She focused the camera on Sheriff Gray and the old woman and snapped a few shots. The sheriff was writing something in a notebook and then motioned for the woman to leave. He didn't have to insist. She tottered off, dragging the pooch on his leash.

The next to arrive was a white van with a flower shop logo on the side. Then another van, this one with two deputies. She had pictures of them, too, but didn't have their names. Yet.

The sheriff spoke to them and they began putting white coveralls on. She ignored them. She only wanted to see Rylee. The bitch had taken everything from her. She would wait until she could see the look on Rylee's face when the sheriff told her what had happened inside. She wished she could be inside the house when Rylee saw the body. She should have put a nanny cam in there. Hindsight is 20/20, as they say. Even if they'd found the nanny cam, she wouldn't have cared. She could buy one at Walmart with cash and it would only add to the fun. "Next time," she muttered.

She leaned forward and focused the binoculars on a car pulling in. It was the Taurus driven by Rylee, who was going by the name Megan Carpenter here. Her real name was Alexandra Rader, Alex Rader's illegitimate daughter. But she would always think of her as Rylee.

She'd taken plenty of pictures of the car and Rylee in the parking lot outside the Sheriff's Office and in front of Rylee's place in Port Townsend. The car's paint had oxidized. Rust spots were already blooming around the pitted wheel wells. That was how much her Sheriff Gray thought of her. She didn't deserve a better car. In any case, she wouldn't need it much longer.

She'd learned about Monique from Michael Rader. Michael had led her to Monique, and Monique had led her to Rylee.

The plan had gone well. She'd befriended Monique and convinced her to find Rylee in Port Townsend and warn her about Michael. Monique had asked her to help and, of course, she'd agreed. Monique would go ahead, and she would come in a few days' time. She needed the time to locate Monique's daughter and obtain the drug she would need to create the perfect crime scene.

She focused the binoculars again. She watched as Rylee talked to Sheriff Gray. He was old and tired looking. He should be retired.

She might help him along. But not yet. There were others she had to deal with first.

She watched Rylee's face closely and was disappointed when she didn't go pale or cry. In fact, the bitch didn't show any emotion. She was either a sociopath or very good at hiding her feelings.

Another deputy had shown up before Rylee. He was guarding the front door. This one was a bruiser. She'd like to meet him in a dark alley. The thought made her laugh. One of Alex's sayings was, "You wouldn't want to meet him in a dark alley." She liked dark alleys. She'd worked in plenty of them when she was on the street. "Never again," she said out loud.

The sheriff and Rylee spoke to the big deputy at the door and then went inside. Now she'd settle back and wait. She'd left plenty of evidence of who the victim was. Plenty to point to Rylee and identify her to the sheriff. But the bitch would probably talk her way out of it. She changed names like she was ordering off a menu. She was slick.

She hoped it wouldn't take long. She still had to get far from here and steal a car. Monique's had, unfortunately but necessarily, been left behind.

CHAPTER FIVE

I look at all the picture frames on the dresser. When I first met Monique, she showed me a photo taken a week before the kidnapping of her daughter Leanne. In it, Leanne was sitting on a driftwood log at Point Defiance Park in Tacoma. She was looking over her right shoulder with a wary but somewhat shy pose. Leanne and her father had moored a sailboat off the point and taken a skiff in for a picnic. This was that picture.

The sheriff said Monique had only been here a couple of weeks. Why did she bring all these photos with her? They must comfort her. I have two photos of Hayden. They don't comfort me.

Another picture frame is lying face down. I imagine it will be a picture of Leanne too. Maybe it was too painful for Monique. I approach the crime scene tech.

"Can I look at that?"

"It hasn't been fingerprinted yet," he says, and turns back toward the bathroom.

I lift the frame while he's not looking. It's a picture of a young woman who bears a strong resemblance to the murdered Leanne Delmont. A boy is in the background playing on monkey bars at some park. She's smiling and clapping. The boy is maybe four or five. The glass is fractured into a spiderweb. I put it back like it was.

Sheriff Gray gives me a cautioning look and clears his throat. He speaks to the tech: "Let her look in the bathroom and we'll get out of your hair."

"Yes, sir." The tech isn't happy but he calls the other tech out of the bathroom. "Don't touch anything. And be careful of the blood."

I already don't like him. I straddle the blood on the carpet like I'd seen the other tech do. I lean forward and try not to touch the doorframe. I feel like a contortionist, and although it's almost a month since I was shot, my chest seizes. Pain radiates out from my solar plexus and runs down both arms, but I have time to see all I want to see.

Monique's body hangs from the shower head. A piece of white electric cord is wrapped around her neck; the end with the plug is draped over her shoulder. She is a short woman and her toes barely touch the tub. Her skin is all in one piece, lying in the tub beneath her. One piece. Like a wetsuit with a wig and face mask.

Her head is slumped to the side, eyes bulging out of the sockets like bloody marbles. There are two teardrop-shaped, blood-filled cavities where her nose should be. Her jaws hang open as if she died screaming. Tony said there are no close neighbors and I didn't see any as I came to the scene.

No one heard her screams.

I feel dizzy, nauseated; my legs are buckling. Luckily, Sheriff Gray has moved up behind me and takes my arm. He leads me back into the bedroom. One of my booties gets blood on it and I hear the tech let out a grunt of disapproval. I almost snap at him but I want to throw up even more. I rush out of the bedroom, into the hall and down to the half bath before I lose it. I gag and retch but nothing comes up. My stomach is in knots.

I pull some toilet paper from the roll, dampen it in the sink, and wipe my mouth. To hell with the techs. I splash water in my face and use more toilet paper to pat it dry. Tony was right: There is no way to identify what's in there as Monique Delmont. Even the hair is so caked and stiff with blood that it's impossible to tell the color. I look in the mirror. Good thing I don't wear much makeup. I return to the bedroom.

"You okay, Megan?"

I'll never eat rare steak again, but I'm fine.

"I'll be okay. I just had breakfast this morning."

My stomach lurches but I won't give the tech the pleasure of seeing me throw up again.

"Good thing you didn't have the greasy bacon, huh?" the tech says, and Sheriff Gray turns on him.

"Deputy, I think you'd better get back to work. I want all the photos and your reports in two hours. Do you understand?"

Both techs say nothing. Their body language says it all. We're interlopers, idiots who have raided their domain. Crime Scene can be that way sometimes. I know Mindy is here somewhere and I want to talk to her. She won't be such a wiseass. I haven't seen Jerry Larsen. He's probably sitting in his van, having coffee until he can take the body.

"Your chest giving you problems again?"

"It only hurts when I breathe." I smile at him. He doesn't smile back. He knows I'm hiding the pain. I won't take painkillers. I can't let my guard down, and those things put me to sleep.

A pewter tray holding several rings sits on top of the double dresser. A necklace with a thin gold chain and a diamond and ruby pendant are next to the tray. An ornate, carved-wood jewelry box is at the other end of the dresser. The lid is open and I can see other precious pieces inside. I don't take Monique for a person to own junk jewelry. Why did the killer leave the jewelry? Because it wasn't a robbery.

"Seen enough?" Tony asks.

I say something that comes out as a croak, so I just nod. We go down the stairs, careful to follow our own steps back to the front door. Outside, Copsey is playing Candy Crush on his iPhone until he sees the sheriff and hurriedly puts it away. If he knew the sheriff like I did, he would have just asked Tony for some tips on the game. Sheriff Gray spends hours in his office playing some game or other.

"I want a sweep of the grounds," I say. "One hundred yards each direction. I want to know how this guy got in here and how he got out."

"Already being done, Megan." Sheriff Gray points off to the right of the house. I see Mindy is in the tree line. She makes a left turn and comes back toward us in a straight line. She's walking a grid.

"Shouldn't she have some help?"

"She wants to do it herself," Tony says. "She saw your police picture in there and she's worried about you. So am I."

I watch her methodical movements. If anyone can find evidence, she can.

"Don't worry," he says.

I feel like I can breathe again. He's a good man: honest to a fault; but, like me, he'll bend the rules a little for a friend. As far as trust goes, I trust him more than most. Besides, he knows me only as Megan. He doesn't know the name Rylee or that I attended South Kitsap High School. And there is nothing on the picture to identify it as South Kitsap. I am being paranoid.

Mindy looks up briefly and waves. I wave back and return to my car.

CHAPTER SIX

I'm going through the motions like a sleepwalker. I'll wake up and find that none of this has happened. Monique will be in Tacoma and I'll be in bed after having drunk too much wine. Or Scotch. But the pain I feel in the center of my chest tells me I'm awake. I'm here, on the road, doing the legwork.

First step, check with all the neighbors. Get names, vehicles, descriptions, anything and everything that can help me identify who was where and when they were there. This is a nice neighborhood, but the yards are too perfectly kept. Too big. I don't imagine any of the owners do their own landscaping. I doubt the killer was here during the day to do their dirty work, so the landscapers would have seen nothing.

Plus, our coroner, Jerry Larsen, was getting into his van as I was leaving and told me he couldn't give me any kind of accurate time or date of death. But his guess was two days, because that was the last time the neighbor walking her dog said she'd seen her. The coagulation of the blood supports that. I remember Tony saying what the woman actually said was that she'd had tea with her. I wonder when that was.

I had the neighbor's name and address: 123 Julianne Lane, Mrs. Perkins. I drive past the house and for another ten minutes I drive around the neighborhood to get a feel for it. I've lived in Port Townsend a couple of years and have never been to this area. The extent of my exploring has been driving to Port Hadlock and Chimacum and back home. Maybe a little downtown to one of five eating establishments and/or bars. Outside of investigations, I don't go anywhere. My last case took me to several islands, but I wasn't sightseeing.

I pull into the driveway at 123. Mrs. Perkins is standing behind the storm door. She is a delicate-looking woman with wispy blue-white hair. She adjusts her large, black plastic-framed glasses and squints at me. The house where Monique was murdered is three long blocks away. There's no possibility this woman saw anything from her house. To be honest, I can't see her walking that far just to take her dog for morning business.

I knock on the door and hold my badge up and identify myself. Mrs. Perkins comes to the door, cocks her head and her glasses slide down. I could burn ants with the lenses. She pushes them back up the bridge of her small nose.

"I'm Detective Carpenter," I say loudly, in case she has problems hearing as well as seeing. "Sheriff's Office."

She doesn't move.

"You just talked to my boss, Sheriff Gray. I'm here to talk about your friend, Monique Delmont." I don't tell her I'm there to ask questions, because I think she'll pull her head all the way into her shell and scuttle out of sight and back into the surf.

"She wasn't really my friend per se."

Mrs. Perkins says this loudly like I'm the person with hearing impairment. This is going to be fun.

She unlatches the door.

"Come in. I'll put coffee on. I drink tea myself, but I make a good pot of coffee. I roast my own beans. That's the secret."

I walk behind her to her living room. She lives in a nice area, but the houses are much closer together than where I just came from. They are also directly across the street from each other. Out of the window I have a clear view of the living room of the neighbor across the way. A woman is standing there, window watching me. She looks a good deal like Mrs. Perkins. Both are in their late eighties, short, white permed hair tinged light blue. Her glasses are horn-rimmed and attached to a silver chain worn around her neck. Both women are wearing what my aunt Ginger called a housedress: a shapeless, one-piece dress with short sleeves. The dress across the way is red with big white flowers. Mrs. Perkins's frock is white with red flowers. I imagine they call each other every morning and come up with the dress code.

Mrs. Perkins catches me looking across the street. "That's Mrs. Guidry. Leona's a widow like me. She's so nosy."

"Did Mrs. Guidry know Monique—Mrs. Delmont?"

"Have a seat," she says. "The couch is very comfortable. My son sent it as a Christmas present. Shipped it from Arizona, where he and his wife and three children live. He works for Amazon. Never comes home much since his dad died."

She didn't answer my question, but I've learned that with some older folks you don't push. They come from a different era when people still visited and talked and got to know each other before they got down to the nitty-gritty. My mom said she remembered her parents and their neighbors or friends actually sitting in each other's kitchens and playing games, drinking coffee or something stronger. I look up again and there is Mrs. Guidry, still glued to her window like a tree frog.

"Nosy thing," Mrs. Perkins says, and makes a dismissive motion with her hand. "Don't pay her any mind. She's like a cat. If you give her the slightest provocation, she'll follow you around. Would you like tea, Detective?"

What I'd like is an answer, but I'll have to play along.

"Yes, please. Can we sit in your kitchen? I find it much more pleasant and less formal." I sounded a little like Betty Crocker just then, but it works. She smiles and crooks a twig-like finger at me to follow.

The kitchen table is made of some dark hardwood and there's a half-finished monstrous puzzle on top. The picture on the puzzle box is that of a fireman wearing only heavy cotton pants and a red fire hat. He is holding a hose, and what she'd completed showed a heavily muscled chest and part of a six-pack. A four-pack, to be exact. There are words at the bottom of the puzzle:

LET ME PUT OUT YOUR FIRE

I suspect Mrs. Perkins keeps herself entertained, although I'm not sure how she sees well enough to do a puzzle.

She smiles and fills a kettle, turns on the burner and comes back to the table. We both sit.

"Maybe you can help me with this puzzle. I've done the darn thing three times and I always get the fireman done first, but this time I can't seem to find some pieces."

Maybe she ate them. I look at the floor. Several flesh-colored puzzle pieces are under my chair. I retrieve them and fit them into place.

"There he is," she says with a huge grin. "Isn't he adorable? I could just eat him with a spoon." She blushes, and her hand goes to her face. "I'm sorry." Then she starts to cry.

I wait her out.

"You must think I'm a silly, dirty old woman."

It passes through my mind, but I want to get on with this. I say, "No. I don't think that at all."

She dabs at her eyes with the tip of a napkin. The teakettle screams like a train whistle. She gets up and takes down what I believe are her best china cups. The handles on the teacups are so small and fragile, I have to pinch them between my thumb and forefinger, and that puts my pinky finger in the air. My mother called that hoity-toity. Pretentious. Lifestyles of the rich and clueless. It is, however, the only way I can hold the damn cup.

I put several teaspoons of sugar in my tea and stir carefully, afraid I'll break the china or spill it. Mrs. Perkins opens a cabinet above the stove and takes down a bottle of Johnnie Walker. She pours several capfuls in her tea and offers the bottle to me. I decline. I'm on duty. And I've spoiled it with sugar already.

She takes a seat. "I have to hide the bottle from Leona," she says. "She has a drinking problem."

I laugh. I can't help it. She smiles and we're friends. Just like that.

"So, Detective, where were we?"

Before I can open my mouth, a Jack Russell terrier is at my feet, staring at me. I like dogs. I reach down to pet him.

"I wouldn't do that," Mrs. Perkins says.

I straighten back up in the chair. The dog is still staring at me. Maybe deciding if I'm lunch, dinner, or just a snack.

"That's Gonzo. He's old. He can't half see. He probably thinks you're Leona. She always gives him a treat. Don't pay him any mind. He'll get tired and lay down."

I ignore him and pull my feet and ankles under the chair. "You were going to tell me about Mrs. Delmont," I remind her.

"Oh, yes. Monique. Such a pretty name. Not like Leona or Rowena. That's my name. Rowena Perkins. Rowena Rafferty when I was unmarried. You can call me Weena. I think 'Mrs. Perkins' is just too much."

I don't need to hear all of this, so I move it along. "Tell me about Mrs. Delmont, Weena."

"Oh, yes. Sorry for prattling on." She stops and takes a sip of her tea and actually smacks her lips. "Ahhh," she says.

I think I know why she really hides the bottle.

"Monique moved into what used to be the old Donaldson place two weeks ago Saturday," she says. "I remember seeing that someone was in the house. It sat empty for more than a year. So I went up to introduce myself. She was so pleasant. And she seemed to be sad. We had tea. She sat right there where you are now. In fact, she helped me with this puzzle the first time."

She stops and takes a bigger sip. Quiet. Looking at the puzzle. I believe she's lost in thought until she picks up a puzzle piece and tries to fit it in part of the fireman's groin.

"Weena…" I say.

"Oh. Yes. I was thinking."

I know what she was thinking about.

"She never invited me over. I thought maybe she kept a dirty house. Yet she was always dressed so nice, I knew that couldn't be. She was beautiful. She said she had two daughters and a grandson. We never talked much about them. She seemed to not want to. I think that's why she was sad. My own son hardly ever calls and never visits. I understood her. I don't know why these kids do any of the things they do. Maybe he's just tired of a needy old woman."

She stops and finishes the tea in one impressively loud gulp.

I push a little. "Did you ever see anyone at her house? Did she have any other friends?"

"That's the reason I told you that she wasn't a friend. Not really. After the first few days she was here she seemed to withdraw and keep to herself. At times her car would be gone, so I knew she'd gone out. But she was usually home. I stopped by about four days ago—Thursday, I think. Yes, a Thursday. I was worried that she might be sick, and when she answered the door, I could tell she'd been crying. I didn't ask. None of my business."

"What kind of car did she have?" I ask.

"I don't know cars. A blue one. My husband did all the driving. I don't need to get out much. I have a gardener once a week and a boy to deliver my groceries. Even my medicine comes by mail. Amazon is a godsend. If I didn't have Gonzo, I'd never get out of the house."

"So you were never inside her house?"

"That's what I told the sheriff," she says.

CHAPTER SEVEN

After two more spiked teas and repeated questioning, I found out Mrs. Rowena Perkins had lied to Sheriff Gray. Her excuse for not telling him right away was that he hadn't asked directly if she'd been in the house.

I call the sheriff. "Are you still on scene?"

"I was catching up with Mindy," he says. "Have you already got something?"

I feel a little bad. When I tell him what Perkins left out of her story, he's going to kick himself for not asking. When I tell him what she left out, he's going to give her hell. She's just an old woman who got caught up in something way out of her comfort zone. She thought she was doing a good thing. She is old enough to know that no good deed goes unpunished.

"Someone needs to come to Mrs. Perkins's house and finger-print her."

"Well, shit."

"Yeah," I say. "She forgot to tell you that she went inside the house. Her dog did too. Here's the Twitter version of what she told me. She smelled something bad and hadn't seen Monique for a couple of days. She didn't talk to Monique but just saw her coming home last Thursday. She and Monique weren't good friends because Monique wanted to keep to herself. She hadn't seen or spoken to Monique since and thought maybe she was sick. When she smelled the rot from the street, she went up to the house. She knocked but the door was unlatched and it came open. She opened the door and nearly threw up. She still thought maybe it was the smell of vomit from Monique being sick, and so she went inside."

"She saw the body?" Tony asks.

I tell him no. "However, she said she saw something hanging from the shower and got out of there. Her dog lapped up some of the blood before she could pull him away."

"Damn it."

I can see the expression on his face. It could be—as it was meant to be now—frightening.

"If you talk to her, try not to yell."

"I'll get her… and her little dog too," he says, and I have to chuckle. At least he's got a sense of humor about this mess.

"Have Mindy call me," I say.

"She's right here."

A beat later Mindy comes on the line. "Hey you. You're like a black cloud. But you keep me in business. We got another nut case here, don't we?"

She's joking but she doesn't know how right she is. Everywhere I go, trouble follows close behind.

"Looks like it," I say.

"We found a recent snapshot of you on the bed. Do you think the victim took it?"

"I don't think so. Sheriff told me where he found it and it sounds like it was left that way deliberately."

"That's what I think too."

"The killer left your picture behind. Stalker maybe?"

More than one, I think.

"Right. I can't get a date but I can get a stalker." I try to make light of it. I don't want anyone to start protecting me. I can take care of myself. I can take care of whoever this is. My way.

"Sheriff called your partner and gave her the information on the victim. Knowing Ronnie, she's got a stack of papers for you when you get back to the office."

She's not my partner. She's a reserve deputy.

"She's good like that," I say.

"Well, what do you need first? The house or the perimeter?" she asks. "We haven't finished inside the house, and Jerry just took the body. I can tell you what I found outside."

It must have been a task to collect the body.

"Zip. No sign anyone came in from the trees behind the house. I checked the windows and the ground under them. No way of telling if anyone was looking in a window, but there are no pry marks. Same with the doors. The front door is unlocked. No sign of a forced entry. I looked from the street and from the trees and there isn't a good angle to see if anyone was upstairs. Also, there are room-darkening shades in both the master and guest bedrooms. The guest bedroom shades are closed. The master bedroom you saw."

"Signs of a struggle?" I ask.

Mindy says there weren't any. Everything was pristine.

"No scuffs in the carpet like she'd been dragged. The only thing I found was a puddle of something wet just inside the bathroom doorway. I almost didn't notice because the toilet was right there, but it smelled like urine. I touched it with a glove and did a very scientific test. I sniffed it. It was definitely urine. I took a sample and I'll check it later. I'm thinking she was grabbed there and her bladder emptied. I found clothes in the clothes hamper. There weren't any blood or urine stains on them."

I fill her in on Weena's story. "I just told Sheriff Gray she said she smelled the stink and came in the house. In fact, she saw the body. Her dog was with her and it was lapping up the blood."

"I'll check for dog hairs," Mindy says.

That gives me another question for Rowena Perkins. I'll have to make another trip to see her.

"Do you think she was going to get a shower when it happened?" I ask. I had almost stepped in it. It was insignificant at the time. I chalked it up to being water from the tub.

"I'm almost certain," Mindy says.

"The bloody smears on the bathroom tile were all leading to and from the tub. Was there a lot of blood inside the tub? I didn't look."

Mindy says something to one of the techs and picks up where she left off.

"There were bloody footprints in the tub, Megan. The body appears to have been skillfully skinned. I would guess a taxidermist or a surgeon. They know their way around anatomy and a scalpel. The crime scene techs will check the bathtub drain with a scope to see if there's anything trapped. They'll take swabs too. Maybe we'll get lucky and find some hair that isn't the victim's.

"But, Megan, there's no way the bloody footprints belong to the victim. I checked the shoes in her closet and she wears a size eight. The prints on the floor seem small but they're so blurred it's hard to tell. Sheriff Gray has her Washington driver's license and she was five feet ten inches. Her killer is much smaller."

It was as bad as I thought. "So you think she must have let her killer in? Or it was someone who had a key?"

"Looks like it, Megan. Was she a friend?"

"No," I lie. "I think I met her once when I was going to school. Name sounds familiar."

My denial sounded weak even to me.

"You'd better be careful. People don't just take random shots like that and leave it to be found unless they're disturbed."

She was right.

"I heard Sheriff Gray on the phone. So the woman who called the police lied about being in the house."

"She was afraid she would be a suspect."

"Sheriff said she's about eighty years old and frail looking."

"Rowena Perkins likes tea spiked with Johnnie Walker and puzzles of half-naked firemen waving a hose."

"Who doesn't?" Mindy says with a laugh. "Maybe they got in a fight over the puzzle."

I think it would be more likely over the Johnnie Walker, but I keep that to myself.

CHAPTER EIGHT

I have to talk to Dr. Andrade's office to find out when the autopsy will be, but I don't think he'll talk to me. During the last case, I called him at home in the middle of the night. I needed to know his findings. He hung up, then called me back and hung up on me again. I'll have Ronnie call him. She's my weapon. She's beautiful, red-haired. Men can't resist her. Women want to be her. Not me, though.

Rowena Perkins is waiting for me at her front door. I follow her through to the kitchen, but I decline tea this time in favor of a shot of Johnnie Walker. It burns going down but I need something to keep from screaming at her.

"You're still not telling me everything, Mrs. Perkins." I use her formal name to let her know I'm not playing around.

She sits with her hands in her lap. Age spots mottle the backs of her hands, and her knuckles are dry and red. I don't think hand cream will help this late in the game.

"I knew you'd be back," she tells me. "You strike me as a very smart girl."

I liked being called a girl much better than being called "ma'am," but flattery will get her nowhere. "What didn't you tell me?" I look around and there's no sign of Gonzo. I imagine he's outside watering the lawn.

"When I saw the body, it shocked me. I must have screamed, because Gonzo yelped and then the poor dear puddled on the floor."

"He peed on the bathroom floor?"

"He's old and I must have scared the bejesus out of him. It's not his fault. I shouldn't have taken him in there."

You shouldn't have been in that house.

"I understand," I say. "I'll tell my crime scene guys so they know it's dog urine."

Her eyes well with tears and then the dam breaks. In between racking sobs she asks, "Are you going to take Gonzo into evidence? I don't think I can be without him. He's all I have since my Stevie passed ten years ago. He's my family. I just don't know what…"

I feel my own eyes tearing up. Her son seldom contacts her and she is obviously lonely. I can relate. I've had little contact with Hayden and I miss him. The dog is Rowena's only friend. The dog and the bulging fireman.

"Rowena, no one is going to take your dog. No one will bother Gonzo or you. I promise." I give her a card with my phone number at the office. "If you have questions, you can call me. If you think of anything else, call me. I'll try to come back and tell you what I find out. How's that?"

She stands and wraps me in a hug and weeps. Her emotions come from the horror of what she saw. She weeps because she's all alone and because I'm kind to her.

I ask one more question.

"Did you notice anything else unusual while you were in that house? When you walked through the bedroom?"

I'm wondering if she saw the two pictures of me laid out on the bed. Especially the laminated one.

She shakes her head.

"Did you see anything on the bed?" I need to know.

She looks at me like I'm stupid. "I was drawn to that smell. That's all I saw, except for Gonzo doing what he… you know."

As I drive back to the office I call Mindy.

"It's dog pee, isn't it?" I say right away.

"Yes. It's dog urine."

"She said her dog 'puddled' on the tile because she screamed and scared it."

"Got it. Thanks."

"I'm going to the office." I don't need to tell Mindy to call if she finds anything. I disconnect and watch the road play out. What I saw in that bathroom will stay with me forever. That my photo was found on the bed will give me nightmares. Someone knows that picture and the one of me leaving the sheriff's office are the same person. Sheriff Gray picked up on it right away.

CHAPTER NINE

I park in the same place as I parked when the picture was taken. I look around for the spot where the photograph was snapped. I remember the angle and make my way toward the firs and cedars that ring one side of the parking area. Here, I think, is the place where the photographer likely stood.

The ground is thick with fir needles. I kick some of them around. There's no telling exactly when the picture was taken, but it couldn't have been more than two weeks ago. The toe of my boot shoves some of the debris around and I'm about to give up when I see something red flash. It's a Camel cigarette butt. The red lipstick is fluorescent red.

Who would wear this grotesque color?

The Jefferson County Sheriff's Office is a no-smoking zone within fifty feet of the building. I take an evidence bag from my blazer pocket and use it to retrieve the butt. I'll give it to Crime Scene to have tested and compared with what they found at the scene. It's more than a long shot and I might have to use my secret weapon, aka Ronnie, to get Marley Yang, the supervisor of the state crime lab, to run the test for me. Marley has a thing for Ronnie. She thinks he's cute in a nerdy way and has gone out with him a few times. Marley drops by the office two or three times a week, using any excuse to see her.

Shoving more of the dry needles around reveals nothing except a PayDay wrapper and a pair of women's black lace panties.

Eww.

I collect the wrapper. I suspect stalking is a hard job and they might have gotten hungry. But I can't imagine someone stalking me and taking off their panties. I might have a naked stalker with a sweet tooth who smokes Camels and wears fluorescent red lipstick. I walk away and then come back and collect the panties too. If they belong to Nan, Sheriff Gray's secretary, I'm going to bust a gut. Nan has done the walk of shame a few times since I've worked here.

I think I remember her wearing that shade of lipstick too.

Ronnie holds the door for me. "What were you doing out there? Did you lose something?"

"Actually, I found something," I say, and go to my desk. I take the three evidence bags from my blazer pocket and lay them on the desktop.

"That's the start of a joke," she says. "A cigarette butt, a candy wrapper, and a pair of panties walks into a bar…" Ronnie giggles. It's not funny. Well, kind of. Lately she's started telling lame jokes. She says it's stress relief. I guess it's better than her incessant chatter about absolutely nothing.

"Did you run the name Sheriff Gray gave you?" I ask.

She's holding a manila folder and lays it on the desk.

"I've run the name through local, state and federal databanks. And the Washington State Department of Licensing. The DOL had a license photo and I've made a copy of the license."

She opens the folder and the driver's license copy is on top. There's a driver's license number, the date the license was issued, the expiration date, the license class, Monique D. Delmont's name and date of birth, a physical description, and her photo. Hard to believe that an entire person's life can be documented on a three-by-four-inch piece of paper.

My high school photo the sheriff gave me is laminated. I wonder about that. You laminate something to preserve it. Why would someone go to that trouble and then leave it at the scene of a murder? I feel my jacket pocket to be sure the photo is still there. I panic when I don't feel it. I check my other pockets. It's in my shirt pocket. I don't remember putting it there. I'm rattled. I can't afford to be this way.

"Sheriff Gray called and said you requested me on this case. Is that okay?"

"Yeah. I mean, yes."

She looks excited. I take a moment to steady myself for the dam burst of words that flow whenever Ronnie is excited.

"I'd be happy to work another murder case. I mean, it's not anything to be happy about. Someone died and that's really bad. But I can't wait to get to work on it. I've already run the records from the name, but what else do you need? Sheriff Gray says I'm not to leave the office. I don't see how I can be much help if I stay at my desk. But if he says not to leave the office, I won't. Unless you ask me to, of course. Then I'll—"

I hold a hand up to stop her. My head is spinning already.

"Breathe, Ronnie." I don't realize I say this out loud until it's out.

"Sorry, Detective Carpenter. It's just that I've been sitting around, doing nothing for so long that I think my butt is going flat. I'm so bored. And I love working with you. I hope I don't sound like one of those, uh…"

"Ass kissers?" I say.

"Yeah. One of those."

"Don't worry. Someone else holds that trophy," I say, and look toward Nan's desk. Nan turns to me like she heard my comment. She probably did. Sometimes it seems like she has super-hearing. It helps with her super-nosiness. I notice she's wearing the same color lipstick as that on the cigarette butt. Come to think of it, the underwear is about the right size too. *Double eww!*

"Do you want me to call Marley?" Ronnie asks.

I hand her the stuff I found in the woods. "I hate to ask." I don't really.

"If he wants me to bring it to him, is it okay if I leave the office to do that?"

I give her my blessing and she gets on the phone.

Nan may have super-hearing, but I have Ronnie.

CHAPTER TEN

While Ronnie chats Marley up, I open the file she has given me. Monique's driver's license photo is a newer one. Her hair is shorter and seems to have lost its luster. Her face looks craggy, as if she hasn't gotten much sleep. Of course, the DOL counter employees take only the worst side of you. Eyes half-closed. Every chin exposed. I'm all but certain they have a contest to see who can take the worst picture.

I close the folder and decide to take the file home to read. With Scotch. I don't like invading the privacy of a friend.

Even a dead one.

*

I throw my purse on the table by the door, kick my shoes off and hang up my blazer. I keep the shoulder holster on. It's become a habit after receiving my stalker's emails. Now I have a better reason. Someone knows who I am. They know about my past. If it's not my stalker, I have double trouble.

A bottle of Glen-something-or-other Scotch beckons. After the first sip they all taste the same, so I'm not picky when I buy it. I pour a generous amount in a plastic cup.

After my ordeal with Alex Rader, I began seeing a therapist. Dr. Karen Albright. The tapes of our sessions might hold a clue to Monique's murder. I take the box of tapes and the tape player out of the bottom desk drawer. I've given up storing them in the top of the closet.

I select a tape, slot it and think back to how I ended up with these tapes of my sessions with Dr. Albright, my therapist. I recollect how Dr. Albright's blue eyes scared me at first. Almost otherworldly. How her office smelled of microwave popcorn. How much I grew to trust her. I was eighteen when I first saw her. Defensive. Closed off like a street barricade. I had never let anyone inside, but I was smart enough to know that everything inside of me—from my experiences to my bloodline—had to be exorcised somehow. I'd been traumatized, and while I couldn't see it in the mirror, others did. Night terrors are traumatic and uniquely embarrassing. You don't know if anyone hears your screams.

Dr. Albright had said, "You'll want these someday."

I refused them at first and told her, "I can't see that happening."

Albright had smiled. "Trust me, you will. The day will come when listening to the tapes will make you even stronger." She put her arms around me. We both cried. We held each other for a long time. I knew it wasn't goodbye forever, but it was the end of therapy that had spanned a year and a half. At that time I was graduating from the university with a degree in criminology and had enrolled in the police academy in suburban Seattle.

I draw a breath, take a sip, and hit the "play" button.

Dr. Albright's familiar and soothing voice comes out of the tiny speaker. I'm immediately back in the days when my life was rewritten, when I was on the run, looking for my mother and the murderer who was my birth father. Karen Albright is digging very carefully into that past.

Fittingly, Monique Delmont is the subject.

Dr. A: What did you talk to Mrs. Delmont about?

Me: I talked about the article I'm supposedly writing. Then I asked about the specifics of the murder of her daughter, Leanne. Apart from her reference to Leanne and her father on a sailboat, she didn't mention a husband. Not once in our time together. I don't know if they're divorced or if he's dead. I didn't ask. I didn't think I could take more of the hurt the parents of dead children live with.

Dr. A: What did she tell you about Leanne?

Me: She said those were really hard times for her. She was embarrassed about some of Leanne's choices and didn't want the world to think she was a bad mother. She had portrayed her daughter as a selfish, indulgent girl who didn't follow any rules whatsoever. She said Leanne was a wild girl from a privileged background and never thought of anyone but herself. Now she's revolted by her characterization of her daughter.

I stop the tape. Leanne's murder was attributed to Arnold Cantu, a serial killer. But I know the real killer was my psycho dad, Alex. Monique and her husband had, at first, resisted the idea that Cantu had killed Leanne because all of his victims were college students, older than Leanne. But there had been a period of time that Leanne had run away from home and stayed at a house not far from the University of Washington campus in Seattle. In other words, in Cantu's hunting grounds. I turn the tape player back on.

Dr. A: Did Monique ever admit she could have been wrong?

Me: Yes. She finally accepted that Leanne was one of Cantu's victims.

Dr. A: That must have been hard.
Dr. A: How did that make you feel?

Me: I felt angry and hurt and I wanted to take her pain away but I didn't know how.

I shut the tape player off again. I thought about my own mother. Did she see me as a bad girl? A wild girl? Did she even think about me? I remember the picture Monique had of Leanne. The one where she was sitting on a massive driftwood log at Point Defiance Park. Leanne was looking over her shoulder at the camera with a wary and somewhat shy expression. I'd found an identical picture on the wall in Alex Rader's home office, along with other pictures of the ravaged dead body of Leanne. Those were some of the photos I'd left in Monique's safekeeping, to be turned over to the authorities. Those were the photos that Michael Rader now had.

I've finished almost half a bottle of Scotch. I put the tapes and player away. I take the gun and put it on the nightstand by the bed. I hope I can sleep.

Before I drift off into a slightly drunken slumber, I text Ronnie to meet me early tomorrow.

CHAPTER ELEVEN

The office is quiet as I wait for Ronnie. She should be here any minute. I've been here since 5:00 this morning. I take another look at the file on Monique's homicide.

Her photo stares at me. She was a beautiful woman. Her kindness showed in the DOL photo even with their effort to make you look lifeless.

The second page blows me away.

Monique has a police record. Among the usual traffic citations—ignoring red lights, ignoring traffic signs, ignoring traffic officers—were two misdemeanor charges for trespassing and disorderly conduct. This is a woman who wouldn't say poop if she had a mouthful. At least, she wouldn't have back when I knew her.

But did I really know her? I didn't take the time. I used her to get information. I used her for her connections to get me accepted into college. I used her money to keep going while I was searching for my missing mother.

I never had a reason to check for a police record. My own record, if I were ever caught, would be off the charts compared to hers. I have killed. Outright. Without regret.

The next pages are police reports for the trespassing and disorderly conduct charges. None of these had gone to court. Charges were dropped. I wouldn't expect any less. Monique had friends in high places. She'd somehow managed to get me into college without me having graduated from high school. Someone had doctored my records for her and I enrolled under an assumed name, complete with fake IDs and a diploma.

One trespassing charge is a little more serious than the other. She broke into an apartment and was caught inside. The apartment belonged to a recent parolee, a man who had abducted and raped a twelve-year-old girl. The report didn't say what she was looking for. Probably evidence of other crimes.

Reading between the lines, I can imagine a judge giving her the benefit of the doubt and scolding her not to do it again. The man whose apartment she broke into was a scumbag. She was a prominent figure. A public figure. She was well known for her work as a violent crime victims' advocate.

Ronnie included some news articles too. The scumbag had kidnapped another little girl while he was on parole. He didn't kill the girl but he was convicted and went back to prison. A second article said he was killed by another prisoner. Prisoners have daughters and wives and sisters too. They don't take well to child molesters or child rapists.

I stop reading. We'll need DNA to prove the body is Monique, but I have no doubt it is. But why was she here? I wonder if she sold her own house and was checking out Port Townsend as a place to move. But she was always more organized than that. She would have found what she wanted first and then sold her house in Tacoma. Her house was beautiful, and I can't imagine her wanting to live in Port Townsend. Of course, that house was huge for one person to live in.

I flip to the next page and find the answer.

Ronnie checked several real estate broker sites and Monique's Tacoma house wasn't up for sale. Ronnie searched the county records for the deed and the house was still in Monique's name. Ronnie checked the deed to the rental house and turned up the Donaldsons' name and a current address in Sarasota, Florida.

She even included a website photo of the retirement community where they lived. In the margin were the telephone number of the HOA and the Donaldsons' direct line. Ronnie wasn't lying when she said she was bored to death.

The next pages are a shock. One page is a photo of Leanne Delmont and a news article of her murder. Another page is a copy of a news article about Monique's work as a crime victims' advocate. The last page is a photo of the youngish woman I saw in the shattered picture frame on Monique's bedroom dresser. It's a graduation photo, and the caption reads something about Gabrielle Delmont and mentions a son, Sebastian. Michael Rader told Monique he would find and kill Gabrielle if Monique didn't confirm that I was alive and tell him where I was staying. I need to find Gabrielle. Ronnie hasn't included any information on her other than the photos. I hope that doesn't mean there is nothing to be found.

I rake the papers into a stack and shut the folder. Why was Monique in Port Townsend? Why that particular house? Is that important? It had a view of the bay. It's semi-private. She didn't make friends, according to Mrs. Perkins. She didn't invite Mrs. Perkins into her house. Is that important? Was she keeping a low profile? I had experience with that, of course. Was she trying to find me? She must have had some reason to come here. Maybe she saw my picture in the paper. If so, why didn't she come to the Sheriff's Office in Port Hadlock? Someone had taken the picture of me there.

Could it have been her?

Ronnie comes in carrying two cups of coffee and a bag with bagels. "Morning, boss."

"Never call me that," I say, but not in a mean way. After all, she brought coffee and bagels. "I'm not your boss."

I am your supervisor, however, so you can suck up all you want.

She sits at my desk and I check my coffee. Just the way I like it. With caffeine. Lots and lots of caffeine.

"I've been going through the info you collected yesterday. Good job."

She smiles and blows the steam across the top of her cup. Ronnie drinks candy coffee. Latte, Frappuccino, whatever. Usually with whipped cream on top. Today she's living dangerous and it looks like real coffee.

"Thank you. Marley wasn't in the lab yesterday. I think he was home sick, but they expect him in today. I held on to the evidence."

"I need you to do something else this morning."

"Okay," she says. "Shoot."

I tell her.

CHAPTER TWELVE

Sheriff Gray is in early too. He looks like he had a rough night. I imagine everyone that was at the scene yesterday must have had nightmares. Just thinking about it sends a shiver through me.

I head for his office and close the door behind me. "I want to take Ronnie with me today. I'm going to Port Orchard to see someone."

Sheriff Gray cocks an eye at me but doesn't ask who I'm going to see. He knows I want to keep it quiet and he's giving me room.

"She's on light duty, Megan," he reminds me. "She's still got a bum wrist."

"I need her," I say.

He's surprised, kind of, but he doesn't ask me why. He knows she is a hard worker and smart.

"You can have her, but don't get her hurt."

Like I would let her. She can do that all by herself. She's been hurt before. It's part of the job.

"I promise."

"And check in with me every hour. In fact, have *Ronnie* call me every hour."

He doesn't trust me. I wouldn't, either.

"I'll tell her."

Yeah. Right.

I leave the cigarette butt and other stuff with Nan. I give her the request form to give to Marley and tell her he'll be in this morning looking for us.

"Where will you be if he asks?" Nan asks.

"It's none of his business," I say. *Or yours*, I think. I know Marley will be disappointed that Ronnie isn't here, but I think he'll have fun asking about the panties.

We leave before Nan can burn me to death with her death star glare.

"Where to first? Port Orchard?" Ronnie asks.

I start the car and glance up in the trees to see if my stalker has taken up position. There's no one.

I asked Ronnie to do some more digging into Gabrielle's background. She found the picture of Gabrielle and her son while she was doing a search for Monique. But she only copied it because she thought the woman and Monique looked so much alike. I never knew Gabrielle's last name. I assumed it wasn't Delmont because she had a son.

Ronnie had done what she called "dumpster diving" and found marriage records for Gabrielle and a birth certificate for her son. Sebastian Wilson was born around the same time that Leanne Delmont was murdered by my biological father. Gabrielle's husband had died when the boy was six months old. She graduated from Portland State University and moved to Port Orchard. Ronnie found an address but the phone number was no good.

Figures it would be in Port Orchard. Most everything bad in my life happened there. It's where Rolland, my stepfather, was murdered. It's where I had to fake my own death and flee. I don't think I look like that girl anymore but I'm not anxious to ever go back there.

"I talked to Crime Scene and they didn't find a cell phone yesterday," Ronnie says as we get on the road. "No phone service at the house, either. No cable. Nothing. Don't you find that strange?"

I did, but I didn't want to get into it. "We need to get Monique's phone records for her home in Tacoma, cell phone, anything." I don't tell her I have the phone numbers memorized. "Also phone records for Gabrielle's nonworking phone. Maybe she and her mother talked recently."

"I already sent a subpoena," Ronnie says. "The records should be waiting for us when we get back. I asked for a hard copy and they'll send it to my phone too."

Anxiety seizes me as I think about returning to Port Orchard. I'm not too worried about someone recognizing me, but Caleb still lives there, as far as I know. I would have tried to look him up if I hadn't brought Ronnie along. Caleb knows what I did, what I'm doing now, and what name I'm going by. I can't risk him calling me by my old name, Rylee. Not in front of Ronnie.

"I've never been to Port Orchard," Ronnie says.

That's good. Make this your last trip, I think.

"I visited when I was a kid," I tell her. "Not much to see."

She's on her phone and starts telling me all the touristy attractions. I let her rattle on. Nothing new there. I don't want to go back to those days. Or to the town, for that matter.

"We could have called Detective Osborne to see if the address is still good," Ronnie says.

"What?" I haven't followed anything she was saying for about twenty miles now. "You mean Clay?"

"He owes us. We solved his last big murder for him. Besides, I think he's kind of sweet on you."

Clay is a sheriff's detective for Kitsap County. He's a hunk but I don't need anyone being "sweet" on me. I'm having enough trouble doing my job; processing my confrontation with my brother whom I hadn't seen for years; and pursuing a relationship with Dan Anderson. I met him during a homicide investigation in Snow Creek.

Gabrielle's last known address is near Veterans Memorial Park, and we're almost there before I relax my grip on the steering wheel.

"Are we going to Tacoma after this?" Ronnie asks.

"Maybe. I need to talk to Monique's neighbors." I still say "I." I'm used to working alone. Ronnie doesn't seem to notice that I don't always include her, but I'm working on it. If I don't, she'll have to get over it.

Ronnie is looking at her phone. "Tacoma has the highest violent crime rate in the state. Two hundred thousand people, and the violent crime rate is almost a hundred people per hundred thousand."

I give her a glance that says "So?"

"Mrs. Delmont may have pissed someone off with her victims' advocacy work."

"That's what we're here to find out."

"Oh. Is her daughter involved in the victims' advocacy group?"

Shut up, please, I think.

"We won't know until we talk to her," I say.

I highly doubt Monique would ever mix her only daughter up in that group.

"Turn left here," Ronnie says. "It's two blocks and then a right."

I don't say anything but I know exactly where I'm going. I lived in Port Orchard once.

I can't tell Ronnie that. In fact, I can't tell anyone.

CHAPTER THIRTEEN

I drive and Ronnie rides shotgun with a phone glued to her hand. It would be okay, but the phone case is Hello Kitty. Last month it was unicorns and rainbows. I follow Ronnie's GPS directions to a modest one-story house. All the homes on this block are fronted by a narrow ditch with thick shrubs and greenery with only a walkway separating each property. So much for privacy. This one is covered with vines and hidden in shrubs, except for a set of concrete steps leading to the front door with no porch, just a concrete pad. Only the front entrance and top half of three windows are visible from the street.

"Doesn't look occupied," Ronnie says.

She's right. The windows don't have curtains or blinds. But we're here now.

Ronnie follows me across a wooden footbridge that leads to a sloping walk made of crushed red brick. I stop in the tiny front yard and listen and smell. Nothing but a pleasant scent of earth and honeysuckle that has climbed the right side of the house to the gutters.

Then I smell *it*.

Ronnie crinkles her freckled nose. She does too.

"Go back to the car," I say as I draw my .45 from the shoulder holster. A nauseating odor of decay wafts over me and I fight back the gorge rising in my throat. I think, but don't say, *dead body*. Ronnie hasn't moved except to draw her own weapon. I waste one second thinking of the sheriff's orders and then say, "Can you go to the back?"

She nods and heads around the right side where there is more room to maneuver.

"And don't get hurt, Ronnie."

She doesn't listen to me, but that should cover me with the sheriff.

I crouch and make my way beneath the windows. I'm not tall enough to look in them. I duckwalk to the front entrance. The concrete steps have a black metal railing leading up to the tiny square pad.

I give Ronnie another half minute to get in position at the rear of the house and then I go up the steps. When I reach the pad, a voice yells from behind the door.

"I've called the police. I'm armed."

So am I.

I take out my badge case, flip it open and yell, "Sheriff's Office. Don't shoot." Of course, I don't have any police authority in this county, but hopefully it will mean something.

Ronnie comes running around the side of the house just as the door opens and a woman who looks just like Leanne Delmont peeks out. My heart is thrumming. For a moment I think I'm seeing a dead woman.

"Mrs. Delmont?"

"Gabrielle. It's Gabrielle. Can I see your badge?"

I hand her my badge but she doesn't look at it. "I saw someone in the backyard. Are they with you?"

I motion for Ronnie to come up on the steps. She does but can't reach her credentials and hold her weapon at the same time because of her injured wrist. I say to Ronnie, "You can put the gun away." She does and then fumbles for her badge case, almost drops it. I see her hands are shaking. I don't blame Ronnie after the month we've had.

"I'm Detective Carpenter. This is Detective Marsh," I say, and hand her Ronnie's badge case.

The woman examines our badges and then us—carefully. "She's not a detective. This says she a reserve deputy. And you're not from here."

Oh, crap!

"Yeah. You're right. We're from Jefferson County, but we're on an investigation. She just got promoted and hasn't gotten her badge yet," I lie. It must have been a good lie, because she hands the badges back and invites us inside.

Now that I can see her, she reminds me so much of Monique that I feel a shiver. I'm going to tell her that her mother has been murdered.

We step into her living room. There is a game box on the coffee table and a sixty-inch-screen television on one wall. The couch is well worn but expensive, leather. Maybe a gift from Mom. Almost identical pictures to those found at the scene fill the walls. There are several photos of Leanne by herself, Leanne with Gabrielle, Leanne with Monique, and the photo of Leanne on the sailboat with her father. I never knew what happened with the father. Monique never spoke of him.

There are also several pictures of a boy. The same one taken in the park: the boy on the monkey bars. It had been facedown, the glass broken, on top of the dresser in Monique's house. There are several photos of the boy at various ages and then a graduation picture. I notice there is only one picture of Gabrielle.

She doesn't invite us to sit down. I take the lead and sit on the couch. I pat the cushion, motioning for Gabrielle to join me. Ronnie stays by the door and remains quiet. Gabrielle looks from me to Ronnie and back to me. She sits, takes a deep breath and lets it out. "This isn't about that god-awful smell, is it?"

I shake my head.

"This is about my mother, isn't it? Something's happened to her."

I nod. "I'm so sorry." Somehow I tell her that her mother is dead. And then she asks the question that I'd give anything not to recount.

"Did she suffer?"

I tell her no, and leave out the details. Dead is dead. Her knowing everything that I do isn't necessary, I don't care what they taught me at the police academy. Grief in small doses is always best. I would know. I lost my stepfather and had to go on the run with my little brother in the space of five minutes. Life doesn't have to suck for everyone. I'll give her more of the details if she asks.

She doesn't.

CHAPTER FOURTEEN

"I saw the guns and didn't know what to think," Gabrielle says.

"We smelled something bad," Ronnie explains.

"Smells like a dead body?" Gabrielle asks.

"Yeah," I say.

"My neighbor's septic tank is overflowing. I've complained to him but he's not going to fix it. I've complained to the city and they haven't sent anyone out. And I think he's a little mental. He has about twenty cats and I think some of them are dead."

I've heard of a "cat lady" but never a "cat man." I don't care if he's crazy; I'm glad I haven't stumbled onto another skinned corpse. The smell isn't so strong inside her house. In any case, if it were me, I'd hold the neighbor at gunpoint until he fixed it. But that's just me.

Ronnie makes chamomile tea in the kitchen while I sit with Gabrielle, who says she's a teetotaler. Ronnie brings back cups and saucers for all of us, but I'd rather drink toilet water than this stuff. I can understand not drinking liquor, but chamomile?

Gabrielle stares down into the liquid in her teacup without speaking.

"I'm sorry about your mother," I say.

She examines my face. I can see a light come on and she sits completely still for what seems minutes. Then she resumes sipping the tea and her whole demeanor changes.

"Can we speak alone, Detective Carpenter?"

"I'll make some more tea," Ronnie says. "Would you like some tea, Megan? She has regular tea too."

I haven't even touched my nasty brew. I hand the cup and saucer to Ronnie and nod. I can't take my eyes from Gabrielle's face. "Yes. That will be nice. No sugar. Give us a few minutes."

"Of course." Ronnie heads off to the kitchen.

Gabrielle motions for me to follow her outside. She pulls the door to behind us and faces me.

"I know who you are," she says.

I feel goose bumps on my arms. I believe her. Monique must have told her something, but what? I say nothing.

Tears start to well in her eyes. "Mom told me all about you. She said you were the one. You finished off the bastard that took my sister from us. I recognize you from the newspaper photo Mom kept. She was in awe of you, do you know that? She said your name is Rylee but you'd probably changed it."

I can't speak. No one is supposed to ever know all of that. I feel fear and anxiety and a little relief. Like popping a blister and letting all the bad stuff out.

"Don't worry. I won't say a word. You're like a superhero to us."

She hugs me and cries in earnest. "You'll get him. My mom believed in you. She didn't deserve to die. She was a great woman. She'd do anything to help anyone. She told me how you'd found Leanne's killer. She told me Leanne wasn't the only one that he'd killed. You gave her all the evidence the cops would need to clear all those murders and help their families.

"And then his brother came and threatened her that he'd kill me if she didn't…" Her lips trembled, and I could tell she was fighting for composure. "It's Michael Rader. I just know it. You find him. I know you'll get justice for her."

When she says this, she gives a smile that is both angry and full of hate. I wouldn't want that smile turned on me. "I will," I tell her, but we both know it won't be justice I'll be getting.

It will be something else entirely.

She wipes tears away with the back of her hand. Ronnie comes from the kitchen and into the living room. I take Gabrielle's hand. "I'll finish this," I say. "I promise." She nods and fakes a smile. A more relieved one this time. I know what it's like to smile and hate at the same time.

We go back in and sit on the couch. Gabrielle says, "Please have a seat, Detective Marsh."

Ronnie has been standing this whole time. Gabrielle called her *Detective* Marsh. I see a glint of pride in Ronnie's eyes. "I made you another cup of chamomile, Mrs. Delmont."

"Please, call me Gabrielle. Mom called me Gabby because that's what I usually am. This has been a crazy day." She takes the tea and I pick up my teacup. No sugar, just like I asked for.

"Gabrielle," I say, "why was your mother in Port Townsend?"

"I can't tell you that. I mean, I don't know. I talked to her on Friday night. She told me she was in Port Townsend but she led me to believe she was on business for the advocacy group. She never said who it involved."

"She called you this Friday night?" According to the coroner, she was killed on Saturday.

"Yes. I gave up my cell phone and bought one of those—what do you call them?—a paid one."

"A burner?" Ronnie asks.

"That's right. I only gave the number to my mother."

Ronnie raises her hand. I am propelled back to a classroom.

"What is it?" I ask.

Ronnie puts her hand down. "I got the phone records sent to me while I was making tea. Mrs. Delmont's phone hasn't made or received any calls for three weeks."

Gabrielle speaks up.

"That's probably right. She called and gave me a new number. We've both been getting crank calls and I suppose she changed numbers to stop them. I got the burner. I haven't had any calls since and turned my other phone off."

"Ronnie, will you call Mindy and tell her to look for the cell phone again? Tell her that Monique used it Friday night to call her daughter."

Ronnie goes outside to make the call.

"You didn't find my mother's phone?"

"Not where she was staying as far as I've been told. Do you know for sure she was in Port Townsend when she called you?"

"I heard a horn blaring in the background. I knew she was somewhere near a ferry landing. She told me she was renting a place in Port Townsend."

"She didn't tell you why?"

She shakes her head. "I thought the call was a little strange. We talked all the time up until about a month ago. Then she called and said she was getting crank calls. I thought maybe it had something to do with her work. Maybe someone was harassing her." She stops talking and looks to be sure Ronnie isn't nearby and lowers her voice. "Do you think it was him? Michael?"

I don't know. Ronnie comes back inside before I can answer. "I couldn't reach Mindy. Can you give me your mother's new phone number?"

Gabrielle gives it to Ronnie, who gets busy on her cell phone. She also gives Ronnie her own burner phone number.

"I didn't know you could get phone records that easy," she says. "I don't know how I feel about that. I mean, if you can get them I wonder about…"

She doesn't have to finish the sentence. She knows that Michael Rader has police connections.

CHAPTER FIFTEEN

Gabrielle sees me checking out her game system and television.

"That's mine," she says. "It gives me a distraction when I need a break from working. I work from home. Medical billing. I should have become a nurse, but I have an aversion to blood. I spend a lot of time on my own. I don't even like the games but with my son gone..."

She's chattering about insignificant things, trying to be brave. She went through something similar when her sister, Leanne, was killed. She probably had to hold it together to keep her mother and father from falling apart.

"Where is your son?"

"He graduated high school and got a job with Starbucks as a programmer. He's a very bright boy. He lives in Maine now and is a bigshot IT guy." She tries to smile.

"Sebastian, right?"

"That's right. He's been gone for a year now. He likes the East Coast. Of course, his girlfriend might have something to do with that. She works for Starbucks too. Did you know they send their employees through college? He got his degree online from Arizona State University and is thinking of going for a Masters in computer science to become a software developer. It's basically what he does now."

I feel dread at what I'm about to say. "Gabrielle, can you go visit Sebastian for a while? Stay somewhere that no one can find you?"

"You think Michael will come after me and my son?"

"He used you to get to your mother."

And to me.

"If Sebastian is in danger, I'll do whatever I have to."

"Do you know if he's been getting these crank calls?"

"He hasn't said anything, but I haven't told him about me and his grandma getting them. I didn't want to worry him, but I'll call him now and tell him I'm coming for a visit."

Gabrielle goes into the kitchen and I hear her on the phone. She comes back. "He's glad to have me visit. I don't know how he'll be when I tell him about his grandmother. I don't know how to tell him."

She seems to be holding it together fairly well for everything we've thrown at her in the last thirty minutes.

"You should tell your son exactly what he needs to know to be safe. He doesn't need to know everything. I'll take care of keeping your mother's business in Port Townsend out of the news. I'll call her landlord and make sure that's cleared up. The coroner might want to talk to you on the phone. Do you have keys to your mother's house in Tacoma?"

She goes into the kitchen and is gone a while. When she returns with a key I can tell she's been crying.

"I don't know how to say this," I start. I know that sometimes it's best just to spit it out. "I couldn't positively identify your mother's body."

"Oh," she says, and looks at her hands.

"That's why I need to go to her house. I have to find something of hers that I can use for DNA testing."

Tears well up again. I don't know what to say, even if I could get the words out.

"We're so sorry," Ronnie says. "Is there anyone we can call to be with you until you make arrangements for wherever you're going?"

Ronnie looks at me, no doubt wondering if it's safe to leave her.

"We'll need a DNA sample from you," I say to Gabrielle. "For a positive identification."

Ronnie takes a DNA collection tube with a swab from her pocket. She always seems to have the right thing at the right time. How does she do that?

"She won't have to go right away," I say while Ronnie collects the sample.

I take my phone out and look up a number. I dial and it's answered on the first ring.

"Kitsap County Sheriff's Office. Detective Osborne."

"It's Megan, Clay. I need a favor."

CHAPTER SIXTEEN

I call Sheriff Gray while we're on the road to Tacoma. "We've found Mrs. Delmont's daughter."

"Is she coming to identify the body?"

"I told her not to. She couldn't possibly identify the body anyway."

"And you're worried about her safety," he says.

Sheriff Gray is a smart guy, an old-time detective. "She's going to be protected until she can get someplace safe."

"No need to tell me where," he says. "You can reach her if you need to, right?"

"Yes. Are you somewhere that you can talk freely?"

What I'm really asking is if he's anywhere that Nan can use her super-hearing.

"I'm in my office. Door closed. And I'll talk quietly. Will that do?"

He's aware of Nan and her foghorn mouth. She tells everyone everything. "Have you heard when the autopsy will take place?" I ask.

"Tomorrow morning, Andrade said. Where are you?"

"We're going to Delmont's house in Tacoma to see if we can find out why she was in Port Townsend. And we'll need to find a DNA sample. We got one from her daughter. The daughter gave us Monique's house key and her permission."

Sheriff Gray stays quiet and I go on, "Ronnie is doing exactly what you ordered. I won't get her into a fight. I promise. And she's been a big help. I'll need her to help me search the house, anyway. And she's the one who came up with the daughter's information."

"You don't have to convince me, Megan. Just keep me informed. You don't have any authority in Tacoma, so don't get in any trouble that I can't get you out of."

Sheriff Gray is more of a father than my stepfather Rolland was—although Rolland really tried to act like a father and I knew he cared about me. "I'll stay out of trouble," I say.

I can't guarantee that, of course. If Michael Rader is in Tacoma, I'm going to end him. I'll worry about Ronnie later.

I have been to Monique's house just the once. I don't want to go there any more than I want to be in Port Orchard, but my past follows me. When this day is over, I might have to call Dr. Albright. She always knows the right things to say to put me back together after I have come apart.

As we cross the Tacoma Narrows Bridge, Point Defiance Park is at the tip of the peninsula. The place where Leanne was kidnapped. Ronnie's GPS directs me toward the outskirts of the city. I let Ronnie's GPS take us all the way to Monique's house.

We arrive and Ronnie's jaw drops. Just as mine did when I first saw it. The Delmont residence grabs the edge of a cliff that overlooks Tacoma and the surprisingly pristine-looking waters of Commencement Bay. It is by far the biggest and nicest house that I've ever seen outside of a magazine. It's twice the size of the rental house where Monique was staying. The front door is huge and all glass. I wonder how anyone can keep such a thing clean.

The first time I saw all that glass, it made me think of Hayden and his dirty little fingers, which would have made a mess of it in about two minutes. The thought of my brother Hayden, the way we'd left things when I last saw him, makes my chest hurt. My heart is as broken as it has ever been, and that's saying a lot. He is the last family I have. I knew he hated me before he showed up out of the blue, in Port Townsend, around a month ago. He agreed to stay the night in my spare room so we could talk it out in the morning. But he left before I woke and left a note telling me he never wanted to see me and I should stop trying to contact him. I held out hope that I could explain things. That he would somehow realize that I was his only family and forgive me for leaving him. I can see how my words hurt Gabrielle today. Monique was her world. But at least she has a son whom she loves and who still loves her. Knowing this, why do I expect the relationship between Hayden and my mother to be any different? Hayden loves our mother. He visits her in prison and knows I don't. He still believes she cares. I don't.

We get out of the Taurus. I look through the window in the garage door. Monique's car is there.

"Does she have another car?" Ronnie asks.

"Did you find more than one vehicle registered?"

"The Caddy is the only one I found. That's the one Crime Scene is looking for at the scene. They didn't find a car there?"

"Let's go inside," I say. I use the key Gabrielle provided and unlock and open the door. That triggers a memory of the first time I saw Monique in person. She answered the door with a look of hesitation. Her hair looked like spun gold and she was wearing big diamond earrings. I recognized her immediately. I'd seen her picture in the newspaper articles I'd found when researching the death of Leanne. Her work with the advocacy group was the way I found her address the first time. I called them and arranged to meet with Monique.

This is all like a replay of the past. I hear Ronnie's shoes echo on the gleaming hardwood floors, just as I'd heard Monique's designer shoes as she led me to a cozy seating area in a corner of the elegant great room. The room is larger than the last two houses my family had lived in. Larger than the entire apartment I live in now. For a moment I taste the amazing almond cookies she made. She gave me coffee with them. I had been eating fruit and granola bars since the day I'd gone on the run. I wanted to get a proper meal, but back then I couldn't because I was running out of time.

I feel that same sputtering urgency now.

"What's wrong, Megan?"

"I was just thinking how hard this must be on Gabrielle," I lie.

"What are we looking for?"

"You start in the bathrooms. See if you can find a hairbrush, a toothbrush. Anything with DNA for the lab. I'll start in the kitchen." I don't say I know that's where Monique spent a lot of time with her laptop and drinking tea.

"I wonder where the bathroom is in this place?" Ronnie walks down a hallway and out of sight.

CHAPTER SEVENTEEN

Ronnie is off looking for the bathrooms. There are probably three or four. She should be busy for a while.

I go into the kitchen and remember a conversation I'd had with Dr. Albright in one of my first therapy sessions. The session comes at me in words and pictures, like a movie. I'm sitting on her couch, breathing in the scent of the flowers in the tall vase.

This time, calla lilies.

Tell me more about Monique, Dr. Albright says.

Her deep-blue eyes are full of concern. *Her daughter is dead,* I tell her. *I'm pretending to be a reporter, asking questions that I know are causing her pain. Mrs. Delmont looks at me closely and asks, "Are you all right, dear?" I wonder what it is that she thinks is wrong with me. I'm good at hiding my emotions. "Excuse me?" I ask in the kindest, most nonthreatening, attitude-free manner in which anyone could ever utter those words.*

She looks at my hands. "You've chewed your nails to the quicks." My hands are in my lap. My fingernails are nearly gone. I didn't realize that I'd been gnawing them to the point of oblivion. I wonder what other ways my anger, anxiety, fear and need for revenge was manifesting itself. I felt I was changing in ways that I both reviled and welcomed. Chewed nails are on the reviled side of the T-chart that makes up my life's pros and cons. "It's just this story," I lied to Mrs. Delmont, and notice one of my fingertips is still wet. I wonder how I could be so unaware of myself. What is wrong with me?

Mrs. Delmont says, "It's been a long time since Leanne was taken from me, but it still hurts deeply. I try to keep busy. I try to help, but in my mind I still see my Leanne and her father on the sailboat, smiling, having the time of their lives. She went missing from the marina and I play that day over and over."

I assure her that she's not alone, that all homicide survivors feel that way. But as the words tumble from my lips, I notice her face tighten. I was trying to be thoughtful, but it came off as condescending. I quickly came up with a lie.

I tell Mrs. Delmont my sister Courtney was murdered. That I grieve for her every day. I don't tell her that I don't really have a sister. That Courtney is my mother and she's not dead. I'm trying to find her.

Dr. Albright asked me: *You told her that you had a sister and she was murdered?*

I said, *I guess.*

Why did you use your mother's name when you spoke about a sister? Dr. Albright asked.

I see where you're going with this, I told her. *I was mad at my mother for the lies, the betrayal, but I didn't wish her dead. Even though I was on the run, I was trying to find her. To save her.*

I remember now how Dr. Albright gave me that non-judgmental look that she is so good at. Letting me decide what I'd had in my mind and in my heart.

You're safe here, she said. *You can say anything you want.*

I told her how Monique's face relaxed and she rested a hand on my knee. *Mrs. Delmont said, "Well then, we're in a sisterhood of unending grief."*

I remember that I didn't want to be in any such sisterhood. Who would? For my part, then and now, I wanted to be in the sisterhood of vengeance and retribution. All of her fundraisers, all of her talk show appearances, haven't added up to anything. Not really. As long as a killer breathes the same air as we do, a victim's family is never free.

CHAPTER EIGHTEEN

I was in her kitchen a very long time ago. It still smells of the almond cookies she served me before she knew the truth about me. I see a plate on the kitchen island with half a dozen store-bought almond cookies on it. I try one. Stale. I eat the rest of it and another. I put a couple in my blazer pocket for later and save the rest for Ronnie.

Monique was old school. People her age grew up sitting around kitchen tables, having meals as a family, talking about school or other interesting things that had happened or will happen, playing board games. After Hayden's short visit I'd broken down and bought a smart TV and watched an old show a few nights ago. In it the mother wore dresses with short, puffy sleeves, a ribbon tied at the waist, lipstick, eye makeup, stiff but perfect hair with half a can of hairspray on it. She never said anything catty. Never argued with her husband. The kids were as perfect as they could be.

And yet I know that beneath perfection sometimes lurks something very disturbing.

I sit at the kitchen table. Magnets hold a calendar on the refrigerator. Monique had been marking days with a big X. The marks ended three weeks ago. There was nothing else to indicate why she was doing this. I take the calendar and flip through it. The only things she's marked are hair appointments. No doctors. No birthdays. Nothing. I don't keep a calendar in my place for this very reason. I don't want anyone violating my privacy.

Ronnie comes into the kitchen. "There's nothing in any of the bathrooms. If she has a brush, she took it with her. Same for any kind of medicine. I can tell you that she touched up her own roots but that's about it. No toothbrush, either. Except for one in the packaging in the drawer. Did you find anything in here?"

I don't tell her I've been lost in the past.

"Nothing yet. You go through the cabinets in here and check again. I'll go to the bathroom and double-check. Then we'll check the other rooms. If she left something telling us why she went to Port Townsend, it's likely to be in the kitchen, bathroom or great room, and I didn't see anything in there."

"Me either," Ronnie says. She begins checking the drawers I haven't looked in. "Look at this," she announces, holding a pink sheet of paper. It's a carbon copy of a car rental agreement.

"I guess I know why we didn't find a car at the scene now," I say, and call Mindy's phone.

Ronnie hands me the rental papers. I put the call on speakerphone so Ronnie can listen.

"Hi, Megan," Mindy says. "How are you? Oh, you ask how I am. I'm fine. It's nice to know you still call even when you don't need something."

"I called with business if you don't mind. Then we can have drinks later and you can criticize me for being a bad friend."

"So, what can I do for you?"

"You didn't identify a car belonging to the victim at the scene, did you?"

"No. We got her license plate number from DOL but we haven't found the car yet. It's a new Cadillac. Do you need the number or have you found the car?"

"We're at Mrs. Delmont's house in Tacoma. Her car is in her garage. But I can tell you what you should be looking for."

"I've left the scene but I can go back."

"That would be great." I don't trust the crime scene guys that were there to let me see what's in the car. Mindy will FaceTime me and show me everything. "We might be a while here." I read the plate number and vehicle description off to Mindy.

"Got it. I don't remember seeing a car like that near there. So don't get your hopes up."

"Mindy, if you find it, can you get me on FaceTime and—"

"I'll show you everything before I call Humpty and Dumpty to collect the car."

"Is that what you're calling our fabulous crime scene guys?" I ask.

"They were actually rude to me," Mindy says, and she sounds miffed. "I've never had anyone not share a crime scene with me."

"Be sure you tell the sheriff. He'll tie a knot in their tails. Besides, one of them was rude to me as well," I say. "Let's cut their tires." This gets a giggle out of Mindy. "Also, I need you to look for the victim's cell phone." It feels strange referring to Monique as "the victim." But that's what she is. Another victim I would have to avenge.

Mindy is very sharp. "You know we didn't find her cell phone, or any other phone, for that matter. So you must have a different phone in mind. I'm guessing she had two phones or someone else's phone."

"You should have been a detective," I say, and give her the phone number for the burner. "I think she called her daughter from it a day or so before she was murdered. The victim had been getting crank calls, or at least that's what she told her daughter. If you can find the phone, it might give me some clue to who else she was calling recently. She only had the new phone about three weeks."

"Any idea why she was up our way?" Mindy asks.

"Not yet. We're in her home in Tacoma trying to find something for a DNA comparison."

"Got it," Ronnie says. She's holding a coffee mug up and pointing to lipstick smears on the rim of the cup.

It's the same color I remember Monique being fond of. Now we have two ways of identifying the body.

CHAPTER NINETEEN

Before we leave the enormous house, I go through the upstairs rooms. Ronnie has searched the bathrooms already, but I go back through those like I'm trying to see if she missed something. I know she hasn't but it keeps her in her place as my assistant. Then I feel bad about thinking that. I'm her teacher.

In the bedroom I find Monique's address book containing the members of her advocacy group. I can hear Ronnie in another bedroom, so I go into the hall as if I just came from the bathroom. I call to her. She comes out in the hall with a look of disappointment on her face. "Can you check this room with me?"

"There's nothing in the bedroom. I even searched under the mattress."

"You check the closet. I'll look under the mattress here." The address book is on the shelf in the closet. She finds it right away and flips through it.

"I've got an address book."

"Good work," I say, and she hands the book to me. "We should be able to contact some of her friends and see what she was up to."

"Where to now?"

"I'll drive while you start calling people in the address book. Start with the ones in the advocacy group."

"What if they ask why I'm calling?"

"Tell them Monique is dead. We suspect foul play. Don't tell them what really happened, but you'll need to ask what she was doing in Port Townsend and if anyone wanted to hurt her. So you'll have to tell them she's dead."

"That sucks," Ronnie says.

"It's going to be on the news in a little bit anyway," I say.

We get in the car and Ronnie gets on her phone. "You're right." She shows me the screen. Monique's name is already on the news stations.

My phone rings.

It's Mindy.

I can barely hear her over the clamor of demanding voices. The reporters have smelled fresh roadkill and they'll pick the carcass clean for days, given the nature of the murder.

"The car has been towed already. I was cruising around and a deputy stopped me. I told him what I was looking for and he said he towed the car away from the marina lot yesterday. It was parked almost in the water."

"The phone?"

"I found the phone under the mattress. One of the crime scene guys fingerprinted it for me and I have it with me. It's covered in black powder but it doesn't look broken."

"We're coming back to the office. Can you meet us there?"

"Hang on a minute," she says to me. Then I hear her say to someone: "If you want a story, you need to go to The Tides and talk to Deputy Jackson. He found an important piece of evidence and a witness." I can hear the clamoring increase in volume and Mindy repeating herself until the background noise stops.

"You didn't," I say.

"Yes, I did."

"We don't have a deputy named Jackson," I say.

"By the time they find out there's no deputy or witness there, I'll be back at the office."

"Slick. See you there." I hang up.

Ronnie looks concerned. "Mindy won't get fired, will she? I mean if the reporters complain to Sheriff Gray."

"Mindy isn't a deputy. She's a contract worker. Sheriff Gray will tell them he will talk to her and that'll be the end of that."

"Cool."

"Ronnie, you should never do that. You could be fired."

"Okay. I promise."

I look over and she's got her fingers crossed. "Start calling those people," I say, and we pull out into traffic. I hope we get lucky with one of them.

CHAPTER TWENTY

Rylee and her red-haired detective friend had somehow gotten to Gabrielle's house ahead of her. *Ronnie*. That's the redhead's name. Before they left, a big guy, he looks like a cop, came and is left guarding Gabrielle. She could kill him with one of her knives, and then do Gabrielle, but that isn't in her plan.

Her plan is to make Rylee suffer. She's begun that already. Tick, tick, tick.

And now there are other places to go, people to kill. Still, she would have enjoyed seeing the look she cut off of Gabrielle's face.

She told Monique that she killed Gabrielle but it was a lie. She only said it to see the horror it caused, payback for the help Monique had given Rylee. Michael Rader threatened Monique several years ago. He told her he would kill her remaining daughter if she didn't tell him if Rylee was still alive. Monique confirmed to him that the bitch was still breathing; not only that, he also recovered all the photos Rylee had taken from Marie's house. According to Michael, there were enough photos to fill a wall. A shrine to his victims. A wall of memorabilia that could potentially put Alex in prison or get Michael a death sentence. She warned Alex about that. But Marie had more control over him. Marie was his motivator. But Marie was dead.

She watches the detective sitting on the porch with Gabrielle. She knows he'll be fucking her before the night is over. That's how policemen are. It isn't a bad thing. Just reality. Watching them together, doing something as simple as sitting on the steps, drinking, not even talking, brings back a flood of memories of her time with Alex. The little time he could give to her. She appreciated every second. She hadn't always been so happy. So safe.

She conjures up an image of his face. His dark eyes were so intense. That was what had attracted her to him. The kindness behind his tough exterior was what made her fall in love with him. He saved her from the streets. Took care of her. Gave her a safe place to live, food, money, whatever she needed or wanted.

She didn't want much back in those days and she needed very little. After all, she'd subsisted on next to nothing in her native El Salvador. Her mother and father and brother were killed by the FMLN guerrilla faction for not joining them during the twelve-year war with the junta government. Her brother and father were killed in a hideous fashion of skinning them alive in public as a lesson to anyone that opposed them. Her mother was repeatedly raped before she was beheaded. She herself was raped and discarded by the guerrilla fighters. Left alone at the age of thirteen as an example. No work. No one dared take her in. All were afraid. She was going through garbage or taking the occasional half-eaten MREs the soldiers had stolen from the US-trained troops of the junta government and offered to her for her favors. She had done plenty of favors, but still she almost starved.

CHAPTER TWENTY-ONE

Ronnie hit pay dirt with one of the phone numbers in the address book from Monique's house. Mr. Bridges was a widower; his wife had been killed in a carjacking. A witness said it was two young women who came up to Mrs. Bridges' car while she was stopped at a light a block from the hospital where she worked in the ER. The same one where she would be pronounced dead ten minutes later. The witness was in the car behind her and said one girl ran into the street waving her arms like she needed help. Mr. Bridges' wife, being a nurse, started to open her door and was yanked out by the second girl, stabbed, kicked and the car was taken. The witness was so shocked, she didn't notice the license plate and was unable to give an accurate description to police when they arrived.

Mr. Bridges joined the advocacy group when he saw it on the Internet and made friends with Monique. Monique had dozens of names in that book and I have no doubt all the stories will be full of needless violence and death.

"His number comes up once on the burner Mrs. Delmont had," Ronnie says. "A week ago he said she called him to give him the number in case someone had an emergency. He was like her second-in-command, and if one of them couldn't reach her, they would call him."

"He's a pretty frequent caller on her personal cell phone too," I say. "Once or twice a week, and the calls lasted thirty minutes or more. I'm glad she found someone for comfort."

"Yeah. It must be horrible to have your daughter murdered. Mr. Bridges told me that's why she started the victim's group." Ronnie's quiet and I think I see tears form in her eyes.

"Makes you appreciate our sad little lives, doesn't it? She was helping with morale and maybe financial support, pushing police departments to do deeper investigations, hounding city officials. But we're tracking the assholes down. We bring peace to them."

"Yeah, we do."

"Did she tell Mr. Bridges she was in Port Townsend looking for an old friend that she thought needed her help?" I ask.

She nods her head. "He said it's not unlike her to do something like that. Sometimes a couple of people in the group will travel to wherever they're needed. Monique always footed the entire bill. I asked him if she rented a car to do this. He thought that was unusual."

"Does she always get a burner phone for these things?"

"I forgot to ask. I'll call him back."

"Not necessary. If it was unusual for her to rent a car and not tell him more than what she did, I think we can safely say it wasn't normal for a woman her age to buy a burner phone, or even know to do it."

"He made it sound like she was afraid for her friend. He blames himself for not insisting he come to help her. I think he was a little more than her second-in-command."

I do too, but I'm really glad that she finally came out of her shell enough to trust another man. I haven't fully done that yet. I once thought I could with Caleb, but when he found out what I'd done to my bio-father and watched me take down another killer, he was sickened. He will always associate his minor part in that with me. I destroy monsters, but I'm a monster to Caleb.

Dan Anderson is the closest thing I have to a boyfriend, and we've only been out a couple of times in the last month. I don't know why, but my gut is telling me to call him to see if he's okay. If he's also been getting crank calls.

"Mindy is going to go through the rental car. Are you still calling people from the advocacy group?"

"Yeah. I've only got a few left. Then I'm going to call Gabrielle and see how things are there. Do you want me to check in with Clay and see if she told him anything she didn't tell us?"

I don't know why, but I tell her I'll call Clay. Maybe I don't want her doing all of my work. Maybe I don't want her getting involved with him and hurting Marley's feelings. Marley is more important to us. To me. Ronnie goes back to her desk, and Sheriff Gray motions for me to come in his office.

"Shut the door," he says. I take a chair in the corner. He leans back in his chair and it doesn't screech. The WD-40 I left on his desk has done the trick. He looks at me for a long time. I keep his gaze and sit still. I'm good at waiting. I'm good because I'm ready for him to try and talk me off the case. Not going to happen. Not even if he gives it to another detective.

He reads my expression, sits forward and lets out a deep sigh.

"You're not going to give this one up, are you?"

I shake my head. Words are piling up and almost spewing out of my mouth. I know to keep it shut. He gets the idea.

"Tell me what you have. I heard you talking about it out there, but I need to know the rest. All of it."

With those last words he raises an eyebrow. He knows I'm going to lie. So I don't disappoint him.

"First of all, you already know that I knew Monique way back when. I knew her better than I told you, but not so well that I can't keep my personal feelings out of the investigation."

That's the first lie, but I temper it with a small truth.

"You know we had Detective Osborne from Kitsap stay with her daughter until she got away to stay with her son in the

Midwest. Indiana. She'll be okay there and was planning to visit him anyway."

That's a lie. The son is in Maine.

I hate lying to Sheriff Gray, but it's for his own good.

And mine.

"Monique left her car in Tacoma and drove a rental here. We have the car in the impound lot and Mindy's going over it. Mindy found Monique's phone under her mattress and she's going through that for us, too."

"Her burner phone," Sheriff Gray says.

I nod. "That's out of character but I can't explain it yet."

"And why would you have Detective Osborne stand by with her daughter? Did you think she was in danger from this lunatic?"

"Better safe than sorry."

"And this has nothing to do with the, you know, that I gave you?"

"I don't see how it could."

My final lie.

Sheriff Gray looks at his watch. "Tell Ronnie to call it a night. You both go home and get some rest. You got Gabrielle safe, so this will keep until morning."

"I'll run her off, but I still have some work to do," I say. I don't know what I can do tonight. The autopsy is tomorrow and all I can do is sit and think.

"Go home," he says.

Not a request.

Maybe he's right. I can think at home with a drink.

CHAPTER TWENTY-TWO

I dial Dan's number as I drive.

"Megan. I was just thinking about you. I must be psychic, huh?"

"Or a psycho. I mean, you *are* dating me."

"We're dating?"

"No. Yes. You know what I mean. We're going out now and again and—"

"I'm just pulling your leg. Don't sweat it."

I can hear something in his voice. I've said something wrong and I don't know what. I'm not good at this dating stuff. I called because I'm thinking about how close to home Monique's murder is.

That and my stalker's last email.

You are a busy girl. But then, you always were sticking your nose in places it didn't belong. I see you're on the hunt again. And this time you're interfering with Clallam and Kitsap County cases. Good for you. I'm sure you'll find your man. Just hope he doesn't find you first. You're not as clever as you think.

The last two lines now make that email seem pertinent to Monique's death and the crank calls she and Gabrielle were receiving. I never met Gabrielle before today, but I knew of the threat Michael Rader made to her mother. The last two lines of that email make me wonder if my stalker and Monique's death are connected.

I'm in Port Townsend. See you soon. Wallace.

P.S. Who's the lumberjack?

It had been signed "Wallace." Wallace apparently doesn't know Dan's name, if that's who he's referring to. I thought the stalker was just after me. Trying to scare me. I even considered Dan could be the stalker. It seemed awfully coincidental that I'd just had a date with Dan before I read the email. Dan knew about the murder cases involving Clallam and Kitsap Counties. But he would hardly have named himself "The Lumberjack."

Maybe Dan was leaving a red herring in the email. Make me think the stalker has noticed him. It would be a good way to throw me off his scent. But it doesn't matter because I have no clue as to who is sending the emails. My suspects for who has been sending them are Dan; Caleb; my brother, Hayden; and Michael Rader. I thought Hayden was in Afghanistan when the email was sent, but then I found out he had been in Port Townsend. For weeks. The email that I thought was from my stalker said, "I'm in Port Townsend. See you soon." And then Hayden shows up at my door the next day. As far as I know, he's still living in Port Townsend, but I can't let myself believe it's him.

I don't know where Michael Rader is. I haven't kept track of him. I didn't really have the means to keep tabs back then. But now I wonder why I didn't when I joined the Sheriff Office.

Good question, I think.

"Megan? You still there?"

It's Dan.

"Does anyone ever call you Lumberjack?" I don't realize I say that out loud, but I'm thinking it.

He laughs. "Lumberjack? That's a good one. I guess I did kind of dress like one the other night. And with the short beard, it's not a bad depiction."

"Lumberjacks use chainsaws," I say, and try to make it sound like a joke.

"Yeah. And since you mention it, when are you going to come by the shop and pick up the piece I saved for you?"

Dan has a cabin up at Snow Creek where he makes wood carvings of bears, lighthouses and eagles in flight, among other things. He's an artist with a paintbrush and chainsaw. He's recently opened a little shop along the waterfront in Port Townsend. He offered me the bear when I was working on some murder cases over in Snow Creek. I didn't take it. In fact, he asked me out, sort of, and I stood him up.

He contacted me again while I was involved in a case a while back and I finally gave in and went out for a drink with him. He said he would bring the bear the next time we went out. Clever way of getting another date. Well, it worked. We went out a couple of times and I grudgingly took the bear. Now it sat beside my desk. I like it, but I don't like the idea of owning things. I have learned to travel light. My whole life until Port Townsend was picking up and leaving at the first hint of trouble. Now I had "stuff." Up until the bear the only "stuff" I had were the audiotapes Dr. Karen Albright gave me when I concluded my therapy sessions with her. But they help sometimes. Help me get the past behind me. Help me with hidden clues about cases in the present.

"How about we meet for drinks and a sandwich tonight?" Dan asks.

Instead of answering, I ask him, "Have you gotten any funny calls lately?"

"Besides this one, you mean?"

He makes me smile. "I mean crank calls. Wrong numbers. Hang-up calls."

"I run a business, Megan. What do you think?"

"Okay. Point taken. But listen, if you start getting anything you think is suspicious, I want you to call me right away."

"Okay. Will you make the bad people go away? I mean, you have a reputation for finding your man. Or men."

He said: "finding your man." Just like the email from my stalker. The stalker probably wasn't Dan, but I wouldn't be able to unhear what he just said.

"Funny. You're a funny man, Lumberjack. Seriously, do you promise to call me if you get any calls like that?"

"Sounds like you care about me. But, yes, I promise. So how about that date tonight?"

I have an attraction to Dan, but I'm not going to get serious with anyone. I can't. It wouldn't be fair to either of us. I'm not a very trusting person, and I've learned the hard way not to get too close to anyone or anything. Like the bear. I'd sell it if I thought he wouldn't find out. He's a nice guy. He deserves a normal girl. That's not me. Anything but.

"The Tides," I say. "Seven, unless I get called in. Then I won't be there."

"Understood, Detective. Sometimes I have emergency carvings, so I may not make it, either."

It's good he can joke. He doesn't take everything I say literally or even seriously. He is easy to talk to. Easy to be around. He doesn't pry into my past. I will be there. Unless I get shot again.

CHAPTER TWENTY-THREE

I park and go to my front door. I left a light on in the entryway. It's off. I look around the street. The other houses have power, so that's not it. I've never replaced a lightbulb since moving in. I draw my .45 anyway.

The door is locked. Someone could have come in and locked the door behind them. I would. My key finds the slot in the waning light and I push the door open. No one jumps out of the dark interior. I go in and try the light switch. It flicks up and down. I have a fuse blown or the bulb is out.

Cursing my stalker for making me feel on edge, I go down the hall and flip another switch in the hall. A light comes on. Relief washes over me and I'm holstering my .45 when my phone vibrates and startles me.

"What?" I say, more angrily than I intend. I don't realize how shaken I really am. I wish, not for the first time, my stalker would show himself. Come for me. Get this over with.

"Megan?"

It's Clay. "I'm sorry, Clay. I had my hands full and couldn't find my phone."

"Understand completely," he says, but I don't think he's telling the truth. "I just wanted to catch you up on that thing in Port Orchard."

Shit. I forgot to call Clay.

"I called Ronnie and she was on her way to the crime lab to turn over some samples."

Go, Ronnie! Yay! She was so competent it was starting to gnaw on my nerves. No doubt she wanted to brag to Marley that she'd found all the stuff herself. I remind myself that I'm the one who threw those two together just so I could get favors from the lab.

"She said I should call you."

"Okay. Did Gabrielle get off okay?"

"She packed a bag and I took her to the airport. Is she a witness?"

"Not really," I say, then feel bad for asking him to babysit. "But she might be in a little danger. I'm just playing it safe." That should make him feel important.

"Glad I could help. I'm glad we could work together again."

He leaves the sentence just hanging there like he wants to say something. I wait. He's a grown man. He can spit it out, whatever it is.

"Speaking of," he says and pauses. "Now that we're not actually working a case together, I've been meaning to ask you something."

Oh, shit. I think I know what's coming next and I don't want to know. I feel a tingle of excitement. Clay is a very attractive man. He's built like a linebacker, but he's at least ten years older than me. Maybe fifteen. And I have a date tonight with Dan. Please don't say it.

"Would you go out for drinks with me?"

Shit. Shit. "Let me think about it."

"Okay. That's better than a no. Call me when you make up your mind."

"Thanks for taking care of Gabrielle." I hang up. Shit.

I stand on a chair and check the entryway lightbulb. It's unscrewed slightly. I screw it back tight and the light comes on.

I go to my office. Everything appears to be as I left it. I get in the closet and find something decent but not too much to wear to The Tides tonight. I pull out a pair of black jeans that I picked up in a second-hand clothing store. The knees are fashionably shredded. I take out a pair of cork-soled sandals but decide to wear my work boots. A dark blue button-down long-sleeve shirt that came from the same store will work under a cheap Levi's blazer. My statement accessory is my gun.

I check the drawer where the tapes are kept. Nothing looks disturbed. I'm getting paranoid. But like they say, you're not paranoid if someone is really out to get you.

The tapes call to me. I have enough time to listen before my date-meeting with Dan. I find one at random, slot the tape and play it.

Dr. A: Tell me about the dream. Tell me about it as though it were happening now.

Me: I'm staying at the Best Western in Kent, Washington. I have an ice pick I've taken from Aunt Ginger's kitchen. My plan is to find Alex Rader and shove the ice pick into his eyes. I drift into an uneasy slumber and dream about the little girl from the rest stop.

Dr. A: Do you know her name?

Me: Her name is Selma. She's running as fast as she can.

Dr. A: Is she running away or toward someone or something? What did you feel?

Me: I don't know. Her feet are bare and bloody, her dark curls streaming back in the wind. I call out to her to hurry, but no sound comes from my lips. She moves toward me, and as she approaches I recognize the look in her eyes. She's terrified of something and she needs my help. She screams.

Dr. A: It must have been terrifying for you.

*Me: The sound is so loud that I close my eyes to try to seal it
from my eardrums. When I snap them open a second later, still
in my dream, all I see is a white and red nightgown lying in
the parking lot next to the well-worn trail to the restroom. I cry
out for her as I hurry to the nightgown. I pick it up and hold
it to my face. The smell is unpleasant, and I know instantly
what it is. I'm taking in the acrid odor of blood.*

*When I pull away, I notice that my hands are bloody. The
dream—no, the nightmare—propels me out of my restless sleep.
I feel sick, scared, angry. I don't grasp the importance of the
dream or why I had it.*

I pause the tape. Monique's blood was drained from her body.
I remember seeing the skin suit in the bottom of the tub, the body
with no flesh covering, and imagine the bleeding must have been
considerable, but all that was left were a few bloody footprints.
I could smell it then. I can smell it now, but I know that's just a
trick of the mind.

The bottle of Scotch in the desk drawer is tempting, but I'm
going to have a drink very soon with Dan.

CHAPTER TWENTY-FOUR

Parking at The Tides is not a task to be taken lightly. There's always some drunk who will block your car in. I park down the street two or three blocks away and walk down some alleys. I've got a gun. I'm a good shot now.

The Tides is a converted warehouse at the end of the dock. It's authentic, not one of those chains that brings in a couple of buoys that have been professionally banged up to look like they've weathered a nor'easter and sun-bleached floats covered in heavy netting, none of which have ever seen sea water.

The building is painted blue and features a broad white and navy stripe on its awning over the door. "THE TIDES" is spelled out in thin pieces of driftwood on the bright red, newly painted door.

Very patriotic.

Looking around at the parking lot, I don't see Dan's truck. I'm glad to be here first. I can sit where I can see who's in the bar. That's not a cop thing, by the way. It's more of a being-kidnapped-and-stalked thing.

I go inside and find a seat next to the massive saltwater tank with a school of clownfish and others I can't name. Hayden would be able to. He is, or at least was, a walking encyclopedia of fish species. He should have become a marine biologist in a perfect world. Ours, however, was not a perfect life or world. He was placed with foster parents after I left. He did well in high school but joined the army instead of going to a college. My fault. If I had stayed with him and supported him, however I could, he could have gone on to live a normal life. I was only seventeen. And I was supposed to be dead. It was the only way I thought I could protect him. I left him with foster parents who would love him. Not as much as I do, but I had thought he would at least have a chance to be normal. I find myself looking around the room, hoping to spot him there in the bar.

The waitress quickly goes to another table. I've hit the point in my life where I'm almost invisible. Service at a bar or restaurant is slow. Talking with the waiter or anyone is nonexistent unless I'm willing to dress provocatively. If Ronnie or Mindy were here, I'd already have a drink.

Dan walks in and gives me a little wave and a big smile. I can feel my pulse pick up and remember the last time we were here and he kissed me. We were in the parking lot, intending to go to our respective homes. The kiss was lingering and I kissed him back. It was one of those rom-com moments where the big hunk of manliness kisses the girl and her knees go weak. I don't like feeling weak. It scares me.

Dan is wearing a red-and-black plaid shirt with the sleeves rolled up on his muscular arms and a red sock hat cocked back on his head. He has on painter's pants, tight fitting in all the right places, and suede Caterpillar boots. With his short brown beard he looks like Paul Bunyan.

He's dressed like this because of our earlier conversation.

Smartass.

He poses in front of me. "What do you think?"

"Where's your axe and your blue ox?"

"In the back of the truck," he says, and merely has to raise two fingers of his hand before a young female waitress smiles and comes our way. We both order Scotch. He orders his neat. I ask for one cube of ice, then change my mind and ask for lots of ice. I don't want to get drunk.

The waitress doesn't even look at me. Her attention is turned on Dan, and as she walks away, she looks back over her shoulder and wags her ass like a happy dog on her way to get our drinks.

"Friend of yours?" I ask.

He grins and it would melt an ice shelf. "Jealous?"

I laugh it off. "In your dreams, Bunyan." Unless I wanted something.

"What have you been up to lately, Megan?"

His voice is mellow and soothing. Sincere. I'm glad I came.

"Busy," is all I say. I don't want to talk about my day. I want to forget it. Just for a while. He seems to read my mood and takes a sip of his drink.

"How about you?" I ask, remembering to be social.

"Same here. I sold four pieces this morning."

"That's great!" I realize I say that a little too enthusiastically. It sounds fake. "So business is good?"

He nods and takes another sip. He seems nervous or uncomfortable. I'm making him uncomfortable. Damn.

He has opened his store and is there part time and at his cabin at Snow Creek the rest of the time. He does his carving and painting at his cabin. He would have massive complaints if he ran a chainsaw all day in town.

"How's the new hire?"

"A high school kid. I think she'll work out, but she has a hard time making change without a calculator. I got a register that tells the change on the slip so she can count it out of the drawer. All in all, I'm happy with her."

"Her"? I hope she's not as nipply as the waitress. "That's great," I say. "I like the business cards you had made. I put one up in the office."

"I'm having my girl build a website for me," he says.

"My girl"? What the hell?

"These younger people have a knack for that kind of stuff. It should be up and running in a few days."

I decide to change the subject slightly. I have questions that pertain to my case and I need to ask them without being too obvious. This gives me the perfect opportunity.

"I guess you put in a business telephone?" I ask.

"Had to since I'm not at the store all the time. Jess takes the orders. Makes out the invoices. Other things."

I'll bet she does.

"Back to the crank calls, please?"

"It's a business, Megan. Some people get cranky if they don't get exactly what they want. I think they're just trying to get a better price."

That's not what I meant. "I've had a complaint of kids crank-calling people from here to Hadlock," I say.

"That's kids for you," he says, and I'm getting frustrated.

"Are you getting them at the store or at home?" I ask point-blank.

"Are you?" he asks. His face has gone serious.

"Dan, just tell me if you've been getting crank calls. Hang-up calls. Anything suspicious."

He's never been this evasive before. I wonder if that's what's making him seem uncomfortable. I say, "You just seem uncomfortable. Is there something you're not telling me?"

CHAPTER TWENTY-FIVE

Dan orders another round of drinks. We sit and don't talk until they arrive. He takes a long sip, puts it down, and takes my hand in his. His hand is rough, calloused and warm. I don't pull away even though I don't like to be touched. The bar is full and conversations tend to be loud depending on how much alcohol the speaker has consumed.

Dan scoots his chair over closer so we can hear each other without being loud. His smile is gone and he looks serious. He reaches into the pocket of his jeans and my heart leaps into my throat. I'm not ready for this. If it's a ring, I'll never be ready for this. I'm thrilled but I'm scared to death. I can't take my eyes from the hand stuffed in his pocket.

He pulls something out and my eyes follow his hand as he lays it on the table in front of me. It's a photo. The one the sheriff showed me yesterday. The one of me coming from the Sheriff's Office. The one found at the crime scene.

"How did you get that?" My heart goes from being in my throat to being on the floor. I'm not exactly disappointed but I'm completely caught off guard.

I know Dan is friends with Mindy but I doubt she would give him a piece of evidence. "Did Mindy give you this?"

He doesn't answer. He still has that serious expression. He reaches into his pocket and takes out another photo. This one is laminated. This one of a younger me, blond, half a smile. I know

Dan couldn't have that one because it's still in my pocket. The only one who has seen it is Sheriff Gray.

He's looking at me questioningly, as if he deserves an explanation. I'm the detective. I'll ask the questions.

"Where did you get these, Dan?" I ask this in my detective's voice. He still doesn't answer. I'm not used to being at a loss for words.

"This one"—I put my finger on the one where I'm leaving the Sheriff's Office—"was left at a crime scene yesterday morning. A *murder* crime scene. How did you get it?"

Instead of answering, he pushes the laminated picture of a teenage Megan—when I was Rylee—toward me. I've never seen this side of him. He's always so easy to talk to. Non-judgmental. Never digging. That's the reason I like him. I don't like this guy.

"What do you want me to say, Dan?"

He breaks his silence. "I want you to explain why these were left in the mailbox at my cabin."

I down my Scotch in one swallow and look around for the waitress. Naturally, she's nowhere around. "I don't know."

"Don't know or won't say?"

"Honestly, Dan, I don't know."

"I saw on the news this morning that a woman was found murdered. The newscaster said you were working the case."

"I am," I say. "Can we just have our drinks? I don't want to talk about work."

"And now you're asking me about strange phone calls." Dan pushes his drink away. He looks angry and concerned and it's not a good look for him.

"I told you why I asked about the phone calls."

"I never thought you'd lie to me, Megan."

"I'm not lying. Yes, I'm working the murder. Yes, I have a case where crank calls play into it."

I don't tell him the calls are probably made by the murderer. I feel guilty for not telling him that he might possibly be in danger because of me. I don't tell him any of that because someone, maybe the killer, has left the photos at Dan's place in Snow Creek. I don't know what connection he's made that is making him act this way.

"Are you in danger, Megan?" he asks.

I want so badly to tell him what's going on, but I don't dare. If I tell him, it will make him more of a target, make him paranoid like me, make him hate me for what I've done to bring this down on myself.

"I can take care of myself, Dan."

I smile. The smile is a mask.

"I don't know why someone would leave these for you."

Before I can pick them up from the table, he puts a hand on them. "I called Mindy."

Uh-oh.

"She said a picture just like this was left at the crime scene." He puts his finger on the office picture. "What's going on?"

"I can't discuss it with you, Dan. The investigation is just beginning and Mindy shouldn't have told you anything."

"Who is the girl in the other picture?" he asks.

"I have no idea. I've never seen that picture before."

He looks at me for several seconds. "It's a picture of you when you were a girl. Don't tell me it's not."

"I don't know what you're talking about," I say, but I can tell he doesn't believe me. I wouldn't, either.

He puts the pictures back in his shirt pocket. "Then you don't need these." He downs his drink and gets up. "I've got to go."

"Dan, wait," I say, but he is halfway to the door. I watch him leave. I wonder how a simple evening drink can turn into an interrogation. Welcome to my world.

CHAPTER TWENTY-SIX

Across the street she can see inside The Tides. Rylee and her man are having what can only be a lover's quarrel. Rylee only shows concern when the man leaves in a huff. He's someone she cares about deeply. She watches him go to his truck and follows, thinking about the similarities between herself and Rylee. Rylee is strong willed. But so is she.

She only made it out of Ecuador because of her extremely strong will, not just to live, but to survive. Those two things were different. One was to barely hang on. The other was to do whatever it took to gain some ground. Because of her cunning, she was able to stow away on an oil freighter. Because of her survival skills, she traded whatever favors she had with the crew and so was brought ashore in America. A little the worse for wear, but alive, her stomach full, hope in her heart.

All she had were the clothes on her back. Little more than rags, except for a T-shirt and a too-big pair of work boots she'd stolen from the crew's quarters. She ended up being sold as a laborer to an abattoir, a slaughterhouse for animals. Her station on the floor was at the end of the line. Cows' heads hung from meat hooks and she would trim off the flesh.

The knives she has now, six of them, blades five to nine inches, each as sharp as a surgeon's scalpel, are irreplaceable. A gift from Alex Rader when he saved her. He said it was to keep her senses sharp and remind her where she came from.

If she closes her eyes, even after all these years, she can smell the stench of blood, hear the impacts and grunts of the cattle as they were put down. She hated the sights of slaughter but it was a job that didn't require identification. She was an illegal. She had none. They didn't care where she came from or where she went at the end of her fourteen-hour shift. They paid in cash at the end of each day.

Her boss at the slaughterhouse took half of her pay for finding her. He allowed her to live in his basement with other girls but charged them rent. His friends paid him to have at her. She was sleepwalking through life. Horror became the norm.

Then her boss decided she could make more money working the streets in Seattle. He dressed her up and put her in his stable of girls. He told her she wasn't attractive. She knew that. But what she lacked in looks she made up for in skills. During that time he got her strung out on heroin. Her life on the streets was tough, but she was tougher. Or so she thought.

Then the craving for drugs became more important than surviving. She lost weight. Her nails and hair became brittle. Then came the arrest and the beginning of a new life.

Now when she looks in a full-length mirror she can smile at what she sees. She has filled out over the years. Breast implants and time at a gym have transformed her once emaciated body into Alex's idea of a beautiful woman. She still didn't see it herself, but if he said it, that was enough.

Then the girl took him from her. When he was gone—murdered by the girl named Rylee—she discovered through an attorney that he had left everything to her. After his death, everything would have gone to his legal wife, with a small amount going to her. It would have been enough to buy a small place of her own. Enough to buy a decent vehicle. But the girl murdered Marie, his legal wife, too. The Raders' wills left everything to her on the wife's death.

Marie knew about her. They even met. Were somewhat friends. She is doing this for Marie as well as for herself, but mostly for him. For Alex. Rylee took everything from them. From her. She cares nothing for what she now owns. She'd give it all up tomorrow if she could have Rylee's head on a meat hook, coming down the line, where she waits to flay that face down to the bone. It is her right. It is her duty. It is fitting that all of his enemies are killed with a knife. That was how Marie died. That is the way they will all die.

She will save Rylee for last.

CHAPTER TWENTY-SEVEN

I walk to my car. I'm caught. Whoever is doing this is using my personal life to get to me. Taunting me. Exposing me. Distracting me from chasing them down. They don't realize they're just fanning the flames. I can always move. Take on a new persona, a new job, a new life. They'll be dead.

When I get home, I go right back to the tape player.

Dr. A: Did the dream have meaning for you?

Me: Caleb told me one time that dreams were messages from your subconscious. I'm more practical than that, but I let him believe that I agreed. I hated lying to him, but I saw the lie as a way to get just a little bit closer to him. So if he was right and I was wrong—and I don't like admitting it—what was that dream, that horrific dream, telling me? Was Selma me? Was Selma my mother? We're both blond, not dark-haired like Selma. Our hair is straight, not the mass of curls of the girl running away from the van.

Then it begins to hit me. I roll out of the bed and go to the bathroom, where I sit on the toilet and cry. I am crying so loudly that I turn on the shower so people in the motel room next door can't hear. In the mirror I see my mother again. Not a ghost or a spirit or whatever, but the essence of her in my face. I don't say the words, but they move from my mind to wherever my mom is being held.

Hold on.
I'm coming.
I will make him pay with his life.
We will be free.

Dr. A: Did you have doubts? Weren't you afraid?

Me: I was only fifteen—sixteen at the most. I'm a girl. I've never shot a gun or hurt anyone in my life. All the odds are against me except the one thing that my bio-dad could never count on. I am determined to be as ruthless as he is.

I put the tape player away. I'm done in. I need to sleep. I need to decide if I can be as ruthless as this killer. The answer comes right away.

Yes, I can.

CHAPTER TWENTY-EIGHT

The next morning, on my way to the office, I think about calling Clay. I was caught off guard by his interest in me the other day. Actually, that's not totally correct. I could sense something there before. And Ronnie said that she thought Clay was "sweet on me." I don't want to encourage that.

I didn't do so well with Dan last night. He walked out of the bar on me and was in a foul mood. No, he was hurt. I don't blame him for thinking I'm lying about the pictures, because I am, and Dan is pretty attuned to my thoughts.

Maybe going out with another detective would be easier. Out with the old, in with the new. Clay might understand when I don't want to answer questions about a case. Or not. Maybe it would be worse. Considering his police background, Clay would be more of a problem to lie to.

I decide to call him. Make it clear that I'm dating someone. Not that Dan will ever ask me out again. But I definitely don't want to date a cop.

I look up the call he made to me yesterday and punch the number. "Detective Osborne, this is Detective Carpenter."

"Hi, Megan. You can still call me Clay, even though I *am* somewhat of a hero. Thanks, by the way, for cleaning up that mess for me."

He is referring to the case last month where I unveiled two serial killers and helped him and another county clear several homicides.

I felt he owed me one. That was why I called and asked him to guard Gabrielle until she arranged to stay with someone.

He asks, "Am I supposed to call you Detective Carpenter now?"

I could hear the humor in his voice. *Shut up, I'm trying to be serious*, I think. "No. Megan's fine."

He's laughing now. It's not really funny. I ask, "So what's going on with Gabrielle? She didn't call to tell me she'd arrived. Did she call you?"

"She didn't call me, but I told her to avoid using that phone and get another one. She'll call you and give you her number. She probably hasn't had time to get one."

He is right, of course.

"I'll have someone go by her house randomly and check it for a couple of days," he adds. "She'll do fine. I told her to contact you or me before she comes back to get the all clear."

"Thanks for doing all this, Clay."

"Hey, I owed you one. Right?"

Yes, you did. You still owe me. "You don't owe me anything. We're a team, right?"

He laughs. "Speaking of which, I wonder if you and Ronnie would like to come have drinks with me tonight. Not as a date. Just coworkers that kick ass and chew bubblegum. I'm buying."

I almost say I already have a date, but Dan may be a thing of the past. And I may have to set up a protection team to keep an eye on Dan now. But I can't afford to piss Clay off because I might need another favor. I say, "Maybe some other time, Clay. We're going to be busy for a while on this."

"Gotcha. If I can do anything on this end to help out, just let me know."

"Thanks, Clay. I will." And I mean it as I disconnect. I wonder how I've gotten so popular all of a sudden. It can't be because of the pile of dead bodies I seem to attract. Maybe it's not being emotionally available? Men seem to like that. And big breasts. I don't have those. But Clay also invited Ronnie, and she can give Dolly Parton a run for her money.

I pull up in the Sheriff's Office lot and can't help looking up into the woods where my stalker was. I think about putting a bear trap out, and an image of Nan with a trap attached to her bare ass makes me smile.

CHAPTER TWENTY-NINE

Back in the office, Nan approaches me and whispers, "Dr. Andrade's office called."

I whisper back, "What about?"

She gets a hurt look on her face. "Well. You should call them."

"I was just about to. Thanks, Nan."

She doesn't know whether to be insulted or pleased. She leaves. That's good. I'm not in the mood to feed her need for gossip today. Ronnie comes to my desk.

"Dr. Andrade called."

"I know. Nan just whispered in my ear," I say. I hear papers being stacked hard against Nan's desk. She has heard me with her super-hearing. I really don't care.

"I've called all the people in Mrs. Delmont's address book. The ones who were answering. I got nothing more than what we have already."

"Clay told me you took the samples to Marley at the crime lab," I say.

"I did. He's got the mug with the lipstick and the things you found outside here, but he doesn't have a DNA sample from the victim yet. He's waiting on the autopsy. He says he can get us pretty quick results. I think he was excited to be working on something like this with me."

"Can you call Dr. Andrade's office and see if they have a time for the autopsy yet?" I don't want to go. I remember what happened last time. The sight of all that cutting triggered some memories best forgotten. Ronnie had weathered it like a veteran. But she's not seen, or done, the things I have.

"I think he already did the post. He's sending samples to Marley at the lab. His secretary said he wants to talk to you."

Me. What have I done now? "Okay, I'll call him. Can you start writing up what we did yesterday?"

She hands me a set of typed sheets. It's the report I just asked for. I don't know how she manages to type so fast with a fractured wrist.

"I didn't put anything in there that can lead anyone to Gabrielle or her son," Ronnie says quietly. "I've got another report with all of that information saved on a thumb drive. I don't want someone getting into my computer."

Ronnie has been sitting at a vacant desk since coming on board. She was originally only here to do a rotation through the various sheriff units. She would have been with us a week at most but my last case changed that. She is still a reserve deputy, but I think Sheriff Gray has other plans for her. She doesn't have her own computer and has had to work off of the office server. I need to get her a password so she can protect her things. I think of doing that because of Nan and the fact that someone is stalking me. Which means they could be stalking Ronnie as well.

"Ronnie, you need to keep alert until this is over. I don't want a repeat of last month."

"That wasn't your fault, Megan. If you hadn't been there…" The shocked look on her face is real. "I owe you my life. Do you think the killer is coming after you?"

I do. I'm torn between not panicking her and keeping her aware enough to not become a victim. She's a grown woman and so I decide to tell her enough to keep her on her toes.

"Let's step outside."

She follows me outside. I want to get a little distance between us and Super Nan. We walk out to where I found the cigarette butt, the candy wrapper and the lace underwear.

"This is where I found that stuff on Monday."

She looks back toward the office. She had seen the picture collected from the crime scene. "The person taking the picture was here," she says.

"I'm guessing. But if they were, look how out in the open this is. Anyone could have seen them." But I didn't.

"They weren't too worried about being noticed," she says.

"Or they didn't look suspicious in the least. We have to consider that the person who took the picture is one of us." I don't know that, and I don't even think that, but I want her to be souped-up alert. The expression that crosses her face tells me I've done my job in that regard. We've already run into that scenario once.

"I don't want to talk much in the office. And I don't want to leave anything out on the desks until we have a better handle on what we're dealing with."

"I understand. I won't make copies until we're ready to go to the sheriff. Have you told him your concerns?"

The sheriff knows what my concern is. He knows I'm going to keep this below the radar if possible. I don't want anyone to put me together with Monique's past. I still don't know where Michael Rader fits in, if at all. He's a wild card. I wouldn't put it past him to be setting me up for Monique's murder. He knows about me. He could be the one leaving my picture everywhere. The fact that Dan has the same pictures worries me.

"While I call Dr. Andrade, I want you to do something for me. As discreetly as possible."

She picks up a notepad from my desk and a pen.

"Michael Rader," I say. "He's a white male, middle-aged, maybe in law enforcement somehow."

She raises an eyebrow at that last.

"Gabrielle gave me the name," I tell her, and that's not a lie. "See what you can find, and this is just between us."

"Of course," Ronnie says.

I call Dr. Andrade.

CHAPTER THIRTY

I was put through to Dr. Andrade immediately. Normally the secretary would have asked questions and said the doctor would call me back.

"Andrade here, Megan."

"You wanted me to call. Have you done the post already?"

"That's what I want to talk to you about. Do you know who this woman's doctor was? Did you find any prescription bottles at the scene?"

"We didn't find anything at the scene. I searched her home in Tacoma and didn't find any prescriptions there, either. Hang on a minute." I call out to Ronnie. "Can you look through the address book for any doctors?"

To Dr. Andrade I say: "Ronnie found her address book and she's looking for doctors now. It may take a few minutes."

Ronnie dutifully flips pages. The address book is quite thick.

"That Ronnie's a firecracker," Dr. Andrade says.

I'll bet he never says that about me.

"Why do you need to know about a doctor? Did you find something I need to know about?" As far as I knew, Monique was in perfect health, except for taking Xanax. I'd stolen her Xanax when I was there a few years back. I thought it would be a weapon. Poison.

Ronnie found a doctor's name in Tacoma. I provide it to Dr. Andrade and he repeats it back.

"I'll give them a call," he says.

"Tell me how she died." I wasn't letting him off the line that easy.

"Exsanguination," he says.

"She bled out."

"Yes."

"Why do you need to talk to her doctor?"

"Megan, it may be nothing. I'd like to check with them first before I commit."

I've caught him making mistakes on his reports before. He has a mind like a steel trap, and just as unforgiving. I need to know what he has. "Tell me what you think. I won't hold you to it. It might have bearing on what I do next."

Dr. Andrade let out a breath. "Okay. Fine. But you understand that there might be a simple explanation. In any case, the cause of death was loss of blood."

I waited.

"There was an agent in her system that I've never run across before. All I can tell you right now is that it has paralytic properties. Like succinylcholine. That's what they use sometimes for surgery."

"Can you spell that for me?"

"I can't tell you what it is. I'm just saying it's a paralytic like succinylcholine."

"Please. I just want to keep it in my notes." He spells it for me. "Do you have any idea how it got in her system?"

"I can't tell you yet. I found a needle mark on the skin of her neck. I've taken a biopsy of the neck muscle where the injection—if that's what it is—was placed to see if I can find the same chemical. I sent it to the crime lab but it'll be a while before they get back to me."

"Were there any other injuries?" I ask, as if being skinned isn't enough.

"I didn't find any broken bones. There were no abrasions or cuts on the skin that would indicate anything other than the skin being removed. I can tell you this: whoever did this is a professional with a blade. I don't know many surgeons who could have done that to her. It had to be a very sharp instrument. I would say a scalpel, but there are indications that it was a longer blade. Maybe six or seven inches. Like a fillet knife. A damn sharp one."

He pauses and I can tell he has something else to say. I wait, not knowing where he's going with all of this.

"Megan, if the chemical is a paralytic like succinylcholine she would have been conscious but unable to move. She may have been alive when her skin was removed. The pain would be so great that she wouldn't have stayed conscious for long, but she might have lived until she bled out."

My heart is still in my chest and my throat tightens. I feel dizzy and take several breaths before the world is back in focus. His words run through my mind like a song you can't stop thinking of.

She may have been alive when her skin was removed.

The bastard paralyzed her and then sliced her skin from her body. It's personal. It's more than that. It's a threat.

To me.

CHAPTER THIRTY-ONE

We're back in the office. Ronnie gives me the address book. I'm going to make the calls she already made and the ones she might have missed. I might get lucky if someone remembers something after the first call.

Ronnie is going to run Michael Rader down. If she can't find him, I can supply things I know about him and tell her it came from Gabrielle.

"Gabrielle didn't give you much to go on. There are forty-two Michael Raders in Washington. Five of them are females. 'White male' narrows it down to thirty-one. 'Middle-aged' I take to mean older than thirty and younger than fifty. There are fourteen that fit. Maybe we can get a better description from Gabrielle, since she gave you the name."

"I don't think she'll be any help. She said her mother told her the name at one time or other and she thought Monique was afraid of the man. She gave Gabrielle the description that I gave you in case he bothered her."

Ronnie pauses and looks up from her notes. "I can tell you that none of the Raders I found have police records. If that helps."

It doesn't.

I know that Michael was a correctional officer. I can call the prison and see if he's still employed there. I can get his personal information from their personnel. I'll tell them I'm doing a background check for a car loan. Or I can have Ronnie do that, but I'd have to tell her what prison.

My phone rings again and I don't recognize the number. "Detective Carpenter," I say.

"This is Gabrielle. Have you found out anything?"

"Not much right now, Gabrielle. How are you doing?"

"As good as can be expected with what's going on."

"I don't need to know where you are; I just want you to be safe."

"Thank you for coming to let me know in person. I haven't told my son what's going on. If I tell him his grandmother is dead, he'll wonder why I'm here and not making funeral arrangements. I'll have to come home soon."

"I understand. Call me before you do any traveling, okay?"

"I'll do that, but can you keep me informed, please?"

"Yes. I have a question. The coroner needs to know what medications your mom was taking. There was nothing at the"—I almost say "crime scene"—"house she had rented. And there were no medicines at her house in Tacoma. Do you know if she was taking anything?"

"She wasn't on any medication."

"Are you sure?"

"She used to take something for depression. When Leanne's killer was… gone, she found she didn't need it anymore. She was busy with her work, and it seemed to be enough. Why?"

"The pathologist found a chemical in her blood. He was just wondering if it was a prescribed medication."

"My mom would never take an illegal drug, if that's what they think."

"I'll tell them what you've told me. They're trying to get an identification of the chemical right now. I'll let you know."

"Okay. This is a new phone. Should I call Clay and give it to him? He was so nice."

Clay? I wonder just how nice he is. "No. Not for now. We will keep it safe. Just call me when you plan on returning and I'll pass it on to Detective Osborne. It's better if fewer people have it."

"Thank you. Remember your promise."

"I will. Is there anything you need?"

"Just this guy dead."

Before she can disconnect I say, "By the way, what did your mom say about Michael Rader? Did she have any contact with him after that one time?"

Silence fills the line as she thinks for a moment.

"No. At least I don't think she did. But he scared her. *Really* scared her. She said you would know more about him than she would."

Monique was right about that. Except I had run from Michael Rader. I'd never faced him. And then I never tried to find him again. It's my fault that Monique is dead. I have to own that.

I ask one more question. "Can you give me a better description of Michael Rader? Any little thing your mom might have said."

"She said you might have a better description than she did. She was pretty shook up after talking to him. All she could think of was that he might come after me and Sebastian."

"That helps. I'll be in touch. If you feel unsafe, you should call me."

She promises and we disconnect. I hand Ronnie the phone number to store in her phone.

Just in case.

Ronnie looks at me expectantly. She's still standing at my desk. I say, "He works at a prison. She can't remember which one, but she thinks her mother said the women's prison in Gig Harbor. He's in his forties."

"That's great. Do you want me to call them?"

"Can you see if you can find a directory first? Maybe you can find something about the prison that will mention him in a news release or other activity."

"Good idea, Megan."

Of course it's a good idea. I've been doing this since you were shopping for expensive clothes or getting your hair styled.

CHAPTER THIRTY-TWO

Ronnie went home at the end of the shift. Sheriff had gone to some Civitan thing and wasn't going to be back. Nan left after looming over my desk, asking if we were getting anywhere with the murder. I told her an arrest was imminent. I figured I'd see myself quoted on the news tonight.

I went home, where I changed into jeans and a Washington State University T-shirt.

I slip my shoulder holster on. I take a kitchen chair and shove the back under the front doorknob. I would put salt on all the window ledges—salt is supposed to repel ghosts—but I don't think it would keep the ghost of my past outside. I've learned from experience that if someone wants in your house, they will find a way. I've done it myself. I also know that no matter how hard you try to keep the past out of your mind, it will come back. Through dreams, or worse, through people.

With a box of wine on the edge of my desk, I fill a plastic Solo cup nearly to the rim. The box of tapes and the player are already out and waiting for me. The little spools on the cassette tape look like greedy eyes, hypnotizing me, drawing me in.

I am getting nowhere with this case. My gut is telling me it is someone very close to Alex Rader. Each clue points to the same person: Michael Rader.

It's evening, and I imagine Ronnie is settled in, having a drink herself. Or watching *The Bachelor*. I don't watch much television except for the news. It's all delusion and lies and I already have enough of that in my life.

I decide to phone Ronnie.

"Megan. I was just thinking about calling you." She sounds excited.

"Did you find something?" My heart beats harder.

"I found a news article involving someone named Kim Mock. He apparently was arrested and charged with murdering a Megan Moriarty almost twenty years ago. He was killed in prison. But the interesting thing is there is a newspaper photo of him being transported from jail to prison. Guess who is transporting him?"

"Michael Rader," I say.

"Not only that, but when Mock was killed in prison, Michael Rader is the corrections officer who found the body."

Of course, I already knew this. I knew Michael had Mock killed by other inmates—or did the job himself—because Moriarty's family began questioning if the police had arrested the right guy.

"That's great, Ronnie. We'll get into it more in the morning. Take some time off and chill. We're going to be busy getting all the paperwork together."

My phone dings.

"I just sent you the picture from the article," she says.

I pull the picture up. It's Michael Rader all right. I came across the same picture years ago after Monique told me about him.

"Good work, Ronnie. I talked to Gabrielle. She remembered her mom said Michael had a brother named Alex Rader. He's a cop. Can you add that to your research list?"

"I'll get on it first thing in the morning. I'm going to have drinks with Marley and I'll find out what the crime lab is doing."

I thank Ronnie and end the call. I've lied to her before but I hate that I do it with such ease.

The tapes with all my secrets call to me and I select one regarding Shannon Blume's murder. I hope to find some answers in the past. If nothing else they help me think of who I was and who I've become. I slot the cassette, refill my wine and wait for the tape to begin.

Dr. A: Why were you in Kent? Staying at a Best Western, you said.

Me: Yes. I wanted to find out what happened to Leanne, Shannon, and Megan. I found a story in the paper about Shannon Blume's murder with a picture of the Blumes' home. A homeless guy named Steve Jones was arrested and convicted for Shannon's murder, but I knew it wasn't him. It was my bio-father.

I remember finding the Blumes' home and how it looked just like it did in the online newspaper article. It was a single-story rambler with white shutters and matching window boxes. In front was a monkey puzzle tree that had grown nearly as tall as the roofline.

Me: There was a photo of Don and Debra Blume in the story. I found the house easily and peered through the window of the garage. Two cars were there. One was a Ford Focus, like the one I was driving. My mother had taught me how to manipulate people. To be what they needed me to be. I thought I would act as though I loved my car or hated it, depending on whatever they said about theirs.

The tape goes silent. I'm thinking of what I want to reveal.

Dr. A: Take your time.

Me: Mrs. Blume answers the door with a wary but kind smile. I tell her I'm with the North Bend Courier *newspaper. I ask if she had heard about our series on Marilee Watson who was murdered last year. I tell her my editor wants me to do a new series about how people cope after a tragedy and ask if I can talk to her and Mr. Blume.*

She said, "You can't cope after a tragedy, Miss?…" She searches her memory for my name, and I hand her a business card I've stolen from the newspaper office.

I say, "I'm Tracy Lee. That's the point of my article. My aunt Ginger was killed in a car wreck and I know it's not the same as what happened to Shannon, but my mom has never gotten over it, either. I'm including my thoughts about that in the article too. But it can't be about me."

I wonder if I remind her of her own daughter. If she thinks I'm too young for the job. If she's just having a bad day. Maybe every day after you lose a child to murder is a bad day.

She says, "It was a long time ago. We really don't like reliving it. I'm sure you can understand that." Of course I did. I hate that I'm opening old, never-really-healed wounds, but I have no choice. I told her it wasn't my intent to hurt her again.

I stop the tape. I have to revisit the Blumes. If they still live in Burien, they would be in their mid- to late sixties by now. Retired. Hopefully at home.

CHAPTER THIRTY-THREE

Wide awake at 4:00 in the morning. I try to go to sleep again but my mind is churning, working the case. I feel like I didn't sleep but only lay completely still with my eyes shut. I give up and take my .45 out from under the pillow on the other side of the bed. I've taken to sleeping in jeans and T-shirt, boots beside the bed at the ready. The stalker started this. The killer has only made it worse. I get up and pad, sock-footed, to my desk.

I left the tape player out, ready to go. I know this is the tape that covers my conversation—interrogation really—with the Blumes about the disappearance and murder of their daughter, Shannon. I don't have to play it. I remember it all like it was yesterday.

Dr. Albright had asked me if it was understandable that Mrs. Blume was hesitant to let me in. I said yes, I understood, but I had to talk to her. I told Mrs. Blume that it was important people learn the truth. And that some hurt never goes away. That others have gone through what she has and she's not alone in her pain.

What I said must have had the desired effect. Mrs. Blume had looked at me and said, "All right," and invited me inside. I felt a tremendous relief. I also felt a little sick for lying to someone about something so tragic, so important.

I remember feeling horrible even relating the story to Dr. Albright.

I lied to Mrs. Blume and said I would have called but with cell phones these days, no one has a landline anymore. Her house was neat, clean, frozen in time. The furnishings, the décor—even the air—felt old. The foyer was devoid of anything personal. A Boston fern the size of a Mini Cooper filled most of the space.

Mrs. Blume said she was making pizza and asked if I wanted to stay for some lunch. Her eyes were very kind.

I was still a little sick from the last food I ate but I said I was starving. That I hadn't eaten all day. And I told her thank you. I'd been there all of two minutes and had already lied to this nice woman five or six times. I had no choice, of course. If I had told her the truth, she probably would have laughed at me and called the police. That would have ruined my plans and have gotten my mother killed.

Dr. Albright asked: "So you continued to lie?"

I told her I wasn't proud of it, but, yeah. I remembered Donald Blume came into the room. He was older than his wife, but he had a nice smile and I liked him right away.

He said, "Doing a story about our little girl." He sat down, sinking into what I assumed was "his" chair, a big leather club chair.

I gave him the same line I'd given Mrs. Blume about the story I was doing. He said it would be a short story, and Mrs. Blume went to get the pizza.

That was when I saw Shannon's shrine. There were nearly a dozen pictures of a girl my age lining the mantel and a large silver urn, which I can only assume held her remains. I don't know why people keep ashes. I don't get that at all. The person is not the residue of their burned-up flesh and pulverized bones. The person is the spirit that was left when she was brutally killed. By my bio-dad.

Mr. Blume said Shannon's death had ruined their lives. He had taken to drinking. Debra had taken to antidepressants until she had to go into treatment.

I told him I was sorry. I didn't know what else to say.

He said he was too and I could see a sheen of tears behind his glasses. He said the short story was that Shannon was everything.

Dr. Albright asked if it helped me to find my mother.

I told her: "You have to understand that I needed these people to like me. I needed them to tell me what they knew. I needed to process all of it and somehow figure out where my mother was being held captive."

I pick another tape out of the box and slot it in. Before I turn it on I think back to that day. We ate pizza. If I think about it I can taste the chicken pesto, but I don't want to think about it. Disgusting.

CHAPTER THIRTY-FOUR

I start the tape.

> *Me: The Blumes started at the beginning. They told me about the kind of hurt that comes from when forced to identify their daughter's body on a gurney through the thick glass of the morgue's viewing room. And they told me how much they regret not telling her they loved her as much as they should have.*

> *Dr. A: That must have affected you greatly.*

Now I know what Karen was really asking was how I could be so callous. I wonder that myself sometimes but I live with it. On the tape I didn't answer her question.

> *Me: I watched Mrs. Blume put a trembling hand on her husband's. She's the stronger of the two.*
> *He asked her to get him a drink and I remember him saying, "And don't be stingy on it, either."*
> *I muttered something about being sorry and told them they at least got some justice. At least the killer was caught and punished.*
> *Mrs. Blume said in a small voice. "That's what they tell us."*
> *The remark was odd and I waited for her to explain.*
> *"Honestly, Tracy," she said, "we never really felt comfortable with the prosecution of Steve Jones, that homeless man, for the*

murder of our daughter. Don't get me wrong." She stopped and looked at her husband. She said, "Don't get us wrong. We don't doubt the prosecution did the best they could, but, well, we sort of believed Mr. Jones's alibi."

I was surprised. I didn't remember what his alibi was and then it came to me.

He'd said he was out drinking and had a blackout. A friend of his, another drunk, had told him the police had picked him up. He didn't remember that. The next thing Jones knew was that he was in front of Shannon's dead body when sirens woke him up.

I asked her who had called the police.

Mr. Blume said it was an anonymous caller. The police tape of the call was lost before trial. There was no evidence that the tape really existed, and who would believe a drunk?

I asked them if they thought Jones might have been set up.

Mr. Blume said they thought someone had tampered with the evidence. The homeless guy was convenient for the murder. He said they were happy about the conviction at first but there were other questions the police couldn't answer. He said Shannon was missing for a week and when her body was found she had a tattoo.

I pause the tape. I remember the tattoo clearly. A heart with the number 16 inside it. Alex's trademark. All of his victims had the tattoos. I continue listening.

Me: Mr. Blume said Shannon would never have gotten a tattoo. He showed me a picture of her taken at a Highline High School performance of Les Misérables. He said she played Cosette. She was beautiful and perfect.

Dr. A: How did you feel about bringing up memories for Shannon's parents? It must have been hard to listen to.

Me: Mr. Blume wasn't kidding about getting into a bottle. When he'd asked his wife not to be stingy with the drink, it had nothing to do with the number of ice cubes she put in it. His head bobbed slightly and his words were beginning to slur. He was getting drunk.

Mr. Blume said something about the detective leaving the tattoo out of the investigation.

I asked Mrs. Blume what the detective's name was. She couldn't remember but would call if it was important. I told her it was important.

I stop the tape and look at my watch. I still have to shower and get ready for work. I check that the chair back is still under the doorknob, then go to the bathroom with my .45 in hand. I lay the weapon on top of the toilet tank, farthest from the door and closest to the shower. I'll play the rest of the tape when I get a chance. So far nothing jumps out at me, but something is circling in my mind like a hawk looking for prey. I'm sure somewhere on that tape Mr. or Mrs. Blume talked about a detective coming to their house but she couldn't recall his name.

I ignore the shower and go back to the desk, naked except for my T-shirt.

CHAPTER THIRTY-FIVE

I feel ridiculous sitting here with just a T-shirt on, but I need to hear the rest of the tape. I remember Mrs. Blume calling me at the hotel later that night. I stop fast-forwarding and hit "play."

Me: I came back to my room and saw a blinking light on the phone. It was a voice mail left by Mrs. Blume. The insistent tone in her voice was anything but calm. She wanted me to call her right away.

Dr. A: That must have been unsettling, Rylee.

Me: I called and she answered on the first ring but now she sounded unsure if she should have called. Or maybe she was afraid to call. She told me the detective I'd asked about had called her. Then he came to their house and asked questions about me. His name was Alex Rader. He told them I was an imposter bent on stirring up trouble.

Dr. A: That must have been a shock. A surprise. Did you think he was following you?

Me: Of course, I pretended to be at a loss why he would say that. But I know I have been an imposter my entire life. But so has he. He's lived among the shadows, doing evil at night. During the day he masquerades as an upstanding citizen. A cop. I know that he's killed all those girls. Maybe others. I know he has my mother right now. I just don't know where.

I asked if they'd told him where I was.

She said, "No. I never trusted or liked him whatsoever. Neither did my husband. He was nothing more than a conceited snot that never gave one whit about Shannon. He said all the right words, but I knew he was just looking for a notch on his detective shield."

I told her that I knew the type all too well. Such a fraud.

I gave her my thanks and our conversation ended with her saying, "I could tell when we talked that you care about Shannon."

I hung up and my pulse quickened.

I remember ending that call, my adrenalin pumping. *Alex Rader was trailing me. I wondered who would find who first? If it was a competition, I intended to win.* Two minutes later I was on the road. Since Alex Rader was a cop, my respect for the cops nosedived that day. My stepfather, Rolland, once said that the police are limited in what they can do, but I know that there was at least one among them—and maybe more—who did what they wanted no matter the price. Going to the police? Mom went there for help and look how it turned out for her. It is one thing of two that I know she and I will agree on. The other is that Hayden must never know what I know to be true. Like Mom, I carry that burden now. I love my little brother too much to have him live a life knowing that his heart circulates poisoned blood.

Like mine.

CHAPTER THIRTY-SIX

I drive on autopilot as if my car knows the way to the office. Leanne Delmont, Shannon Blume, Megan Moriarty. They are all victims of Alex Rader. They are on my mind. I wish I could avenge them again. I have killed Alex Rader, the serial killer. I have killed Marie Rader, his assistant and motivation to continue the killing spree. I thought I had cut the head off of the snake, but now it seems to have grown another.

I have to figure out who is finishing what those two sick, psychopathic assholes started.

I pull into the Sheriff's Office parking area and automatically look up into the trees. Nan is out at the edge of the lot with a cigarette in one hand and a cell phone in the other. She sees me and hurriedly crushes the cigarette under the toe of her shoe and gets off the phone. As I get out of the car she walks past me.

"Good morning, Detective Carpenter."

"Morning, Nan," I say. I want to call her Nannette, her real name, but I know it bugs her and I don't need to piss her off.

She goes inside and lets the door slam behind her. I go over to where she's crushed out the cigarette. It has the same color of lipstick on the filter as the one I sent to the lab for testing. But it's a Virginia Slim, not a Camel. I bag the cigarette butt.

Ronnie has beat me to work. She's typing on her computer keyboard like a concert pianist. I motion for her to come to my desk.

"Did you have a good time with Marley?" I ask.

"All he did was talk about science and things I'm barely familiar with. I felt like I was out with Bill Nye the Science Guy."

We both chuckle. Marley looks nothing like Bill Nye but he definitely had the science guy routine down.

"I had him send his lab report directly to me," Ronnie says in a whisper. "The DNA on the coffee mug matched the body. The DNA we took from Gabrielle suggested she was the daughter of the victim. The DNA from the items you found out in the trees wasn't in the database. It's an unknown. Marley was a little angry that he had to check it, but I told him I found it and put your name on the request form. I told him you said it was a waste of time but I had a hunch."

I like this girl more each day.

"Thanks, Ronnie. At least we have the DNA on file in case something else turns up." As I say that I can't help but feel I've jinxed myself. I don't want anything else to turn up because I don't want anyone else to die.

"I've got something else that I'd like him to run." I hand her the bag with Nan's cigarette butt. "It needs to be eliminated from the other things I—you—found out there. If those things belonged to Nan, she won't have DNA on file, either, but he can tell if that butt matches the other butt. If it does, we can probably pitch all that stuff."

Ronnie grins mischievously. "So you've got Nan's butt in a bag and you want Marley to look at her butt to compare it to another butt?"

"May the best butt win," I say, and Ronnie giggles. It isn't that funny, but it kind of is.

"I checked on Alex Rader," Ronnie says. "He was a detective with King County Sheriff's Office. He disappeared a couple of years back. No trace of him."

I'm surprised. I thought his body would eventually be found. The smell would draw attention. Marie had found him. I wonder what she did with his body. I know they found hers, because they made a big fuss over it, since Alex was a cop. One of theirs.

"His wife, Marie Rader, was found brutally murdered in their home. The detective I talked to said they suspect Alex might have killed her in a rage and fled. No one's heard from him. They don't have enough evidence to issue a warrant."

And they never will. "Were the murders anything like ours?" I ask, knowing they were nothing like ours.

"I told the detective we were working a case where the name Alex Rader was mentioned. It's not a totally uncommon name. I told him we'd get back to him if we had anything linking our case to their Alex Rader."

"It's probably nothing. I'm more interested in finding Michael Rader. Any luck there?"

Ronnie finds a photo on her phone, a face shot of a man, forty to fifty years old, craggy features, dark hair and eyes that look evil. "This guy was a corrections officer."

All I was able to find out was that Alex Rader had a younger brother, Michael. I only saw a photo of him in a news article.

"He was last at the men's correctional facility in Monroe," she says.

"Where is he now?"

"He moved six months ago. I haven't been able to find out where. I didn't want to call the prison without talking to you first."

"How did you find out he moved?"

"I checked utility companies around Monroe," Ronnie says. "I got an old address but there were no bills for the last six months. I assume he had the utilities turned off."

CHAPTER THIRTY-SEVEN

Michael Rader is in the wind. To find him I'd need Sheriff Gray's help. He could call the Snohomish County Sheriff's Office and check Michael out. The Monroe Correctional Complex is in that county. But to do that Sheriff Gray will want to know why I'm interested. I don't want to tell him more about my past.

I doubt he would have hired me if he knew everything about me. I know *I* wouldn't. I think that's because, deep down, I feel like a fraud. Dr. Albright warned me that it would be a lifelong battle and I might never fully believe that I am a good person but that the sins of my past don't define me.

Maybe I'm wrong about Michael Rader. Maybe the sins of *his* past don't define *him*. I'm sure he killed Kim Mock in prison, but he did it to protect his brother. He threatened Monique Delmont and got all the evidence I had given her against his scumbag brother. The evidence proving Alex was a serial killer. He must have found Marie's body after I killed her. I don't know how he could have known about me unless Marie or Alex told him about my mother and about Alex being my father.

"I'll talk to the sheriff," I say. "He knows the Snohomish County Sheriff and can get more information than we can."

"What should I do?"

"Call Mr. Bridges again. The guy from the victims' advocacy group. See if he can remember anyone in particular that Mrs. Delmont talked about." I'm hoping he mentions the names Blume and Moriarty. I want to get into those cases and find the dead girls' parents again. I want to see if they've also had hang-up calls. Part of the evidence Michael Rader took from Monique were pictures of their murdered daughters.

Ronnie hurries off and I take a deep breath before knocking on Sheriff Gray's door.

"Come in," he says, and I can hear a desk drawer closing.

When I enter, I can smell hamburgers and onions. I'm sure if I look in his drawer there will be a greasy bag full of the stuff. He's got a smudge on his chin. I don't point it out. Who am I to judge? His wife does enough of that to the point he has to hide his food like an alcoholic hides his bottles. Burger-aholic. That's him.

"You look like hell," he says.

I try to perk up. I don't do a good job of it.

"Sheriff, I need your help with this case," I tell him. I shut the door behind me and take a seat across from his desk.

"You're biting your nails again, Megan. What's wrong?"

I take my finger away from my mouth and wipe it on my slacks. I grip my hands in my lap and take another deep breath. I don't know how much I should tell him. I don't know *what* to tell him. I don't know because I might walk out of here in handcuffs.

He beats me to the punch. "This is to do with the picture I gave you, isn't it?"

I can feel my eyes water and I don't want to cry. I really like this man. I love my job. I love that I'm making a difference. Helping victims. Getting justice. Maybe in the form of vengeance, but justice all the same.

I nod. "I need to tell you some things. I hope you don't hate me when I'm through. The picture you gave me is me when I was sixteen. I was going to high school in Port Orchard."

He doesn't say anything. I notice some hamburger grease around his mouth and I know I'm deliberately distracting myself. I take another breath.

"I'm not going to quit this case," I say.

He nods. He knows he's not going to stop me.

"I'm being stalked by a man named Michael Rader."

Having said it out loud feels like a weight taken off my chest.

He doesn't ask why. He says, "What can I do to help? I assume this guy is part of your investigation."

His offer knocks me down. I expected him to take me off the case a long time ago. But he knows what this means to me. I tell him about Michael Rader's visit to Monique's house several years ago. I tell him of the threat he made to kill her daughter, Gabrielle, and her grandson. He doesn't ask how I know this but I'm sure he will someday.

"Are you sure it's him?" he asks.

"I had a kind of date with Dan Anderson a couple nights ago. Dan had both pictures. The one of me leaving here and the older one from high school. He said someone left them in the mailbox at his cabin. They were the same pictures you have."

"Do you think Dan is in danger?"

"I don't know. Can we spare anyone to keep an eye on him?" I ask.

"And you don't want Dan to know about it. Am I right?"

"He's already pretty pissed at me because I wouldn't tell him anything. If someone could just keep a loose watch on him, it would be great."

"I'll get a car out there."

I can breathe again. This is going better than I thought.

"Dr. Andrade said he found a chemical substance in Monique's system. A paralytic agent. He can't identify it yet. He thinks she may have been drugged and was alive when they did that to her." I can't say the words. I don't want the mental image again.

"Yang is working on it?" he asks.

"Right. And the coffee mug with lipstick we found in Monique's house matches the DNA of the victim. The DNA sample we took from Gabrielle matches, too, so we can now say it's definitely Monique Delmont."

I feel myself tear up again. I wonder if I'm doing the right thing here. Maybe I should beg off the case and let someone not emotionally involved investigate. The answer is no. I can't even if I wanted to.

"You think this Michael Rader is a good enough suspect to have him picked up?"

"Not yet," I say. I don't want him to know I'm coming for him. I don't want anyone to know what I did to his family. I don't want him found.

Ever.

"But there are some other things I didn't tell you about Monique."

"I'm listening," he says, getting the bag of hamburgers out of the drawer. He offers me one. I gobble it down before continuing. It may be my last meal.

CHAPTER THIRTY-EIGHT

I go back in the office and round Ronnie up and head to the car. I didn't ask Sheriff Gray to contact the sheriff of Snohomish County just yet. I'm afraid Michael will still have friends in the area that might tip him off that I'm looking for him. The good-old-boy network.

Now that I've put most of it out there for the sheriff, I'm not so worried about questions of how I know any of this.

"Where are we going?" Ronnie asks, getting in the car.

I start the engine and a thick cloud of smoke belches out of the tailpipe. "First, tell me what Mr. Bridges said."

She takes out her ever-handy notebook with its fancy leather cover and flips to a page she's marked. "He gave me some names. Most are recent victims' families."

"I want to hear the ones that are three or more years old."

"Okay." She flips some more pages. "Monique's daughter, Leanne, was murdered—"

"I know about that one," I say a little too quickly.

"Did you know she didn't believe the guy they caught was the killer?"

"I may have known that," I lie.

"Did you know that she thought two other murders were tied to her daughter's murder?"

I act surprised. "Two others?"

"A girl named Shannon Blume and a Megan Moriarty, both sixteen when they died."

"Did you look them up?" I am hoping she did.

"I've got the case number for each, the parents' information and the names of the detectives working the cases. Both cases happened almost twenty years ago. Right around the same time as Leanne Delmont."

"Where?"

"All in King County. Including Leanne."

"Who were the detectives?" I ask, like I don't know. "Are they still around?" I know we can't talk to him.

"A Sheriff's Office detective. Alex Rader." She says this with emphasis.

"The same Alex Rader that they think killed his wife? What was her name?"

"Marie Rader," ever-ready Ronnie says. "She was wheelchair-bound. He's the one who disappeared and was never heard from again. Don't you think it's odd that his brother has done a runner too?"

I agree. It only adds to my suspicion that Michael is our guy. "Do you have an address for Shannon Blume's parents? Do you know if they still live there?"

She has the address already pulled up on GPS and I hear that grating robot voice give directions. We head that way.

As I drive I remember where I first heard the names Shannon Blume, Megan Moriarty and Leanne Delmont. After my stepfather was killed, I fled the house with Hayden and we discovered that I had a key to a safe-deposit box in a Seattle bank. In that box I found several envelopes. Letters, newspaper clippings and a gun. One of the envelopes was marked in my mom's handwriting:

For my daughter's eyes only.

Another was marked for Hayden:

For my son's eyes only.

And it was in that letter to me that I found out the truth my mother had hidden from me until that day. I destroyed the letter, not wanting Hayden to ever know, but I remember it word for word.

Honey, I have lied to you. I lied because it was the only course of action to save you, save me, save Hayden.

She told me that the man we'd been running from our entire lives wasn't some jilted boyfriend or a stalker. He was my real father. Alex Richard Rader. A police detective. A serial killer. He'd tried to kill my mother but she told me she was the victim who got away.

If you decide to try to find me alive—I know I can't stop you—you will need to follow his trail. Look into the victims' pasts to find me.

Two things stand out immediately, now, as I remember her letter. My mom wrote that I had seven days to find her. Seven days between when the victim was kidnapped and killed. The other thing is her words. *Look into the victims' pasts to find me.* It's as if she's giving me clues to solve this case. Is she telling me there's a deadline too? And should I look into Monique's past or my own? I was a victim too. I was another one who got away.

CHAPTER THIRTY-NINE

It's a two-hour drive from Port Hadlock to Burien by way of the Bainbridge ferry. I originally found Don and Debra Blume's address in a library. I searched the Internet for Leanne and Megan. I tried to find Alex but he was a ghost. Now Ronnie had the address from police reports of Shannon Blume's death. The GPS guides us right to the house.

I pull up in front and it looks just as it did when I last visited. According to Ronnie's search engine, Don and Debra Blume still reside here.

"What reason are we going to give for why we're here?" Ronnie asks.

"I'll take care of it. Just follow my lead."

We go to the door and I ring the doorbell.

I hear someone inside saying, "Be right there." Probably Mrs. Blume. I am right.

Mrs. Blume answers the door and she looks ten years older than I remember from a few years ago. I've changed my hair, gained a little weight, and I know she'll mostly look at my badge. I'm still nervous that she'll recognize me.

"Can I help you?" she asks.

"Mrs. Blume?" I ask.

"Yes."

"I'm Detective Carpenter. This is Detective Marsh. We're with the Jefferson County Sheriff's Department. Can we ask you a couple of questions?"

"Of course. But excuse the house. I haven't done any cleaning today. Come on in."

She leads us into the same room where I pretended to be a reporter with the *North Bend Courier* doing a story on how people cope after a tragedy. She may have aged, but her house is still spotless. I don't see a sign of her husband, Don.

"Is Mr. Blume here as well?" I ask.

She indicates for us to have a seat, but I continue to stand. Ronnie has her notebook out and ready.

"Mr. Blume isn't here," she says, without elaborating.

I don't know if they've split up, he's died or maybe he's in rehab. It doesn't really matter, as long as he wasn't murdered.

"We hate to bother you, but we're working on a burglary case."

She looks around uneasily. "Not around here. We have very nice neighbors and I've never seen anyone suspicious."

"Nothing to be concerned about, Mrs. Blume. We're just checking out some phone numbers we found in a suspect's cell phone. One of them is your number."

Ronnie shows me the number on her notepad, but I have the number memorized. I tell Mrs. Blume the number and she looks shocked. I feel relieved. Probably no one has been here.

"That's our phone number, but I haven't been burglarized."

"We know. We checked with your local authorities before coming out."

That's a lie, but it seems to settle her down. "Why don't we have a seat?"

We all sit and the concerned look returns to her face.

"Mrs. Blume, the phone call only lasted ten seconds. It was probably misdialed. We still had to check with you personally to make sure you haven't been getting suspicious calls. You know: people calling and hanging up, crank calls, that kind of stuff."

"No. No. Not that I'm aware of. My husband used to sit on his phone and butt-dial people, but he hasn't had a phone for quite a while now."

"Can you tell me where your husband is?" I ask.

She looks at me in an odd way and I can see the flicker of a light coming on behind her thick glasses. I've changed my appearance but my voice hasn't changed. "You don't have to tell me. It's not part of what we're doing. I'm sorry."

"No. I'll tell you. He's in a nursing home. It's been over a year now. I wasn't able to care for him anymore here."

I don't want to bring up the past, especially since she's dealing with another tragedy. I can understand why she's aged. But I need to know if Rader has been back.

"Mrs. Blume, do you have children?"

She recoils as if I've punched her in the stomach. "We did. Not anymore."

"Mrs. Blume, I'm so sorry to bring back sad memories. But I have to ask if you've been contacted by anyone saying they are investigating that case?"

"Not for a long while. A detective came by and told me he was looking for someone pretending to be a reporter. I didn't like his looks. I didn't tell him anything and to this day I don't think he was really a policeman."

He was a serial killer, so her instincts were good. She's still looking at me. I can see wheels turning. It's time to end this. I hand her my card. "If anyone calls or comes by asking about that case, please call me."

I have an idea. "Detective Marsh, can you pull up the picture of Rader?"

She does and shows it to Mrs. Blume.

"Have you ever seen this man before?" I ask.

She studies it. Looks up at me, not Ronnie. "Does this have something to do with the burglar?"

"Maybe," I say. "Have you seen him before?"

"No. I've never seen this man. Is he dangerous?"

I'm already scaring the wits out of her, but I say, "We suspect this guy of doing home invasion burglaries. You know: pretends to be someone so they can get in your house. So please don't let anyone inside that you aren't sure of."

She's still looking at me in that odd way.

"We're sorry to have bothered you," I say, and we go to the front door and let ourselves out. I try not to run.

On the drive back to the Sheriff's Office, I can't stop thinking about how Dan and I left things. That's the problem with having a relationship. I always avoided them until Caleb came along, and after he broke my heart I thought I was finished with them for good. Apparently not.

"Why don't you call him?" Ronnie asks.

Why don't you mind your own business? "Speaking of calling someone, why don't you call Marley and see what he's found on the drug from the autopsy?"

CHAPTER FORTY

I get back to the office and on the computer. I search the Internet for Alex Rader, Michael Rader, Steve Jones, Kim Mock and Arnold Cantu. I print out everything I find.

Steve Jones, a homeless man, was found guilty of killing a complete stranger, Shannon Blume. He died, beaten to death, in prison. I didn't find anything showing that Michael Rader was in that prison at that time, but he could have been.

Kim Mock was found guilty of killing his girlfriend, Megan Moriarty. He was stabbed to death in the chapel of the prison. Michael Rader is the one who found him. Now Michael Rader has done a runner.

Arnold Cantu, convicted serial killer, confessed to killing Leanne Delmont. He was confessing to a lot of murders. They believed him and the case was closed. Monique wasn't sure they had the right man. She thought they'd done a cursory investigation.

Alex Rader was the investigator.

Now Monique Delmont, a woman who helped me over some very rough patches—who helped me become the woman I am—is brutally murdered. Anyone the Raders touch ends up dying. Technically, I'm a Rader. I've killed before.

Technically, Hayden is a Rader also. But he's the kindest, gentlest boy—man now—that I've ever met. He's had a very messed-up life, but he's overcoming it. Without me. Maybe in spite of me. He's been visiting our mother in prison, the one who betrayed us both and lies as easy as breathing, but his foster parents gave him a good role model and a good life.

Sheriff Gray has already left and I don't think what I've found is worth calling him at home. I say good night to Ronnie. She's going to meet Marley to get the results. He's being bullheaded and won't give them to her except in person. That's not very professional for the supervisor of the crime lab. But he's putting all my stuff in front of the line, so I won't complain.

I put all the printer sheets in a folder to take home with me. I want to find the tape on Megan Moriarty. Ronnie has an address for Mr. Moriarty, her father, but I hesitate to talk to him again. He's a letch but he seemed genuinely broken over the loss of his daughter. This case has been nothing but pain for me. And for all the ones in the path of Hurricane Alex.

Dan hasn't called. Not even to yell at me. On the way home, I drive by Dan's shop downtown. The front of the building is all windows with stands displaying all of his carvings. No lights are on inside. His truck isn't there unless it's parked behind the building. I slow down and think of stopping. I don't want these feelings. Just when I'm starting to get comfortable with the idea of dating, my past has to get in the way. He's not from my past. Maybe not my future.

I make it home, park and watch the front of my house. I left the light on in the entryway and it was still lit. I make a mental note to buy lightbulbs and replace the whole damn bunch of them.

I look around before getting out and then look up and down the street. The usual cacophony of noise from people and a car down the street playing music.

I take my key out, draw my .45 from the shoulder holster and then try the door. It's locked. I feel silly for having a gun in my hand to enter my own house. While I've got the gun out, I think of going down to the loud car and introducing myself. But I don't. I don't need to attract the attention.

Inside, I feel uneasy. The last couple of months have been hard on me. One murder after another, being shot, watching Ronnie get kidnapped, receiving emails from my stalker and now Monique brutalized by someone from my past. And there's Hayden suddenly showing up and offering only a tiny hope of reconciliation. I don't even know where he is or have a number to contact him. Maybe he's safer staying away from me.

I'm almost one hundred percent sure my stalker and the killer are the same person: Michael Rader; but then, could it be someone else that Monique angered? I can't count that out. And apparently she had mentioned Megan Moriarty and Shannon Blume to Mr. Bridges in the advocacy group. She talked about them enough for him to remember their names. There's no telling what hornets' nest she poked.

It's still early. I hang my blazer in the closet. I shrug out of the shoulder holster and hang it on the back of the chair at my desk. I take all the research I brought home, spread it across the top of my bed and go back to the desk. The bottle of Scotch and a plastic tumbler are in a drawer with two packs of Cheetos. I have dinner.

I open another drawer and take out the tapes and player. I know which date I want. I slide it into the player and pour a generous amount of amber liquid in my cup and open both bags of Cheetos. It might be a two-bag tape, with a lot of amber waves of grain.

I stuff Cheetos in my mouth and go find a paper towel to wipe the orange stuff off. I hit the "play" button.

Dr. A: Tell me about Megan Moriarty. What did you find out?

The tape hisses as I pause. I'm thinking. Gathering the information.

Me: She's another pretty blond. Sixteen.

Dr. A: The same age as Leanne and Shannon.

Me: Yes. Megan Moriarty was on the cheerleading squad at Kentridge High School

Megan lived in a suburb further south of Seattle. I don't think I would have liked her. I know that it's wrong. For some reason I never liked the girls on the cheerleading squad. They were so over-the-top in their self-indulgence that if you weren't a mirror they'd never look at you. At least, they never looked at me. Caleb Hunter said I was way prettier than the six girls that considered South Kitsap their personal turf.

There's a longer pause on the tape this time, but Dr. Albright doesn't interrupt my train of thought. The Cheetos, however, do. I can't stand to be messy. I shut the tape off and go to the bathroom. I wash my hands and face. When I look in the mirror, I think of my mom. Every year I look more like her. Every time I have that thought, I'm reminded of Hayden. I wonder if I can find him. I wonder if he's in Port Townsend. I don't know if tracking him down is a good idea, but tomorrow I'm going to try and find out where he lives. I need to know that he's okay. But surely, if I didn't know he was back in the country, much less in town, no one else will know. He'll be safe. Probably. My mother might know, but there's no way I'll open that wound again.

CHAPTER FORTY-ONE

The gun is next to me on the nightstand. I close my eyes but I can't get Michael Rader out of my mind. The picture Ronnie showed me reminds me too much of my bio-dad, too much of me, too much of the genes we share. I wonder if there's a DNA strand specifically for killers. If gene splicing, like I saw on a Twitter video clip, can replace that malignant gene with a normal one.

My mom said to look in the past. If it was meant to be a clue maybe it meant Michael Rader's past and not mine. I give up trying to sleep and take the gun back to my desk. I lay the gun down, get on the computer and skim through the news articles and blogs about the Moriarty case and Mock's death in prison. I pause and stare at a picture of Mock. He looks bewildered, sitting next to his defense attorney.

In the picture's background I see Dan Moriarty—younger but out of shape. Next to him is a woman with her hands pressed against her chest as if she's holding her breaking heart inside. Megan's mom. She has those same haunted eyes that I saw in Mrs. Blume. No mother ever gets over such a loss.

Next, I scroll down and read one of the articles. The headline is:

MOCK SUCCUMBS TO INJURIES

The article gives me a recap of his crime and a better sense of who Kim Mock was as a person. He was eighteen years old when he was convicted and given a life sentence. He was moved from the juvenile justice center in Seattle to the men's correctional facility in Monroe. I remember Monroe as a sleepy prison town east of Everett, Washington. As I read, it is as though I'm in a race to capture every detail I can in one giant gulp. He was considered a model prisoner there, teaching other inmates how to read and write. He even led a Bible study group.

The article reads:

On Tuesday Mock was in the prison chapel when an assailant stabbed him with a knife made from a flattened and sharpened spoon. Mock was taken to the infirmary, where he died after surgery. His attacker was never identified. The prison was on lockdown for twenty-four hours, but is operating normally today.

At the bottom of the piece, mention is made that there *was* a pending investigation into Mock's death.

I move further down the computer screen. The follow-up article is so brief that if I blinked at the moment it passed in front of me I would have missed it.

REVIEW INTO MOCK DEATH COMPLETE

Once again, I see the name of the guard who found Kim Mock stabbed to death and alone.

Michael Rader.

Ronnie had found an old address and possibly a phone number for Michael. I need to verify he's still there. Back when I was hunting for his brother, I found that Alex wasn't listed anywhere but water records. I need to ask Ronnie if she checked that.

A benefit of being in the Sheriff's Office is that I am tied into the city and county databases. One of the things I can now access is the department of water records for bills and usage. They will also show if he transferred his water service. It's just possible he lives in such a remote area that there are no utility services of any kind. Some people live rough in the county. I think of Snow Creek. Still, it's something I can do.

But there are only a few computer stations that have IT permission to access those records. One of the stations, luckily, is mine. At work only. I'll check it in the morning.

If that doesn't reveal where Michael is living, I'll ask Sheriff Gray to call the sheriff of Snohomish County and make some inquiries. If Michael isn't working at the prison or living in the county anymore, there must be a reason. He doesn't have a warrant issued for his arrest, so he hasn't been caught for the murder of Kim Mock or others.

I put the tapes and player away. The empty Scotch bottle goes in the trash with the Cheetos wrappers. I'm a little hungry but I don't want to eat. My stomach is queasy. I need sleep.

CHAPTER FORTY-TWO

In the morning, the hot water from the sputtering shower relaxes me. Washes the bad stuff away. The body wash Ronnie suggested smells and feels wonderful compared to the bar of Dial soap I normally use. It's lavender scented and so I use it for shampoo as well.

I dry off and go to the closet. My usual lineup of blazers and slacks await me. I think of buying some new clothes. New shoes: sensible low-heeled ones instead of boots. But the places I go sometimes aren't conducive to that kind of footwear. Also, I've ruined several blazers searching inside burnt-out husks of buildings, wading through mud and oil or chemical spills in creeks. What I have is practical. I think I might want some off-duty clothes that are more up to date. Not necessarily feminine, but something more eye pleasing.

I get dressed, slip on the shoulder holster and a blazer, remove the chair from the door and head off to work. It's early but I'm starving. Cheetos don't stay with me long. I head for my favorite breakfast place.

Hudson Point Café is open early and it's very popular with tourists and locals alike. The view from their outside seating is of Port Townsend Bay with its sailboats and cabin cruisers. I know the cook and I order two sausage and egg biscuits for myself, a pancake with bacon and whipped cream for Sheriff Gray, and two poached eggs embedded in light buttermilk biscuits on a bed of spinach for Ronnie. I'll eat her biscuits if she doesn't want them.

As an afterthought, I order two rashers of bacon and three large coffees to go.

The drive to the office isn't long, but I consume both sausage and egg biscuits and half my coffee before I arrive in the parking lot. Sheriff Gray's and Ronnie's cars are there.

I carry everything inside and go right to the Sheriff's Office. Nan looks up. She's smelled the bacon.

"We have a meeting. Sorry, Nan. I didn't think you'd be here early," I lie. Then I see the plate with three glazed donuts on her desk, so I don't feel too bad.

Sheriff Gray's not on the phone and Ronnie is in his office.

"Close the door," I say to Ronnie, and put the box of goodies and coffee on his desk. "We're having a meeting," I explain and give them their breakfasts. "I see Nan's already here. I forgot to order something for her," I say. It's a lie. I don't want to encourage Nan to talk to me. The feeding-a-stray-dog rule applies here.

"I brought donuts," Sheriff Gray says. "She'll be okay."

Ronnie opens her bag and smiles and we all chow down. Tony sighs, leans back in his chair and proudly displays his whipped-cream mustache.

"You have something on your lip, Sheriff," Ronnie says.

I think, *You have your whole breakfast on your face.* I should have had the cook put the boss's meal in a bowl. But that's unkind. It's only a mustache, after all.

He looks around for a napkin. I've forgotten napkins. He opens a drawer and brings out a small stack—no doubt from McDonald's—and hands them out. We all sip our coffee. It feels nice to take a breather. For once, I feel comfortable with other people. We've become a team. I still have trust issues, but they will never go away after the life I've lived. Still, it's nice to let my guard down long enough to eat.

Sheriff Gray wads up his bag, tosses it in the trash basket beside his desk and looks at me. "What gives?"

"Can't I just be nice and bring breakfast?"

"No."

I look at Ronnie and she grins.

"Okay," I say. "I want to fill you in on yesterday."

"And?" he asks.

"And ask a favor."

"Shoot."

"I don't know how much Ronnie has already told you…" I begin, and Ronnie smiles. "What's going on?" I ask.

"Tell her, Ronnie."

"Tell me what?" I ask.

Ronnie looks ready to bust. "I'm released back to active duty tomorrow. And that's not all."

She pauses, staring at me with a stupid grin. I want to slap it out of her. I don't like anticipation and we have business to discuss.

"I've been permanently assigned here. Tony—Sheriff Gray—asked for it. And…"

I try to look excited to hear what else, but I'm truly just anxious for her to spit it out. I have things to do, people to track down and punish.

"…and he's going to hire me full-time as a deputy," she says. Then she does something that I always hate to hear from women: she squeals like a schoolgirl. "Can you believe it?"

No. Yes. Maybe.

"I'm really happy for you, Ronnie. You deserve it. You'll make a good addition to the office."

I think that about covers all the nice things I'm expected to say. I even mean some of them.

Sheriff Gray adds his platitudes, but he means them, and turns to me. "Now, what's the favor?"

"Before I tell you, when are you planning Ronnie's official hiring ceremony?"

"Next week. She'll need new uniforms. And she'll have to get some other plain clothes. I think I'm going to assign her to you for training."

"As a detective?" I ask. I'm not really surprised.

He gives me a defensive look. "I thought you'd be happy."

"I am. I mean, that's great." I shake Ronnie's hand and this time I say, "Welcome aboard."

"Thanks, partner."

Don't get cocky.

"I was asking because I want to get Ronnie an assigned log-in for the computers. And I want her to have access to all of our resources and databases. I have something for her to do this morning but it can only be done on your computer or mine."

"Already done," Sheriff Gray says. "Before I went to the Civitan meeting Wednesday."

"Oh. Well, the favor I want to ask is this." I tell him about Michael Rader's deeper involvement per my conversation with Debra Blume on Wednesday. I don't tell him about my past knowledge of this scumbag. "He was, and still might be, working at the men's correctional facility in Monroe. Ronnie tried to track him down and she thinks he no longer works there. I'm going to check the utility records this morning to see if I can get a forwarding address and confirm the last address, but I—*we*—need to know if he still works there. I thought if he doesn't, he must have gotten in trouble. If he has a record with Snohomish County of any kind, you can find out."

"So you want me to call the sheriff and not the prison because he might still be working there and tip your hand?"

I nod emphatically. "Plus you have a working relationship with the sheriff, don't you?"

"We've had a few drinks together at conferences. I don't know him well, but enough to believe he can keep his yap shut."

CHAPTER FORTY-THREE

I leave for my office and hear Sheriff Gray on the phone asking for the Snohomish County Sheriff. Ronnie comes to my desk.

"You should have access to the database of the Jefferson County Public Utility District," I say, and pull my chair out for her to sit at my computer. "Go ahead and log in and we'll see what IT has given you."

Ten minutes later, we have the information on Michael Rader's water account. I don't have to instruct her. She catches on quickly, intuitively. Like me. She pulls up the monthly bills, his account information, payments, payment types: whether check or credit or cash. She finds his address from six months ago and where his account was transferred one month ago. His address is in Clallam County, a small town called Silent Ridge about thirty minutes south of Port Angeles. It sits along the Elwha River running north from the Olympic Mountains into the Strait of Juan de Fuca, the Salish Sea.

We try to find the town itself, but there is very little information except that the Elwha River hiking trail is a popular destination and the trailhead is in Silent Ridge. No population given. The road from Port Angeles ends at the trailhead.

I can't imagine why a city boy like Michael Rader would move to such a remote spot unless he wants to kidnap hikers and kill them. The Olympic National Forest would be the perfect dumping ground for a serial killer.

Ronnie pulls up the map and we find a GPS designation for the address Rader's last payment was made from. The Google

Map isn't very helpful. It's only fifty-eight miles but will be an hour-and-a-half drive to maybe find a dead-end road and a lean-to. Michael Rader would know how to disappear.

I have to decide. Do I go an hour and a half on a wild-goose chase north to maybe find Michael Rader, or do I go two and a half hours south to Kent to find Dan Moriarty? I decide to go to Silent Ridge. I'll call Dan Moriarty, but I may want to have the Sheriff's Office there do a welfare check on him first.

The sheriff makes my decision easier when he calls me into his office.

"Snohomish County doesn't have a criminal record of Michael Rader," Tony says, "but they do know of him. The sheriff said he got into a little trouble at the correctional facility and quit his job about five months ago. He's had a few problems in town. Drunk and disorderly. But he's never been arrested because of where he works. He said they give those guys a lot of slack since they work with the worst of the worst. He gave me the same address that Ronnie had on him. Do you want me to have someone go by there and see if he's still living there?"

I call Ronnie into the office and we shut the door. "We found a bill he paid a month ago. It was sent from Silent Ridge in Clallam County."

"Silent Ridge?" Sheriff looks dubious. "There's not much housing around there, Megan."

"I didn't think so. I still want to look."

"Take Ronnie with you. What can I do?" he asks.

"Can you call the crime lab and see if they ever identified the paralytic chemical they found during autopsy?"

"They haven't called you yet?"

I shake my head and he gets up and calls Nan in. She comes right away.

Something she only does for him.

"Nan, didn't you say the crime lab report came in?" he asks.

"I put it on Detective Carpenter's desk yesterday," she says.

"That's fine," he says. Nan waits but sees he is done and leaves. I shut the door behind her.

"I don't have a report," I say. I can't believe Nan would stoop to being malicious even though I haven't exactly been nice to her. It's something I would do. Good for her.

"I'll call the lab and get the report sent to me directly and a copy will be sent to your phone."

"Thanks, Sheriff. We'll call if we need anything," I say.

Before we leave, Nan stops us. "I did put the report on your desk yesterday. You must have put it in with some other files," she says.

"Probably," I say. "Thanks, Nannette."

*

I take Anderson Lake Road west to SR-101. I stop at the Wendy's in Port Angeles to re-caffeinate myself. Ronnie asks for a water.

"If you're going to work with me, you need to start drinking big-kid stuff, Ronnie." I order a coffee for her. She takes the coffee and asks for three creams and three sugars.

It's not coffee anymore. But it's a start.

I drive west on 101 and turn south toward Silent Ridge Road. The houses are thinning as we take the wide curving highway south now, and soon there are farm fields and then into the forest we go. I'm beginning to feel like Little Red Riding Hood going to meet the Big Bad Wolf. And I forgot my axe.

"Are we going to call the Clallam County Sheriff and let them know we're here?" Ronnie asks.

I give her a blank look. If we get into a shooting situation, I'll call them. When you're dealing with someone like Michael Rader, it's better to sneak up on him. Then shoot him and leave quietly. But that won't work with Ronnie along.

"Are you sure there are no warrants for his arrest?" I ask, fingers crossed.

"I checked. Nothing," Ronnie says.

"Do you have body armor with you?" I've taken to wearing my body armor, or keeping it handy in the back seat. Shoot me once, shame on you. Shoot me twice, shame on me.

"I wasn't issued any yet," she says.

My fault. I should have asked this long ago. I'll make sure we fix this today.

"I have an extra on the back seat. Put it on over your shirt." I don't really have an extra, but technically she's still on light duty and isn't supposed to be out in the field. If she gets killed, Sheriff Gray will be pissed at me.

Ronnie looks at me. "You aren't wearing any."

I'm tougher than you, I think.

"I have some in the trunk," I lie like the expert I am. My mother taught me this. I didn't learn how to sew or cook or iron. I learned how to lie. Thank you, Mom. This skill seems to come in handier than the others anyway. I can always follow a recipe to cook. Not so with telling a believable lie.

Ten minutes later, Ronnie has slipped on the vest and tightened the straps. We see a sign:

HISTORIC HUMES RANCH CABIN
5 MI.

And another sign:

ELWHA RIVER TRAIL
3 MI.

Ronnie is on her phone, of course. "The Humes Ranch Cabin was built in 1900 by William Humes. He was on his way to the Klondike but liked the area along the Elwha River so he and his brother settled there and built the cabin. It's three miles from the Silent Ridge trailhead. Maybe we can stop by there on our way back to the office?"

I don't say it, but I'm thinking, *Maybe. If we're still alive.*

CHAPTER FORTY-FOUR

I turn into the parking area for the trailhead and back into a space. There is one other car with no occupants in sight. I saw a couple of dirt roads angling off of the main road on the way but there are no signs or mailboxes. I imagine if anyone lives out in the sticks like this, they use a P.O. box in town.

I get on the radio and have Dispatch run the Oregon license plate of the other car in the lot. It comes back to someone with an Oregon address. It's not stolen. I have Dispatch run the name for wants and warrants. No warrants and the license is clear. The plates come back to the correct vehicle.

"What now?" Ronnie asks.

"Wait here." I get out and look around. Nothing but forest for as far as I can see. No noise that would indicate a human presence. I get back in the car. Damn. I didn't really think it would be this easy, but I'm not looking forward to the long drive back. Still, I decide to check some of the side roads for signs of recent traffic. Maybe there are campgrounds or cabins that are unmarked?

I pull out.

"We're going to check some of the side roads. You watch your side and I'll check this one." *And look for someone holding a sign that says, "I'm a serial killer."*

I drive down one bumpy dirt side road after another and all roads end at a turnaround. I'm on my fourth road, if you can call a path of tire ruts through the grass a road, when I hit pay dirt. I slow and see a stump of a 4x4 wooden post that's been sawed off six inches above the ground. This must have been for a mailbox or a sign marking the campsite.

The bark-and-cream-colored motor home is set back a couple of hundred feet from the road. The color blends with the trees and is almost hidden by towering red cedar and pine trees. If anyone is inside, they have seen me. So now I have two choices. I can drive on as if I'm out for a ride on a deserted side road in the middle of nowhere. Or I can stop down the road a piece and go to the door. If it's not Rader's place, I can tell whoever answers that I'm a lost hiker and ask for directions to the trailhead. If it's Rader, I can ask for directions to the Monroe Correctional Complex and expect some fireworks. But I'm not really dressed like a hiker. I regret not getting Ronnie body armor before I left the office. But I'm here now and I don't want to risk losing him.

"I'm going to check it out," I say. "Stay here and cover me. If there's shooting, call for backup."

"I'm not staying here," Ronnie says, getting out. "You don't even have a vest, Megan. Do you?"

Okay, you go in front of me. Human shield.

"I'm going to knock," I say. "Get back in the car. It's an order."

I hope he is smart enough to believe that we wouldn't come to get him by ourselves. I hope he doesn't know that I'm not that smart.

Ronnie stays with the car and I question my sanity as I walk down the rutted path that leads to the motor home. I'm extremely calm given the fact I might come face to face with a man who wants to kill me. The only downside of this is that if he's home and I have to shoot him, Ronnie will see it all.

There are deep, wide tire tracks where the motor home was backed in, but they look old. There are several more narrow tracks, from car tires, criss-crossing the wider tracks. He's brought a car too. Sensible. The motor home has been there awhile. A canvas rollout shade is extended by a door with a small set of metal steps. There is a small foldout picnic table and one stadium chair next to the side of the motor home. A charcoal grill is near this. No garden gnomes or lanterns strung up that would indicate an older couple. There are waffle-soled prints from heavy boots around all of this. The boot prints lead to the back of the motor home and I follow them. This is where the car was parked but it is gone now.

I look at the door and the top edge of the motor home to see if any cameras have been set up. Nothing. If I was a killer on the run, I would have set up some type of warning system. I look back along the path. I've left boot prints in the softer dirt. My boots are size six. His are size eleven. Maybe he does have an intruder system: shoe prints.

And I've just left the intruder alert for him.

I go back to the car and Ronnie gives me a questioning look.

"I think this is the place," I say. "Looks like he has a car and has gone somewhere. Maybe getting supplies?"

Maybe killing another victim.

"What do we do now?" she asks. "Should we have Clallam County try to locate him? There aren't many towns between here and Port Angeles. Or do you want to go back through some of the little towns ourselves and hope to spot him?"

Neither. I open my car door and find a leaflet on the floor. One of the church groups left it under my wiper blade one night. My soul needs saving but not today.

"Wait here," I say, and go back to the motor home. This time I step off to the side of my previous shoe prints, being careful not to leave another set.

I stick the leaflet in the crack of the door where he'll be sure to see it. If it's not Michael Rader's motor home, the occupant won't think someone was snooping around. I then circle around the motor home, staying on the already bent grass. There are no windows or doors on the back side except for a driver's-side door.

There is a large window at the back but it has heavy shades drawn. I would have to jump up to look in any of the cab windows.

I go back around to the door with the steps and knock. I wait and knock again. No answer, and I detect no movement inside. I use a trick I've learned from one of the patrol deputies. I begin knocking with the side of my fist on the door and keep the pounding up for a full minute. I wait thirty seconds and start again, this time beating even harder for several minutes. This usually causes some type of response. Last week I served a robbery warrant in Port Hadlock where I used this technique. The guy, even knowing he had the warrant issued for his arrest, came to the door and yelled, "WHAT?"

There's no response and I look at Ronnie. She's been watching to see if there's any movement. She shakes her head and holds her hands up at shoulder level. I don't know if she's saying *What are you doing?* or *Nothing has moved.* Either way, I can tell she's expecting me to come back to the car, but I have a different plan.

I try the door latch and it doesn't give. There is a metal tent peg on the ground by the grill. I stick the point of it in the crack by the latch and pry open the door.

I don't have to look back at Ronnie to know she's about to shit her pants. I'm committing a burglary. I don't know if she will ignore this, but I don't care at this point if it helps me find Michael Rader.

I draw my weapon and announce "Sheriff's Office" loudly for Ronnie's benefit and then open the door. I peek inside quickly toward the front and again to the back. No one shoots. I go in.

The motor home is more tricked out than Ronnie's place in Port Townsend. Michael has some money, for sure. There's not many places to hide in the back except for a bathroom. I check up front, crouched, gun out. No one is hiding. I crack the bathroom door enough to see if someone is inside. It smells of something strong and I know the smell but can't place it. I'll get back to it.

I call Ronnie on her cell.

"What are you doing?" she asks. And rightly so.

"Just keep a sharp eye out. If you see that I'm getting company, honk or call me back." I hang up before she can say anything.

I put on latex gloves and go to the cab to look for anything identifying the owner. The visor above the driver's seat has what I'm looking for. Vehicle registration. The motor home is a lease vehicle. I look in the cubbyholes and glove box. There is one pay stub. Monroe Correctional Complex. For Michael Rader. It's seven months old. He made good money, but not enough to buy this luxury motor home. I'm guessing that, new, it would go for at least $300K.

I start at the cab and move to the back, searching cabinets, under mattresses, under the built-in stove, the bathroom. I find no weapons, ammunition or any gear. There are men's clothes and a pair of Wolverine boots in the back bedroom, where the curtains are drawn shut.

I go to the bathroom again. The smell is strong but not unpleasant. Then it hits me. Almonds. I look in the cabinet under the sink again and find a container the size of a round Morton Salt box. The label identifies it as rat poison. I take the container out and don't have to sniff it to recognize it as the source of the smell. There are granules in the sink and on the small countertop. Mixed in with this are black seeds that remind me of apple seeds.

I notice the top is not pushed down securely. I pop it open and inside I find a dozen or more small syringes. One is loaded with some type of thick, dark liquid. Either Michael is a diabetic or he's mainlining cyanide.

I take a bag out of my pocket and collect a loaded syringe. I take another bag and collect some of the rat poison from the container and another bag for some granules and seeds from the countertop. Before I leave the motor home I look around to be sure I left the place as I found it. I don't see anything to collect for DNA comparison but remember a piece of some type of fruit or vegetable I didn't recognize in the refrigerator. It is cut in half and in a plastic bag. Part of it has been bitten off. I put that bag inside a bag of my own. Then I go outside, use my blazer sleeve to wipe my footprints from the metal steps. I open the grill lid and see something has melted on the grate. I pry it loose. It's melted plastic with a needle on one end. A syringe. I collect it and head back to my car. It's in the trash so fair game as far as evidence goes.

CHAPTER FORTY-FIVE

We get back in the car and I show Ronnie what I've found.

"Let's go to the crime lab. I want Marley to tell me what all of this is and see if he can get DNA from the mango- or avocado-looking thing."

"That's not either of those things," Ronnie says, looking at the bag with the fruit in it. "It has seeds like an apple."

"I've never seen anything like it," I say. If this stuff is what paralyzed Monique, and if the DNA matches any found at the scene, he's as good as caught. Anything that happens when I find him will be legal. I'll make sure of that.

I give Ronnie the lease information for the motor home. It's leased out of Seattle. Long term. Lease-to-own. She calls the lease agency and they have the same address in Silent Ridge. The woman she talked to said Michael made a substantial up-front payment, in cash, of more than half of the cost of the vehicle. That explains their lack of a background check to verify the address is real.

I call Sheriff Gray and explain what we've found.

"Tell me you were in there legally," he says.

"Of course," I say. "The door to the motor home was open and I was concerned for his safety. There are bears in those woods and they frequently find their way indoors. I was doing a welfare check."

It's lame, but he doesn't question it.

"I need you to contact the sheriff in Snohomish again and find out exactly what went on with Michael Rader," I say. "Ronnie found out the motor home is leased but he paid over half of it down in cash. It's a luxury motor home."

"I see."

"And when I looked in the bathroom to see if Rader was alive, I smelled a chemical that I thought to be cyanide. Rat poison was in view." After I opened the cabinet, that is. "And there were syringes sticking out of a container of rat poison. One of the syringes was loaded. I'd like to know what the chemical is that was found at the autopsy."

"Sorry," Sheriff Gray says. "I should have told you. Nan found the lab report on your desk."

Of course she did.

"There was a chemical in it that Yang identified as cherimoya. It's made from the seeds of a fruit. The fruit is supposed to be very tasty and is edible, but the seeds are poisonous."

"Are the seeds black? About the size of apple seeds?"

I hear him flipping through some pages. "Yes. Yang sent me a picture of the fruit and the seeds. You want me to send it to your phone?"

"Please. I found some type of fruit in the motor home that I didn't recognize and the seeds in the fruit were the same as some that I found in the rat poison container."

Just then my phone dings. I pull up the photos. It's the fruit and the seeds I collected.

"That's exactly what I found," I say.

"The report doesn't say anything about cyanide, Megan."

"I'm more interested in the seeds and what's in that syringe. We're on our way to the crime lab."

I hang up. I don't drive through any of the towns on the way to the crime lab. It will take two and a half hours to get to Olympia as it is, and another two hours to get back to the office. The day will be shot. Ronnie calls Marley and puts it on speakerphone. He answers on the first ring.

"Crime lab. Supervisor Yang," Marley says in a deeper voice than I remember him having. He knows it's Ronnie's phone and so he can't resist reminding her how important he is.

"Marley, it's Ronnie."

"Oh. Hello, Ronnie. I was busy and didn't recognize the number."

She looks at me and cuts her eyes. "Marley, I know you must be super-busy, but I have some good news."

"I heard," he says. "You're being hired full-time. Congratulations."

"Oh, phooey," she says, with a fake pout on her lips. "I wanted to tell you myself."

"You still can. How about dinner tonight and we'll celebrate your good fortune? My treat."

She looks at me again. I mouth, "Go ahead."

"That sounds nice. What time?"

They gab some more and I point to the evidence bags.

"Marley, I have a favor to ask. I know I'm always asking, but this is for a big case I'm working with Detective Carpenter and it will really help me."

"Fire away, Detective Marsh," he says, and I want to puke.

She tells him about the things I found in the motor home in Silent Ridge. She doesn't tell him I broke in and searched, so that gives her extra points. He seems to hesitate and I think he might really be busy, but then she says the magic words.

"I would really appreciate it, Marley. I'll owe you one."

Now he doesn't hesitate. "I'll hold you to that, Red."

Red? I give her a look like *What the hell?*

She giggles. "Dinner tonight. You pick the place. We're on our way to the lab. We can talk about it when we get there."

"'We'? Who's coming with you?"

"Megan is. She's my training officer, you know."

"So you're going to be partners, huh?" he says.

"I hope so." She looks at me. I don't respond. I want to say that's not up to me. But it really is. Outside of working with temporary trainees, Sheriff Gray doesn't make you take on a partner.

"Will you need a DNA run?" he asks.

Shit. I forgot about running the DNA. That will add an hour or two to our time if we wait for it. I nod my head.

"Yes," Ronnie answers. "But only if it's not asking too much."

"I'll make the time," he says. I think he would eat a bowl of glass for her.

"Red?" I ask when she hangs up.

"It's better than what he wanted to call me. He started calling me Yin," she says, rolling her eyes. "He says I should come work at the crime lab. We would make a good team. Not going to happen."

I don't get it for a second, then I do and I regret it. It's fitting. They're about as opposite as you can get.

"You can take lead when we get to the lab. You've got a good connection there, Red."

CHAPTER FORTY-SIX

It's a long drive to the lab, made even longer by Ronnie's never-ending chatter. I make an excuse to let her go in by herself, and when she's out of sight I call Sheriff Gray.

"Are you at the lab?" he asks.

"Just got here."

"I got some interesting news about Michael Rader."

I hear his chair squeak shrilly, a door close, then another creak as he sits down. "Here's what I was told," he says. I know he's leaning back against the wall, because the springs in his chair are screaming, *I give up! I'll pay you to get up!*

Like duct tape, WD-40 only goes so far.

"Rader has worked at a couple of maximum security prisons around the state," Tony says. "He was at Monroe for the last twenty years. He came under suspicion a year ago when there was a rash of prisoners having medical issues. Such as breathing difficulty, muscle weakness, rashes, heart issues. One prisoner who was nineteen years old and in perfect health dropped dead from a heart attack. Ninety percent of these individuals were under the supervision of Michael Rader before developing the conditions. Rader was also handy with his night stick. Of the physical altercations between prisoners and staff, Rader accounted for sixty percent by himself. It was well known that if Rader was required to break up a disagreement or fight among prisoners that he was bringing an ass-kicking with him."

He sounds about as delightful as his older brother, Alex.

Sheriff Gray goes on: "He was investigated by the prison's internal affairs office and was being watched closely. Not closely enough, as it turns out, because four prisoners died in a one-week period. The autopsy showed they had ingested some type of poison. That was six months ago. A full investigation of their deaths was launched by the prison. Rader wasn't a clear suspect in any of these deaths so he was just kept under scrutiny. Then the story got around that Rader had words with each of these prisoners.

"Were these reliable sources—the stories—or prisoners that already had a grudge?" I ask. I can't believe I'm asking this because I want him to be guilty. Yet, if he was abusive to prisoners, they may have set him up to get even.

"It was other prisoners talking at first and then two guards came forward and admitted that Rader had been involved in breaking up an altercation in the cafeteria. The four prisoners were the main ones fighting and two of them went to the medical office with cuts on their heads. The two guards admitted that they'd lied for Rader and said the prisoners did that while fighting, but the cuts were from Rader's club. He'd asked the guards to cover for him, but Internal Affairs put the screw to them and they gave him up."

"So why wasn't he arrested for aggravated battery?" I ask.

"You'll like this," he says. "The video from the cafeteria on the day of the fight somehow disappeared. The guards then changed their stories and said they'd only implicated Rader because they were being threatened by the investigators. Both guards were suspended, but Rader was still untouched.

"He put in for a transfer to another prison. His reason was that he was being harassed by Internal Affairs. The superintendent turned down his request and assigned him a desk job away from the prisoners. Rader quit."

"So that's it?" I ask. "They're not going to pursue him for the deaths. The murders?"

"Megan, I want him to be guilty as much as you do. But there was no physical evidence and there was no way to prove Rader had brought poison into the prison."

"What was the poison?" I ask, though I already know the answer.

"Cyanide. They found it at the autopsy, but by the time they knew it was a poison that killed them, the cells had been cleaned out and other prisoners were in them."

"And there were holes in the video when they checked to see if Rader went in their cells before they died?"

"Yes. Rader will never get a job with corrections again. Or any law enforcement agency, for that matter. He was suspended twice for excessive force but both times it was only a day or two and a fine. It pisses me off that no one put the word out on this guy. He could have been living here, pulling the same kind of shit on anyone that got in his way."

I can hear anger in Sheriff Gray's voice. I'm pissed off, too, but for a different reason.

"If Marley finds what I think he will," I say, "I should have enough to take him into custody."

Sheriff Gray goes quiet. Not good.

"What?" I ask.

"Megan, even if the lab says this is the same type of chemical that was in Delmont's system, it won't prove he poisoned her. You don't have anything showing motive. Why did he kill her?"

I can't tell him everything I know. I don't dare. If I don't, a murderer will walk free. Rader will win again. But even if I spill my guts, it will only hurt my getting a warrant. I'll look as bad, or worse, than him.

And there's the fact that Rylee was never found. She's supposed to be dead. The only thing I can hope for is a DNA match that positively puts him at the scene of Monique's murder. I need to go back and search the motor home again. Look for any type of knife.

If he's home, he'll fight. If he does, I can take a dying declaration from him. My word against a dead man's.

I zone back in. Sheriff Gray is calling my name.

"Sorry, I was just thinking."

He's quiet again. Long enough to worry me.

"Sheriff?"

I hear his chair squeak. He's sitting up. "Megan, when this is over, we need to have a talk."

I don't ask about what. I know. I hoped this day would never come.

"Thanks for trusting me," I say.

"No problem," he says.

Before he hangs up I ask, "By the way, did you ask the Clallam County Sheriff if there were any murders like the Delmont case?"

He sighs. "I'm not stupid. I told him about our case. If he had anything, he would have told me."

"Right," I say. I don't think he's stupid. I just want to be sure.

CHAPTER FORTY-SEVEN

Marley Yang is walking Ronnie to the car. His hair is more stylish than the last time I saw him. His clothes a cut above his usual Macy's menswear. He gives me a knowing smile and comes to my window.

"I knew you'd be wanting to know," he says, "so I'm delivering it verbally in person. I'll send the report tonight, but Ronnie said you needed to know right away and she didn't think she'd remember everything."

I almost laugh out loud but choke it back. Ronnie is a manipulator. Maybe as good as me. "Okay."

"First of all, I'm not even going to address the black lace panties. I have them if you want them back."

I don't. It was mean to send them, but you never know if it's evidence until it isn't. Except in this case.

"The cigarette butts have two separate DNA. Neither DNA matches any of the other evidence. I sampled the lipstick on the coffee mug Ronnie found in the victim's permanent residence. Good catch, by the way."

When he says this he gives Ronnie a big smile. No doubt he thinks flattery will get him to third base. He's not even on the bench yet.

He sees I'm still waiting for him to tell me about the fruit.

"I've positively identified the fruit as *Annona cherimola* or simply cherimoya. You find it in Central America. Colombia, Ecuador, Bolivia, Chile, Peru or tropical regions. Spain, even. It's known as custard apple because of the very sweet taste. It doesn't grow around here and it would be almost impossible to try."

"You're saying the thing was brought in here from another country?" I ask.

"You can probably buy it on Amazon," Ronnie adds.

"She doesn't mean *from* the Amazon," Marley adds, and grins as if he's made a joke. It's not funny.

"The skin of the fruit is what's important, though," Marley says. "If it is crushed and put into liquid form—say, like the loaded syringe Ronnie found—it is highly poisonous and has paralytic properties. Like anesthetic only more potent. The liquid in the syringe is a match for the chemical we found in the victim's system. Like I said, it has paralytic properties that would render someone unable to resist. Enough of it would kill. I'm trying to get a baseline for the exact amount it would take to cause death. I'll let you know when I know."

I hate to ask this. "What about the candy wrapper and the melted syringe?"

He gives me an unhappy look. "The candy wrapper didn't have DNA. The syringe, however, had trace amounts of the same chemical as the loaded one Ronnie found. If there was DNA, it was destroyed by the heat when it melted."

"Cyanide?"

"The rat poison is cyanide. The granules collected with the seeds is cyanide—rat poison. There was no cyanide in Monique Delmont's system. There wasn't any cyanide in the syringes."

Ronnie beams at Marley. "He's so smart."

Marley actually blushes. "I've got to get back."

I nod and he turns to Ronnie. "Still on for tonight?"

"You bet," she says. "Megan should come too."

"I wouldn't want to be in the way." The minute I say it I know it's the wrong thing to say. I should have said I'm coming down with Ebola.

Anything plausible.

"You won't be in the way, Megan," Ronnie says. Her eyes plead with me to come to her stupid dinner. Marley's eyes are warning me not to interfere with his third-base play.

"I'll be there," I say. I can piss Marley off now. He's Ronnie's project.

"Marley is going to call with a time and place and then I'll call you," she says to me. "This is so exciting. I'm getting promoted and my two best friends are going to help me celebrate."

Besties? If that's true, she's worse off than I am.

"We need to head back to Port Hadlock," I say. "Thanks for the quick work, Marley. You are a genius. I knew we could count on you to help solve this case." Some of that is true, but the rest is smoke and it doesn't hurt to say nice things now and then. Especially if it gets you favors in the future.

Marley gets a peck on the cheek from "Red" and I put the Taurus in gear before I vomit. I drive away from the crime lab thinking about what I might have missed today. It will be late when we get back to the office and Ronnie is celebrating her hiring as a deputy tonight. I will have to spend some time in the office typing out the affidavit for the search warrant and it will mean tickling some words.

Not outright lying.

"Marley is so sweet to buy the dinner tonight," Ronnie says.

"Sheriff Gray always has a little party in the office when we hire a new deputy or staff person," I say. "He'll probably do it the day you're sworn in."

"Thanks, Megan. You're a good friend."

"I need you to call one more person, Ronnie."

"We didn't go see Dan Moriarty. I've got his number in my notebook."

Next she'll be finishing my sentences. "When you call, put it on speakerphone. I'm going to let you do all the talking. It's good experience." And I don't want to chance him remembering me. I don't think he will, because he's only interested in a woman's body and not her voice.

Ronnie looks up the number and dials.

A thought hits me just then. *No cyanide in her system. Or inside the syringes.* So why were the syringes hidden in with the cyanide? Why was the rat poison there in the first place? The obvious answer to the presence of rat poison was rats. But a motor home that expensive shouldn't have an infestation.

"Hullo," the voice answers Ronnie's phone. He sounds sick, or drunk or both.

"Mr. Dan Moriarty?" Ronnie asks.

"Yeah. Who's this?"

"I'm Deputy Marsh with the Sheriff's Office. I want to ask a few questions."

"Deputy?" He sounds a little freaked. "What is this? I haven't done anything. I'm obeying the court restriction for house arrest and staying home. You can check my monitor."

Ronnie looks at me.

"I can see you're at your home, Mr. Moriarty. That's not why I'm calling. I need you to answer some questions." She can't ask why he's on house arrest because she's supposed to know that. Besides, it's not important.

She sounds more authoritative. Less unsure. He's a captive audience and prone to answer any question put to him, thinking we are part of the people monitoring him. I wish Ronnie could look up the reason for the house arrest but I'm driving and she's on the phone.

"Mr. Moriarty, I'm looking into a case where phone harassment is taking place."

"'S'not me. Someone sayin' it's me?"

"No, Mr. Moriarty. I need you to listen. Okay?"

"Okay."

He still sounds drunk or drugged. He didn't sound this way back when I talked to him about his daughter's murder. He was on a health kick that time. Getting in shape and all that. I wonder what's happened.

"Mr. Moriarty, I know your daughter was killed many years ago."

He says nothing, but I can hear his breathing become heavier and faster. I hate this part. Bringing the past into someone's life when they've already been hurt beyond understanding. But it's necessary.

"Did you receive hang-up calls before that happened?" Ronnie asks.

"What?" He shifts the phone around and I hear it thump where he lay it down. "Why does that matter now?" He says this as if from a distance. He sounds sober now. He's on speakerphone himself.

"It's important. That's all I can say right now. I want to know if you had hang-up or strange calls back before that happened."

Ronnie is being persistent. Firm. That's good.

"I told the cops back then."

"Tell *me*," she says.

"Okay. Okay. Yes. There were a bunch of hang-up calls. I thought they were for Megan. But later my wife left me for another woman. I know they were for my ex. Every time I answered, they'd hang up in my ear. The bitch. Sorry. Sorry."

"No. I'm sorry, Mr. Moriarty. Have you had contact with your ex-wife?"

I wonder where Ronnie is going with this. I haven't tried to contact Mrs. Moriarty. She wasn't in the picture when I was trying to find Alex Rader. It was an oversight.

"No. She died a couple of years ago. Cancer."

"You have my condolences, Mr. Moriarty. Have you had any strange calls recently? In the last six months or so?"

"I don't talk to nobody. I mind my own business. I stay indoors just like the damn judge… excuse me… like the judge ordered me to. I keep the ankle bracelet on and have to stay near the phone. It's hard taking a damn shower—excuse my language—with that thing on my ankle. I can't even pull my jeans up over it half the time."

"Mr. Moriarty," Ronnie says, like a patient parent to a child, "you didn't answer my question."

"No. I haven't had any strange calls. Unless you count you people checking up on me all the time. I have to take the phone to the bathroom with me. I'll be glad when this is all over."

"So no hang-up calls? No wrong-number calls? No salespeople?"

"Well, sure. Those damn telemarketing people drive a man crazy. All the numbers are from New York or Texas. It's always some damn foreigner wantin' to sell me Viagra. I don't know anyone outside of Washington and I quit answering numbers I don't know. Unless they're local from you guys. Why? Am I supposed to? Am I in trouble?"

"You're not in trouble unless you're not being honest with me."

"I swear I'm telling the truth."

"You have a good night, Mr. Moriarty. If you have any problems, call the Sheriff's Office and report it right away."

"Should I ask for you?"

Ronnie looks at me and I shake my head.

"No. Just the Sheriff's Office. Good night."

She disconnects. "How did I do?"

I give her a thumbs up. I'm trying hard not to laugh. I was afraid to go and talk to this guy. Now I'm glad we didn't. But I think Ronnie could have handled him either way.

She turns in her seat, looks at me and I swear she looks like she's sixteen and going on her first date. "Megan, what do you think about me being hired?"

I don't know what to say. "I'm happy for you."

"No. I mean, how do you *really* feel? Am I cut out for this work? I know I didn't get off on the best foot with you. And I don't always wear the appropriate clothes. And I may be a little too friendly with some of the guys. And—"

"Cool your jets, Red," I say, and smile so she knows I'm not making fun of her. "You will do fine if you look, listen and learn. So far I've had very few things to criticize you about. And you've learned from those things. You may want to tone down your attire because each day is a surprise. I wear crap business clothes because of what I've done and seen. You might have to go in a house with a dead body that is crawling with maggots and flies, or arrest someone with lice or crabs, and not the kind that come from the bay."

She chuckles at my unintentional humor. It makes me lighten up a bit.

"What I'm saying is you're going to be fine. I'd work with you any day. I think I was a little harsh at first myself." I hold out a fist and she bumps it. I can see her eyes begin to water and it makes mine start. It's like seeing someone yawn and you can't help but yawn. I bite my tongue to distract myself. I'm her mentor, after all, and I can't show weakness.

Actually, she *will* be fine. She's seen me at my worst and kept her counsel. Not because she's a suck-up but because she believes in the job the way I do it. Almost. I still will keep her at a distance about some things. I won't ask her to do the hard things. When I kill Michael Rader, she won't be party to that.

CHAPTER FORTY-EIGHT

She watched the Taurus stop on the road earlier and considered killing Rylee then, but the redhead was in the car with her. She knew she could take Rylee but they were both armed. She hasn't gotten this far by taking unnecessary risks.

Rylee is a killer. She overcame Alex and his wife, killed them outright, and at first she put that down to dumb luck. Rylee is anything but dumb.

She herself found Michael Rader's motor home a month ago and has kept an eye on him. He really should have installed a better lock on the door. But he mistakenly believed if the police came for him they would have to play by the rules. A bunch of them would show up and sit for an hour or more waiting for troops to arrive. Then an hour or more waiting for a search warrant before making entry.

She isn't a cop; Rylee is anything but a cop. The badge doesn't change the killer in her. Rylee has the instinct of a hunter. It is an instinct she saw in her old country. She has that instinct herself.

She saw Rylee break into the motor home. She watched her bring out the little plastic bags of planted evidence. She watched her find the syringe in the grill outside. All of it went just as she had planned.

Watching Rylee work over the last couple of years has changed what started out as pure revenge and turned it into something else. She doesn't want to believe someone got the better of Alex. She believes Rylee just got lucky. She hates Rylee but she is coming to

respect her. When Alex died, it was all she could do to not go after
Rylee and kill her. Something, call it instinct, made her wait and
watch. That instinct has kept her from making the same mistake
Alex did with Rylee. Rylee is a force to be reckoned with. But
then, so is she. It will be interesting to see Rylee realize she's been
outmatched and to watch her die slowly and painfully.

She wonders what Rylee thought of the pictures she sent to
the lumberjack.

"What do you think, Michael?" she asks the body lying in the
shallow grave. "What? Nothing to say? You were so chatty when
I caught you sleeping. You were offering to help me kill the bitch
and then begging for your miserable life." She kicks Rader's severed
head into the grave. "You were nothing like your brother. Always
losing your head."

She kicks the scalp in with the body. "You might need this."

She isn't worried about Rader being found. Rylee has focused
on Michael just like she knew she would. And while Rylee was
running all over the state in search of the families of Alex's victims,
it gave her time to tweak her plan to take Rylee down. Monique
Delmont was only a nudge to push Rylee along her current path.
But it wasn't needed in the end.

In fact, the snipe hunt she manufactured for Rylee is almost
over. She will have to leave more clues for Rylee to find her prey.
Michael was the perfect bait, the perfect scapegoat. A self-serving,
greedy, murderous asshole. He only killed Kim Mock and Steve
Jones in prison because, if Alex had been caught, the trail would
have also led to Michael. Michael had partaken in some of the rapes
and tortures. The brothers had shared everything. Even Alex's wife,
Marie. Of course, Alex wasn't aware that Michael and Marie were
having sex while Alex was at work. She found out because she and
Marie became close friends. Marie knew about her arrangement
with Alex. Knew he was sleeping with her. Marie didn't really mind.

When Rylee killed Alex and Marie, it panicked Michael. He collected the evidence, the pictures from Delmont, but not to keep Alex's name clean. In fact, he was going to plant the evidence in such a way that he himself wouldn't be under any suspicion. But it was already too late for Michael. He was already under a magnifying glass by the prison internal affairs office for illegal use of force and one death. He'd gotten away with two others. He had a sadistic mean streak and took it out on a captive audience.

She kept track of him. She knew she would kill him, but she needed him until now. He unknowingly played his part and now Rylee will be blamed for his death.

She picks up the two severed fingers from the ground and puts them in her pocket. These will be her last message to Rylee and a nail in Rylee's coffin.

But there is one last thing she has to take from Rylee. If she does this right, Rylee will be blamed for more than one killing.

CHAPTER FORTY-NINE

I pull into the office parking lot and my eyes are drawn to the woods. I can't help it. Marley said the DNA I collected from the items out there had no bearing on the case. The DNA wasn't in the database and there were no fingerprints. The Sheriff's Office is a non-smoking area. So everyone goes outside to smoke. I saw Nan out there. I couldn't imagine a reason for the women's panties to be there, but in this day and age, anything goes.

Sheriff Gray's car is still here and I know he's waiting to see me. I don't want to go in. I'm not ready for The Talk.

"I'm going to drop you here and head home," I say to Ronnie. "I need to get a shower and change clothes."

"You don't have to dress up for dinner," she says.

I'm not planning to. It's hard to hide a shoulder holster under a dress. I know this is the point where I ask what she's going to wear and make girl talk, but I don't know how to pull that off with someone who really knows me. Someone who knows I have only one nice pair of jeans and a couple of nice blouses.

"Can I bring a gun?" I ask, and she giggles.

"Of course you can. I know you never leave home without it. I'll have one too. That case last month taught me a lesson, believe me."

"You just passed your first lesson, Red. By the way, what do you think of that for a nickname?"

"Honestly?" She cocks her head.

I nod.

"I hate it. But it makes Marley happy. I just hope it doesn't catch on. I don't want to get stuck with it. You know how cops can be."

I know. "Do you want me to tell him it's not appropriate to call you that?" I offer.

"Would you?"

"I'll tell him nicely."

I'll say, *Quit calling her Red, you dumb shit or the sheriff will have your ass. That's sexual harassment.* Marley is a by-the-book kind of guy. If he hears "sexual harassment," his butt will pucker.

Ronnie gets out of the car and I roll down the window. "You still need to let me know where the party is and when."

She comes back and leans in the window. "I'm going to make him take me to The Tides. How about seven?"

"Perfect."

She walks toward her car, turns and waves. I wave back and smile like I mean it. I hang around to make sure Sheriff Gray doesn't come out and stop her before she leaves. When she's safely away, I take off. I'm halfway to Port Townsend when I call the sheriff's cell phone.

"Megan. Where are you?"

"I'm at home," I lie.

"Oh. Okay. We need to talk sometime. How are you feeling?"

I wonder why he's asking this. Maybe he thinks I'm grieving over Monique. I am, but it's not debilitating.

"I'm fine," I say. "We'll talk soon. I promise. I'll tell you everything," I lie again. I wonder if he's just checking to make sure I haven't fled the state. I wonder how much he really knows. He's a very smart man. He was an excellent detective. Better than I am. Maybe.

I change the subject. "Are you coming to Ronnie's party tonight?"

"Party?"

"Yeah. Marley is buying her dinner and they've invited me to attend. I'm inviting you. Please say yes."

I don't want to interfere with their date. Yeah, right.

"When and where? I'll call the wife. I'd ask Nan but she left early. Has a date."

"Oh, darn," I say, and smile. "Ronnie is making him take her to one of our favorite places."

"The Tides."

"Yep. Seven o'clock."

"If I don't show, tell her I'll see her at work. I always have a little gathering and cake for new employees."

"You did that for me and it was a nice gesture," I say, meaning every word.

I hang up and pull up in front of my place. I do my usual routine: check the lighting, the neighborhood, listen, watch for a minute or two, draw my weapon and get out of the car.

I'm weary from driving today. I worry over what I'm going to have to reveal to Sheriff Gray. What he will think of me. What he might do. I like him more than almost anyone, and I trust him the same. But I don't really trust life not to dunk me in a shit bath. After all, when it comes down to it, a murderer is a murderer. I'm as steeped in causing death as my bio-dad. True, I didn't make the people I killed suffer. They were all predators. Their victims were innocent. They are dead just the same.

The shower is barely lukewarm when I get out. I look at the time; I didn't realize I'd just about run the hot water tank dry. Plus I don't have much time to dry off and dress before I head to The Tides.

I resist listening to a tape of the sessions with Dr. Albright. I hated them at first. Each one dug a knife in my heart and made my head hurt. Now they are becoming addictive. I realize how far I've come since my Rylee days. I'm not as angry all the time or disappointed in the world. I'm starting to open up a bit.

But when I do, something always happens that drags me back down into the muck. A good example: the serial killings I dealt with last month. They forced me to become Rylee again. It was that or allow these monsters to take more victims.

I don't want to carry this weight anymore. I want the life I see Sheriff Gray or Ronnie or Dan living. To live in a bubble. That's not who I am. I will never be able to let my guard down that much. I'm a sheepdog. I keep the wolves at bay. I feel my eyes water with the realization that my place in life is to be a killer. I fight back the tears. I don't have the luxury of feeling sorry for myself. I know that if I had my life to live over I would still be where I am. It's in my genes. *Literally*. I'm a monster. But the good kind.

CHAPTER FIFTY

I log in to my personal email account. There's the general junk mail, advertisements. There is also an email from Dan. It's from early this morning. There is nothing in the subject line. It is short and makes me feel worse. The email says:

Megan, I don't think we should see each other for a while. I can't be with someone that doesn't trust me. Be well.

Dan.

My emotions are mixed. Relief beyond words that Dan's all right collides with the stinging hurt of his rejection. I want to cry, but I push the feeling down deep inside my already overcrowded prison cell of emotions.

I dress the way I feel. Typical work outfit and shoulder holster. It reminds me that I'm always on duty. No time for an outside life. Maybe I deserve it. I truly, deeply long for a conversation with Dr. Albright. Even if she can't fix what's wrong, even if I don't feel much better after talking with her, she still has a way of putting it all together in an understandable way and not the helter-skelter jumble of mixed emotions I feel now. I promise myself I'll call her tomorrow.

I stick a toothpick in the crack of the closet door. It's a precaution my mother taught me. If anyone opens the closet the toothpick will fall. I leave my bedroom and entry light on. I go through my place one more time to check the window locks. If you're not careful, someone can get in.

I should know.

I check the street. It looks normal enough. I use the flashlight on my phone to look inside the car before I get in.

I drive to The Tides. The parking is full, as usual. I can put a paper placard on the dash declaring the vehicle as "SHERIFF'S OFFICE." I don't want the attention, so I find an empty parking spot two blocks away and walk.

Ronnie's Smart car and Sheriff Gray's truck are parked almost in front of the bar. They both display the "SHERIFF'S OFFICE" placard on their dashboards. He must have given Ronnie one. I look around for Dan's truck but don't see it. If he knows I'm going to be here, he won't come. I wonder if Ronnie has invited him.

Probably not.

I go inside and see a group from the office have pushed tables together. Mindy Newsom, Marley Yang, Sheriff Gray, Deputy Copsey, Deputy Davis, Nan, even Jerry Larsen, the coroner. Ronnie looks up and beams a smile at me. Mindy has saved a seat between herself and Ronnie and pats it.

"Get over here, girl," she says.

I take a seat, see the slightly inebriated faces around me, and decide I'm having only one drink. Maybe a big one, but just one. My resolve lasts almost as long as it takes to down a Scotch.

Sheriff Gray orders another round, and when they come, he stands. "I know we have a celebration planned for Ronnie's official swearing in, but I think now is a good time to make an announcement." He raises his glass and everyone around the table raises theirs. "Ronnie, will you please stand."

Ronnie doesn't look uncomfortable at all. I would be looking for a door about now. She looks around at the faces and then settles on Sheriff Gray's.

"Reserve Deputy Veronica Marsh came to us last month during her rotation to various units of the department. I assigned her to shadow one of the finest detectives this department has ever seen, Megan Carpenter." He puts his hand alongside his mouth like he's revealing something he doesn't want anyone else to hear, but I know he's going to blast me. That's a tradition as well.

"Ronnie has survived the fire. If Megan didn't break her—or get her killed—then she deserves to be one of us."

There's a round of clinking of glasses and Tony continues. "It's highly unusual for anyone to be hired before completing the rotation process, but soon-to-be Deputy Marsh has been kidnapped and beaten and suffered a broken wrist, all in the line of duty when she and Megan brought down a serial killer."

He holds his glass out to Ronnie.

"Tomorrow you will be sworn in as Deputy Marsh. I'm proud to have you on the team."

Glasses are clinked in salutes all around and Tony orders another round.

Marley is drinking more than his share. I imagine he's disappointed that it wasn't the romantic dinner he planned, but to his credit he acts like the night belongs to Ronnie. And it does. He's being a gentleman and that might make points with the object of his desire. I feel a little chastened by hoping he doesn't get lucky. If he and Ronnie consummate the relationship, it won't be long before one or the other grows tired or complacent and my connection with the crime lab might dry up. I know that's selfish. I don't care.

Where I'm sitting I can see out of the big picture windows of the bar toward the bay. It's dark out and the yellow sodium streetlights only create shadows. I think I see something move across the street and my hand automatically feels for my gun. I watch for several heartbeats but there is no more movement, if there ever was. Maybe a food wrapper was caught by the wind and sailed just out of reach of the streetlights. Maybe someone is going to their car. I feel silly for being so hyperalert.

I really need to talk to Dr. Albright.

As the evening winds down, Copsey and Davis are the first to leave. They have duty early in the morning. Like I don't. Mindy stays but I wish she doesn't. She wants to discuss my love life or lack thereof. It's not a good subject right now. Sheriff Gray stands.

"Come on, Mindy," he says. She got a ride with him. "Megan." He looks at me. "My office. First thing in the morning."

I nod but he doesn't settle for that. "Okay. Your office. First thing, Sheriff."

I would call in sick except for the case.

He seems satisfied and leaves with Mindy. That leaves me, Marley and Ronnie. Marley clears his throat a couple of times.

"You're not getting sick, are you?" I ask him, and get a dirty look.

"It's about time I got home too," Ronnie says. "Marley, thanks for the dinner and sharing my celebration. You're a good friend."

His lips form a tight line at the word "friend." "My pleasure, Deputy Marsh."

Nice recovery, Marley. Now finish your drink, make like a fly and buzz off.

"I guess I'll head home too," I say. "We have an early day tomorrow."

"I'd like to talk to Ronnie alone for a minute if that's okay," Marley says.

I want to argue but just then I see Dan's truck going past the window. At least, it looks like his truck. "See you in the morning," I say to Ronnie. "Thanks for all the help today, Marley."

He nods without taking his eyes from Ronnie. She hasn't had as much alcohol as I've had so she should be safe from Mr. Yang. I leave a large tip and then leave The Tides. Outside I check the parking lot and look up and down the street. Moths flutter around the lights. I hear a car door slam somewhere and a dog barks.

The bark sounds happy. A loved one has come home. It would normally make me smile. A happy thought. This time it doesn't lift my spirits.

Dan's truck is gone and all I think about is the email. I want to be mad at him. He thinks we need time apart but he doesn't know what I know. Time apart won't help anything unless it's forever. I can't think about that. I've lost so much already.

I walk the two blocks to my Taurus. I've had plenty of opportunity to buy a personal vehicle but for some reason I stay with the Taurus. It's like me: messed up but serviceable.

I sit in my car with the engine running but don't go home. I'm thinking of waiting for everyone to clear out and then going back to The Tides. I'm a little hungry and there's nothing at home to heat. Not even cereal. The milk expired a few days ago and is almost cottage cheese.

Everyone at the party had somewhere to go afterward. Somebody to go home to. Even Ronnie had Marley, who is crazy about her. I have my gun and my tapes. I've had two boyfriends now. Both have abandoned me. My own brother hates me. I like to think I'm a superhero. Like Superman hiding behind Clark Kent's fumbling persona. Unable to form attachments because the bad guys would use it as a weakness. Come after my friends if I had any. That's what happened to Monique. She was caught in my black cloud where monsters are real.

"Stop." I look startled. I don't realize I said that out loud. I've had more to drink than I should have. That's why I'm so morose. My life doesn't suck. Not really.

I put the Taurus in gear and the transmission hesitates, then clunks as the gears mesh. That makes me smile. Maybe I've got some miles left on me too.

I drive by Dan's shop. No lights are on inside. No truck. I step on the gas and head home.

CHAPTER FIFTY-ONE

I wake up with a bad taste in my mouth and my throat is burning. I didn't sleep well. I don't remember the dreams but they were unsettling. I blame the burn in my throat on the jalapeño poppers and the bad dreams on the Scotch.

My gun is on the nightstand. I've kicked the sheet off the end of the bed. I have to pee.

I finish my morning business and as I'm getting dressed I remember part of a dream. In it, Dan was with Hayden. They both looked serious and I had a feeling they were going to do an intervention with me. In the dream, they said I was a liar and they were going to make me tell the truth. I was angry at being called a liar even though I knew it was true. That memory brings back the anger and anxiety of being trapped between a guy I really like and a brother I love and telling the truth to either of them.

It's early but I drive by Dan's shop downtown. It's out of my way and chances are he won't be in yet, but I have to see that he's okay.

The shop isn't open yet. A couple of vehicles are parked along the street. The owners are probably in the coffee shop that opened just around the corner. It's called Dilly Dally. Stupid name, but I heard the coffee's good. I slow down and think maybe Dan will come in for coffee. I stop and get a half dozen coffees. The owner looks like Elmer Fudd in the Bugs Bunny cartoons. He's staring at my chest while he talks. That should get me coffee for free, but I don't say anything. Staring at my less-than-ample breasts may be the best thing that happens to him today.

Dan doesn't come in. I stall and ask for creamer, sugar and napkins. Dan still hasn't come in by the time I get all that and pay. The creep is still looking at my chest while I get my change. I don't leave a tip. He's gotten all he's going to get from me this morning.

I drive by Dan's one more time. He said he hired a girl but there's no sign of activity. I'm not threatened, just curious. I drove by the shop before I went to The Tides last night and he wasn't at work. I'm pretty sure it was his truck I saw driving by The Tides last night. I wonder where he was going.

I have to quit thinking about my personal life. That's the problem with having one. It's hard to stay focused. That is part of the reason I resisted taking Ronnie on as an intern. Now that she will be full-time, I think it might change the flow of things. On the other hand, it may be easier if she gets some of the workload, if I ever get a workload. In the last three weeks I've had two burglaries that weren't actually break-ins. In both cases they turned out to be false reports. They had rented something from a rent-to-own store and reported it stolen to avoid paying. Sheriff Gray calls those places "rent-to-steal" stores. Plus I've had a handful of domestic abuse incidents.

That's another reason to avoid relationships.

At work, I see Sheriff Gray's truck and Ronnie's Smart car. Nan's Batmobile is there. A jet black '69 Cadillac with huge tail fins and black leather interior. She's lucky to get three miles to the gallon.

I go inside with the box of coffees and hand one to Nan and Ronnie. I must be the last person to arrive at work for once. Ronnie seems happy but I can see the headache lines beside her eyes. I go back to my desk, take the lid from one of the coffees and blow across the top. I hear my name called, pick up another coffee and take it to the sheriff. I set the paper coffee cup on his desk.

"Shut the door and have a seat," he says.

I shut the door but don't sit. "I really have something to do this morning," I say.

"We need to talk," he says before I can come up with what that something is.

"Okay." I sit down. I don't intend to have the talk this morning. Or any morning if I can help it.

"What's going on with you?" he asks.

"What do you mean?" It's always good to answer a question with one of your own. Sometimes the other person will answer their own question.

"I think you know this killer personally. I think it has something to do with that old picture of you. I think you are hiding something and it is eating you up. I think you don't trust me."

He doesn't know how right he is.

"I can't tell you everything right now. I will, but not right now." I change the subject. "You know I had an argument with Dan a couple of nights ago?"

He nods but says nothing.

"I think it's Michael Rader who left the pictures for Dan. I knew Monique Delmont from around the time that high school picture was taken. I suspected Michael Rader of being a serial killer back then, but I never had proof. Michael thought I had the proof. He knew I was looking into his past. He threatened Monique back then to tell him where I was or he would kill her daughter."

"Gabrielle."

"Right. Gabrielle. I think Monique found the proof and Rader killed her." This is all made up but it sounds good. "He's coming after me but he wants to kill the people who helped me try to track him down back then. That's why I had Gabrielle move away and why I've been talking to the other people he might be after."

"And you didn't think I should know about this?"

"This is something that I started a long time ago. I wanted to get a handle on it before I told you. You think I don't trust you, but you're the only person I *can* trust."

If you knew the whole truth, you would have to arrest me.

Sheriff Gray looks at me for a long time. He takes something out of his desk drawer. It's another copy of my high school picture.

"This was left under my windshield wiper at my house."

I feel a chill run up my spine. I never thought Sheriff Gray might be in danger. Rader knows where he lives. Of course he does. It is hard to find out where a cop lives if you're a civilian. But for a corrections guard it would be easy.

"And this article was in a Ziplock bag." He takes out the newspaper article that has my picture on the front page. The one that says my stepfather, Rolland, was found murdered and my mother is missing. The article says the police are looking for me—Rylee—and Hayden. I'd never told Sheriff Gray about my family. He didn't know I had a brother. He never asked. And Rylee was dead.

I look at the article. I hope my expression says I've never seen it before, but I'm too shocked to see it again. My face feels frozen and my pulse beats in my throat and temples. He folds the article up around the picture and sticks it in his shirt pocket.

"Sheriff, I—"

"I checked into this, Megan," he says. "You don't need to tell me about it. But you do need to tell me if you're in danger. And if anyone else is in danger. I'm the sheriff, you know. I have a duty to protect people. You do too."

I feel like my life is coming unraveled. I got myself into this situation by not tracking down Michael Rader after I knew he'd threatened Monique. I knew he was onto me and looking for me. I thought I could just disappear, create a new life for myself. But this is what I should have expected. Rader hasn't given up as easily as I did. He isn't finished with me.

Plus, if Sheriff Gray found out this easily, what does Dan know? Did Rader leave a newspaper article for Dan? Does he plan to expose me as well as kill all my friends?

I can't breathe.

I feel the coffee coming up in my throat and run for the restroom.

CHAPTER FIFTY-TWO

I'm in the women's room, leaning over the toilet. My stomach and chest hurt and I feel like acid has been poured down my throat. I don't hear the door open but I hear the click of shoes coming toward me.

"Megan, are you okay?"

It's Ronnie, thankfully, and not Nan.

"I'm fine," I say, but the words are strangled. I can barely push them out.

"You don't *look* fine. I'll get you a washcloth."

I hear her open a cabinet and then the faucet turns on. She comes back with a wet cloth. I take it gratefully and wipe my face, then put it on my forehead and the back of my neck.

"You had a lot of Scotch last night," she says.

I grab onto that thought.

"Hangover," I say.

"Maybe you should go home and take care of yourself. I can come by and check on you."

The sincerity in her voice is real. I've never had anyone really take care of me before. Not even my mother. I took care of myself when I was sick. Hayden was my mom's golden boy. If he sneezed, she was there with a tissue and taking his temperature.

"I might do that, Ronnie. I feel bad."

And I do. I feel bad about everything. I have to fix things. I know who the killer is. I didn't go after him as hard as I should have. I am worried about Dan now. Not only that he may be in danger but that he may know. He may truly hate me. He may be struggling with the decision whether to turn me in or just turn me away.

Rader left the picture and old-new article under Sheriff Gray's windshield wiper outside of his house. His way of saying he's not afraid of the police.

Or me.

And another frightening thought hits me. What if Rader knows about Hayden? I bend over the toilet and retch, but all that comes up is more acid.

"Megan," Ronnie says. "I'll get you home."

"No," I say too forcefully. She is being kind and I sound like the bride of Frankenstein. I know I should tell her everything I can so she can protect herself. But I think if I find Rader and end him, this will all go away.

"I'll be okay." I manage to croak out the words. "We have work to do. I'll get some rest before your swearing-in ceremony. I promise." If Rader doesn't kill me first.

I go to the sink and wet the washcloth again. I wipe my face and look in the mirror. I don't really care how I look but I have to pretend to be getting better.

"There," I say, and force a smile. "All better. Thanks."

I can see that Ronnie's not buying it, but she doesn't say so.

"I may need you to do something for me," I tell her. "Let's go to your desk."

Her desk is further from Nan's. When we get there, I pick up her phone and keeping my back turned toward Nan, I call Dan's work number at the shop. I get an answering machine and leave a message for him to call me. Then I remember he has some girl working for him. I call back, get the answering machine again. I add that his employee should call me right away if Dan's not there. I hang up.

Ronnie is giving me a curious look. "Dan's not at work?"

"I don't know. He's not talking to me."

"You used my phone so he wouldn't recognize the number calling?"

She's smart.

"I guess," I say. My throat is feeling a little better. Good enough to speak clearly anyway. "Can you call his cell phone?"

She calls and hangs up before it goes to voice mail. I think he might not answer if he's outside working on his carvings with the chainsaw. I have her call again. He doesn't answer. I call from my own cell phone. No answer. The voice mail answers and I hang up.

It's 10:00 in the morning.

He should be at work.

"Let's go," I say.

"Are we going to see Dan?"

"I have to see Sheriff Gray first."

I go to his office, rap on the door and enter.

CHAPTER FIFTY-THREE

Sheriff Gray gives me a reprieve until Ronnie's hiring ceremony is over this evening. I promise I will answer his questions. I've already applied for a search warrant for Michael Rader's motor home and he said he will contact me when it's ready to serve. He talked to the judge and was promised an arrest warrant as well. I don't want to arrest Rader, but this will cover the bases.

We get into Port Townsend. Dan's store is closer than his cabin. I push through a couple of yellow traffic lights. The Taurus hugs the ground better than most of the marked police vehicles and I take advantage of that as I round corners. I pull in front of Dan's shop, which is facing the bay, and I try to tell Ronnie to stay put but she's out of the car.

The front of his business is a glassed-in showcase where several of his carvings are displayed. A grizzly bear stands twice the size of the one I have at home. Lighthouses, some painted red and white like a barber pole, some more traditional with the whitewashed tower. Eagles, cranes, wolves, buffalo. He's been very busy.

I look through one of the panes of glass in the door and can see the sales counter. The place looks empty. I try the door and it opens. I tell Ronnie to go to the back and I go in. I move ahead and see a teenage girl holding a rifle. She's holding it like she's aiming it at someone who is just out of my sight.

I don't wait for Ronnie to get in position. Weapon in hand, I move slowly and deliberately toward the armed girl. She's turned where I can see only the side of her face but she's clearly not more than a teenager. Lustrous black hair hangs over her shoulders and down her back. She's about my size. I point my .45 at her. I don't want to startle her into firing the rifle. I speak in a conversational voice.

Sheriff's Office. Don't turn around. Please put the weapon safely on the floor, ma'am. That's what I should have said. In truth I yell like a whole SWAT Unit, "Drop it, bitch!"

Instead of dropping the rifle, she turns toward me, rifle still up and at the ready and I feel my finger tightening on the trigger. I let up at the last instant. I can see the "rifle" is made of wood and is painted.

She turns facing me. Her eyes are big as full moons. Her mouth is working like she's a fish out of water.

I remember the name Dan gave me for his employee. "Are you Jess?"

She tries to talk but only a croak escapes her lips. She nods her head up and down, then looks at the wooden rifle like it's a snake and throws it away.

I re-holster my .45 and show her my badge. "I'm Detective Carpenter. Sheriff's Office. My partner is at the back of the business, so I'm going to let her in. You stay here so she doesn't do anything." I've been in the shop once, so I know the way to the back door.

"You mean like you just did?" Jess asks. She's recovered fast or she's just a smartass.

"Yeah. I thought that was a real gun." I'm embarrassed but I would have been even more so if I'd shot her.

I bring Ronnie through after having her holster her weapon. I don't tell her I almost shot Dan's helper. I introduce Ronnie as a detective. It's easier than giving her whole title and having the person think Ronnie is a rent-a-cop.

"You scared me to death," Jess says. Her hand is on her chest. She's not scared. She's being a drama queen.

She's Native American. She's seventeen, a high school senior, and beautiful. She and Ronnie will get along just fine.

"Jess, I called and got the answering machine. Dan isn't answering his phone, either," I tell her.

"You're *that* Megan Carpenter. Dan's girlfriend. He's told me stories about you."

She seems to be in awe, so I don't correct her about the girlfriend comment.

"I need to find Dan. Do you know where he is?"

She looks up and around like Dan might be on the ceiling. "He's not here."

I can see that. The back of the store is one room with a long workbench but there are two doors. An entry door and a wider delivery door.

"Do you know how to get in touch with him?"

"He's not at home?" she asks.

I want to slap her, but I don't. "Jess, I really need to find Dan. Do you have any idea where he is or how I can reach him?"

She shakes her head. I feel my hand making a fist.

"What would you do if there was an emergency? Who do you contact?" I ask almost calmly.

"I'd call the sheriff. But you're already here."

I look at Ronnie for help but she's got her hand over her mouth, hiding a grin.

I go to yes-and-no questions. "Has he been here this morning?" It doesn't work.

"He was here yesterday. He left me some instructions for today. All I do is run the register and take phone calls."

She's not doing very well at taking phone calls. I wonder if I was that dense at seventeen. I decide I wasn't. Not even when I was six. I didn't have a chance to make a mistake. It might have cost a life. Like just now when I almost shot her. And I may yet.

I let Ronnie take over the questioning. Jess may still be seeing the bore of my .45 in her mind. Ronnie is less threatening.

"You can call me Ronnie," she says, and gives Jess's hand a shake. Ronnie's been working on her grip. My idea. Her handshake used to be like water running through your hand. She's up to a Nerf ball.

"Is Dan coming in to the shop today?" Ronnie asks.

"He was supposed to be here when I opened. I have a key just in case he runs late."

"And what time did you open?" Ronnie asks.

"Six thirty. Well, six forty-five or so. The key wasn't where he usually leaves it and I had to hunt around. He's always here before me, but I think he left me a note last night telling me what to do this morning."

"Can we see the note?" Ronnie asks.

Jess goes behind the counter and retrieves a piece of notebook paper. She hands it to Ronnie. She's probably still pissed at me for putting a gun in her face.

Ronnie hands the note to me. It's handwritten.

Jess, take care of the shop for me until I return.

I'm not an expert on handwriting, but it looks like Dan's perfect hand. I show it to Jess and ask, "Is this his handwriting?"

She shakes her head. "How would I know? *You're* his girlfriend."

My hand makes a fist again and I shove it in my pocket. "Have you tried to call him?"

"When?" she asks.

"Today?"

"No." She looks at me as if I've asked her to calculate the earth's distance from the sun.

"When was the last time you saw him?"

"A couple of days. I don't know."

"How many days?"

"Yesterday morning."

"Yesterday morning what time?"

"What's with all the questions? Is he in some kind of trouble? Am I going to lose my job?"

Ronnie makes me proud. She reaches out and grabs Ms. Moonbeam by the shoulders. "He's not in trouble with us. But you may be if you don't start answering our questions." She says this forcefully and Jess seems to snap out of her childish games.

"I don't know where he is. Honest. He was here yesterday morning when I came to work. I was here about six thirty and I left around five thirty yesterday. He was still here when I left. His truck was parked around the back. I haven't heard from him since yesterday when I left work. He never said anything about not coming in today. I came to work at six thirty this morning and his truck wasn't out back. I don't know if he's coming to work today or not, but he's usually here before I am."

"Was the front door locked or unlocked when you got here this morning?" I ask.

"I thought it was locked still. I used a key to get in but I don't know if it was unlocked or not. I thought I locked it behind me. That's why I was so scared when you yelled at me. The front and back were supposed to be locked."

"Call him," I say. He's not answering *my* calls. He was really ticked off when he left me at the restaurant. But he may answer for Jess. She hesitates only a split second, then pulls a phone from the back pocket of her skin-tight blue jeans. She calls and listens. After a dozen rings her expression becomes quizzical. She hangs up before I can stop her.

"It didn't even go to his voice mail. That's really strange," she says.

CHAPTER FIFTY-FOUR

We're back in the Taurus. It's not like Dan. None of this. I haven't told Ronnie about the little fight we had the other night. It's none of her business but it is quickly becoming necessary.

"I notice you had Jess call Dan," Ronnie says. "You don't think he'll answer if he knows it's you? Did you have a fight?"

"We went out for drinks the other night and I had one too many."

I don't know why I'm lying.

"He got mad because you had too much to drink?"

"It's not important, Ronnie. We just need to find him."

"Megan, if I'm going to help you, I need to know what's going on. I don't understand why we're looking for Dan. Was he a friend of Mrs. Delmont's too? You haven't told me much about why we've talked to these other people. And I think you're keeping things from the sheriff."

Ronnie's been a big help. More of a partner, really. But I don't know how much I can tell her. She's intuitive. That's the problem with not telling her enough.

"I'm going to tell you something that only I and the sheriff know. That means if you tell anyone I'll have to kill you."

She can tell by the look on my face I'm not kidding.

"You know you can trust me." She already knows some things that I haven't told anyone else. She saw me basically assassinate the guy last month who had shot me and was going to rape her. I shot his balls off while he was still alive. He was a rapist and a murderer. He got what he gave.

"Okay, I trust you," I lie. "I knew Monique Delmont. I had more of a friendship with her than I let on. I've been in her house before."

Ronnie gives me a hurt look. I lied to her.

"I haven't talked to her for several years and I didn't know she had any idea I worked here." That much is the truth.

"The picture of you coming from the Sheriff's Office," Ronnie says. "It makes sense now."

"I don't think Monique snapped that picture," I say. "I think the killer wants me to know he knows where I was." This doesn't explain why I would think Gabrielle is in danger, so I say, "I never met her daughter but I figure the killer is crazy and killing people even remotely connected with her. And me."

"Why would the killer be after *you*, Megan?"

Yeah. Damn it. I improvise and hope she doesn't see through the lie.

"Maybe the killer's not specifically after me. Maybe it's all about Monique. Dan showed me the picture that Sheriff Gray found at the scene. That's what we argued about. He said it was left at his store and he wanted to know what was going on. He knows we're working on this murder and wanted to know if the picture was connected. He wanted to know why the killer would send him one. I couldn't tell him."

"I wish I had told him something. Anything. He could have gone somewhere and stayed out of the way, like Gabrielle, until this is over."

But I couldn't chance him finding out about my past. Now he's basically missing and maybe I'll lose him.

"You did what you thought was best, Megan. I know you and you wouldn't put anyone in danger. I don't know why you want to keep this so secret, but whatever. I'm in."

I could hug her. But I don't really like people touching me. And that goes both ways.

"We need to take another little ride," I say.

"Dan lives over in Snow Creek, doesn't he?"

I put the car in gear and carefully pull into traffic. "Can you keep trying his phone?"

She does.

I check with Dispatch. The patrol keeping an eye on Dan's business haven't seen him. I take State Route 20 to Discovery Bay, where I turn south on Highway 101 until it circles back north toward National Forest Service Road 2850. On a map it looks like an unnecessarily circuitous route, but it's the quickest way to cover the almost twenty-five miles to Dan's place.

Ronnie's GPS navigates until I tell her to turn it off. I know the way and the female voice on the iPhone is starting to get on my last nerve. I know with the GPS off Ronnie will have to fill the silence, and she doesn't disappoint.

I tune her out. I have my own thoughts and worries. I berate myself for not sharing my concern with Dan last night. I could have insisted he stay in a motel out of town. Or even at my place. Somehow I can't see Dan on the run. He's not like me. Especially if he thought I was in danger. I don't know him that well, but I believe he'd protect me with his life. I would do the same for him. I can't say that about many people.

Snow Creek Road is just ahead and I look north toward the area where several people had secluded cabins and even a farm or two. They are all separated by almost a mile, and hundreds of yards from the road on winding hard-packed earth tracks. They have almost complete privacy. I remember the last time I was here, a teenage daughter had murdered her entire family. Another woman had kept the desiccated corpse of her girlfriend in her cabin for years for company. Maybe total seclusion drives you mad. Feelings of being alone turn to imaginings and that turns to fear. The only way to work off their mania is on each other.

Another downside of the seclusion is that no one would hear you if you were in trouble. Dan works on his chainsaw carvings here, but you can't hear the noise until you get close.

I reach the turnoff to his house and smell smoke. I can see the fog of it settling in the trees but it isn't unusual for people to burn garbage out here.

"Someone has a campfire," Ronnie says. "I hope they're being safe. I don't want to be in the middle of a wildfire."

I don't, either, but I'd drive through it to see if Dan is okay. "Get on the phone and tell Dispatch we've got heavy smoke here. See if they have reports yet."

Ronnie is on the phone with Dispatch as I hurry down the dirt lane. I can see Dan's house dead ahead. It isn't on fire, but the smoke is heavier here.

"They say they don't have anything, but they're sending a chopper up to check the area out and they're notifying Fire."

I pull in the drive and immediately see the source of the smoke. "Call them back and tell them to send a pumper."

Someone has made a huge bonfire of Dan's wood carvings. There must be over a dozen pieces piled almost six feet high. Flames are shooting three times that high. Dan's truck is parked twenty feet from the bonfire and I worry about it catching fire or exploding.

I know Dan keeps several foam fire extinguishers handy, but I don't think it will be enough. There are two extinguishers on his small, covered porch. I grab one of these and Ronnie grabs the other. I pull the pin. It's heavier than I thought. I've seen them used at the academy but never used one. I do remember one of the instructions. I yell at Ronnie over the roar of the fire, "Ronnie, sweep from side to side at the bottom and work your way up."

Ronnie pulls the pin and holds the heavy extinguisher under her arm with the bad wrist and moves toward the fire, squeezing the handle. White foam bubbles off the scorched wood.

I see Ronnie has this as under control as it's going to get until the fire department gets here. "I'm going to find Dan," I say, and run to the house. The door is cracked open. Dan doesn't do that even when he's home. He lives out in the sticks but that doesn't mean there are no thefts. I go inside still holding the fire extinguisher.

It's not a large place. The front room serves as living room and kitchen. A small bedroom and bathroom are at the back. There's nothing in the front room. I go behind the counter that separates the kitchen from the front room and nothing is amiss. I see the bedroom door is shut.

I put a hand against the surface of the door. The door is cool to the touch. I push it open and go in, extinguisher hose at waist level, ready. There's nothing. Dan's bed is messed up where he slept in it. I've never been in his bedroom before. I check the tiny closet. There are several more lumberjack-type shirts, worn jeans, canvas coveralls, boots, shoes and one blue suit with a white button-down shirt on the same hanger.

The bathroom gives nothing away. A toothbrush, toothpaste still open on the sink. The towel is still damp; the shower has been used recently.

I turn to go outside to help Ronnie when I see something on Dan's pillow. It's the laminated picture Dan had of me as Rylee. I stick it in my pocket. No blood is on the mattress or pillow. No blood is in the bathroom or any area I've been through.

And no sign of Dan Anderson.

I rush back outside and spray foam around the fire, but these extinguishers have no chance of putting down the conflagration that threatens to eat everything in sight.

Then I hear the familiar sound of fire trucks not too distant. It couldn't have been timed better. Both extinguishers are running out of foam.

CHAPTER FIFTY-FIVE

After the firemen arrive I squeeze the Taurus around their equipment and park on Forest Service Road 2850 a safe distance from the blaze. I sit in the car with Ronnie, watching the flames rise above the trees. We might have saved Dan's house by acting so quickly, but all of his carvings will almost certainly be ash. I think of the bear he carved and gave me and of how I moved it because it was in my way. I can be mean-spirited sometimes. I need to value things more, but I grew up moving from one place to another and leaving everything behind at the drop of a hat. I learned not to get attached to things.

Ronnie sits with her arms crossed over her chest. We both smell of smoke. We have the windows down and smoke drifts our way when the wind changes direction.

"Maybe someone is mad at him for something else entirely and set the fire? Or maybe it started on its own. Spontaneous combustion." She doesn't sound like she believes it. Neither do I. The fire was meant to draw me here. Of that I'm sure. Well, I'm here. So what next?

"I think we may have saved his house at least, Megan."

I don't say anything. She's trying to make me feel better. It doesn't work but I'm grateful anyway. Here she is, sitting with me, when she's to be sworn in shortly at the Sheriff's Office. Sheriff Gray must be losing his mind, wondering where we are.

"Call the store again and ask Jess if she's heard from him."

Ronnie calls Dan's shop and gets the voice mail. She leaves a message that Dan or Jess should return the call right away. She says it's a police matter. As she does this my phone rings and I dig it out of my pocket.

It's Dan's phone number.

"Where have you been?" I say a little sharper than I intend to. He doesn't answer. "Firemen are at your place." Still no response. I'm starting to get a little miffed. And then I feel a chill. I ask, "Who is this?"

A synthesized voice comes over the tiny speaker. "Do I have your attention?"

What the?… "Who is this?" I ask, but I know who it is. Rader. "Where is Dan?"

"He's with me. He's alive. For now."

"Why are you doing this? And why are you using a voice synthesizer? You think I'm recording this call."

"You know why, Rylee."

"I think you have me mixed up with someone else," I say.

Ronnie leans toward me trying to hear. I push her away.

"Oh, I don't think so," the robotic voice says. "I've been following your career closely since you murdered Alex and Marie. I was there when you drove your aunt's car into the river. Did you get the present I left for you at your friend's house?"

I assume Rader's talking about Monique. But something about the way he's using words is different. For one thing, there was that pause between the last words. It feels like the words are being read from a teleprompter. I saw a deputy playing with a computer program that did that. It could change the voice to anything. A man, a woman, cartoon characters, celebrities.

"Why do you care about Dan? What is he to you?"

"He was yours. And now he's mine. An eye for an eye. That's what you do. Right, Rylee?"

My breath catches. Alex Rader, serial killer, said those words to my mom. He told my mom she belonged to him. That *I* belonged to him. And he was going to have me. But Alex Rader is dead.

"I did believe that once," I say cautiously. I don't want to go into details with Ronnie sitting right here, but the person calling obviously wants to rub my nose in it. "Let me talk to him."

Rader, or that damn program, laughs. "I know your friend is in the car. Let me speak to her."

Asshole. He knew I wouldn't do that. "What do you want?"

"I've got what I want from you. You understand? I've taken two of *yours*."

"Listen to me, Michael. I don't—"

The laughing starts again in that peculiar Siri way. "You don't know who *I* am, but I know who *you* are, Rylee."

I'm quiet, thinking furiously. He's lying. Trying to confuse me. Or he thinks I'm recording the call and he's trying to keep his name out of this. But if it's not Michael, then who? Maybe there's another brother I don't know about. A son. Maybe one of Marie's kin.

"I know you're the one who's leaving the pictures. First at Monique's and then at Dan's."

"I left something for Sheriff Gray. Did he get it?"

He's talking about the newspaper article.

"Rylee, Rylee. You're wasting time and you don't have much left. *Dan* doesn't have much. He's alive now, but I think I'll carve him like the bear he gave you. I've never used a chainsaw before. Sounds like fun."

"Listen to me, Michael. If you let Dan go, unhurt, I won't track you down and show you real pain. You know I can do it. I won't stop until I find you. Do you hear me?" I feel more than anger or hate. Rage has taken me to a new plane.

"Feel better? You know I'm watching you. I'm coming after you. And your friends. You won't know when or where I'll take one again. You can only be certain of one thing. In the end I will kill you, Rylee."

I shouldn't have pushed his buttons. I realize too late that he might kill Dan sooner. "Let me talk to Dan," I say into a dead phone.

I drop the phone on the seat. Ronnie is silently watching me. I don't know how much of the call she could hear, but even a little is too much.

"You should have recorded the call," Ronnie says.

I struggle with this for only a second.

"No need to."

"Why not?"

Good question. I didn't have an answer. I take the phone back out and bring up the last number. "If I give you the number, can you track it?"

"I can try."

I give her the number and she gets busy on her phone. "No luck," she says. "I can try getting the last cell tower it pinged when we get back to the office. If we're going back, that is."

I have no choice but to go to the office and hope Rader calls again. He's playing with me. He won't kill Dan until he's finished torturing me.

CHAPTER FIFTY-SIX

"This isn't the way to Port Hadlock," Ronnie says.

"Pit stop."

"Are we going to Port Townsend?"

"Yes."

To her credit she doesn't ask why. I have a feeling that Rader wasn't just toying with me during the call. He was giving me a clue. I step on the gas until I reach the town limits. I drive past Dan's shop just on the off chance that someone is there, or I see something out of place.

Nothing.

I pull up in front of my place. Everything seems to be the way I left it this morning. Rader knew about the bear in my bedroom. He was wrong about its location. I'd moved it near the door a week ago. But he said it was by my desk.

I want to go in alone, but Ronnie ignores my order. We have to work on that. I open the door and go in. I immediately see the bear is not by the door. My weapon is in my hand, and when I look at Ronnie, hers is as well. Some things are just reflex.

I whisper at Ronnie to stay by the door and keep an eye out in front. She nods. I mouth at her, "Don't shoot me." Probably not necessary, but better to put the idea in her head just in case.

I clear the kitchen and then go to the bedroom. The bear is on top of my desk. It's facing me. There's something rolled up in its mouth.

I want to see what it is, but I clear the bathroom and closet first. Then I go to the bear. I pull a glove from my pocket and slide it on. A piece of paper the size of a dime coin wrapper is rolled up and stuffed in the bear's jaws. I lift it out of the mouth and feel something inside the paper. My blood runs cold. My imagination runs wild and I suddenly don't want to see what has been left for me.

Ronnie calls from the front. "Megan. Are you okay?"

Stupid question. If I weren't okay, I wouldn't be able to tell her. I'm not used to working with a partner yet, but it's good to have someone checking on me. I know if I don't answer, she will come back here, and I don't want that.

"One more minute," I say.

I unroll the paper. A severed finger falls out of it and lands on top of the desk. My pulse quickens. There is something written on the paper but my attention is drawn to the bear's mouth. Dan carved the bear with a wide-open mouth. Another object is stuck deep in its maw. I take my phone out and use the flashlight to see. It's another finger. I use an ink pen on the desk to pry it out. Both digits are long and thin. Almost like a woman's hand, but there is dark hair on the knuckles. I know they are not Dan's and my heart slows. His fingers are much bigger and calloused. A sense of relief washes over me even though I know they belong to some unfortunate soul.

I take a baggy from my pocket and use it to pick up the fingers and turn the baggy inside out to hold them. I put the baggy in my pocket. I unroll the note again.

Rylee. You know where I am. Tonight. After dark.
Come alone or I will kill him. Bring a weapon and I will kill him. Tell anyone and he will die. If you don't come, you'll never find me. I'll find you.

I hear footsteps in the hall and stuff the note in my blazer pocket. Ronnie comes in and gives me a questioning look.

"It's okay," I say. "No one is here and nothing is missing." It's not a complete lie. Nothing was taken. Something was left behind. "Let's go to the Sheriff's Office. See if you can track down Dan's phone."

Before we leave, I check all the windows. They are locked. While I lock up, I examine the lock and the dead bolt. I don't see any marks on the locks where a tool scratched it. Someone is good at picking locks.

On the way to the office I drive by Dan's again. It's closed up tight. I didn't expect to find Dan there. I don't know Jess's last name or her cell phone number. It would be useless to call her anyway. She's as dim as a broken lightbulb.

"Ronnie, I need you to do something you may not like." She doesn't respond and that's good. "Sheriff will know about the fire at Dan's cabin, but I don't want him to know I got a call from Dan's phone. Or that we checked my place. Understand?"

"You're going to need his help."

"I want to catch this guy. I don't want to scare him off."

"The phone call you got was him, wasn't it?"

I nod.

"He wants to meet you."

I say nothing.

"He left something in your place, didn't he? I mean you've got some strange tastes, but I don't think you would put a three-foot-tall bear on top of your desk."

Ronnie's smart. I keep forgetting that. "I want to do this on my own," I say.

"Because of your friendship with Monique Delmont."

"Yes," I say, but mostly because I want to skin Michael Rader.

"I'll keep quiet about this if you do something for me," she says.

I wait. I think I know what she's going to say and the answer will be no.

"I want to go with you."

"I don't want you to but okay. You do exactly as I say, though."

"I will. We make a good team, Megan. I don't want you to get hurt knowing I could have done something about it. I couldn't live with that."

You can't live if he kills you. I don't plan on taking her, but I appreciate her sentiment. She's a lot like me. Only not as good a liar.

CHAPTER FIFTY-SEVEN

We get back to the office. I don't automatically look into the trees for a stalker. They've made their play. It's time for me to make mine.

Ronnie is using her technical genius to try and locate Dan's phone, or the location it last called from. Sheriff Gray is out of the office. Most likely getting a cake and drinks for the after-swearing-in ceremony.

I sit at my desk. My mind is on fire. I'm afraid for Dan; I care more for him than I realized. I would give anything for him to not be involved in this. I would trade places with him. I know Rader doesn't want that. He wants me dead but he wants me to suffer. It wouldn't hurt so bad if I didn't care. If I never had a relationship. My friends and family are my Kryptonite. I try to think of someone who is precious to Rader. Someone I can take and hurt and make him suffer. The two people I know he cared about are dead. I killed them.

Even if I knew of someone he could be manipulated with, I don't think I'm quite that far down the rabbit hole. But I'm getting there. I have an idea.

"Ronnie, are you getting anywhere?"

She looks up and I can see by the look on her face that she has found nothing.

"I have an idea," I say. "I know you looked into Michael Rader. Do you think we can find any relatives?" She already knows about Marie Rader being murdered and Alex dropping off the map. Looking for family is something I failed to do.

"I can try," she says. "I'll check the obituaries. There are next of kin on those."

I hadn't thought of that. "Also, can you see if we have finger-prints available on Michael Rader?" I'm pretty sure they would have been turned up by the crime lab when we left the container of rat poison. But it's worth a try. I want to compare the fingers I have in my pocket to the fingerprints. I don't know why. I doubt that Michael would cut his own fingers off, but he's half past crazy and full of anger. I don't blame him. I only wish I thought of it first. I have no idea who these fingers belong to.

Ronnie will be sworn in tonight. I can't be here. I will be at Rader's motor home. My hands are shaking. Not from fear, but from anticipation. I have to find Dan and free him. I have to find Rader and end him. I know Rader's had time to set traps. His motor home is in the perfect setting. Secluded. One way in and one way out. If he sees anyone but me, he'll kill Dan. Of that I have no doubt.

It's been unseasonably warm for March but the sun still sets at the same time. It will be dark in an hour. I don't want to be late. I get up and start for the bathroom, which is down a hall. Ronnie looks, then goes back to staring at her computer. There is an exit in the back of the building just down from the bathroom. I reach the bathroom and open the door. Then shut it loud enough for Ronnie to hear. I creep down the hall and gently open the door. It opens soundlessly.

I shut the door quietly behind me and make it around the side of the building to my car. Ronnie's sitting in the passenger seat of the Taurus.

"Okay. You can come," I say. "But remember, you will do what I say, when I say."

"Where are we going?" Ronnie asks.

"Don't ask."

*

I drive to Anderson Lake Road and take it to SR-101. The drive will take an hour and a half at least. I have that long to figure out how I'm going to ditch Ronnie. She doesn't need to be part of this. I can't protect her and get the job done.

We're outside of Port Angeles.

"We're going to the motor home. Is that where he's going to meet you?"

It's dark so I say, "He said there would be a signal. A flashlight on and off in the woods. On your side. You have to duck down. I'm supposed to come alone. If he sees you, he said he'll kill Dan."

Ronnie scrunches down in the seat where she can barely see out. "I won't let him see me."

You're damn right you won't because you won't be with me. Up ahead I see the signs.

HISTORIC HUMES RANCH CABIN
5 MI.

And the other:

ELWHA RIVER TRAIL
3 MI.

I drive a mile or so past these and say, "Hey, did you see that?"

Ronnie scrunches down further. "No. What?"

"I saw a light off in the woods. On my side. He thinks he's being cute." I slow down and pull onto the shoulder.

"What do we do?"

I say, "You can get out of your side. The interior lights don't work. I pulled the fuse when I got the car." I did. There's no sense in giving yourself away with a light coming on at the wrong time. "Stay low and go into the trees. I don't think he can see you. Stay in the woods unless you hear me call out."

"What are you going to do?"

"I'll sit here until you're in the woods. Then I'll go across the road and see what's what." I take my gun out of the holster and lay it beside me on the seat. "He said not to come armed."

"No. You can't go out there without a weapon."

I look at her. "I have to. Besides, you have my back."

"Don't do it. There must be another way."

I wish there was. I wish I could take her with me. Rader warned me to come alone. I plan to. I'm going to kill him and I don't want a witness.

"This is the only way," I say. "It's now or never. If I don't go, he'll kill Dan. We're committed."

"Oh, this is bad. I'm going to get killed before I become a deputy," she says, and cracks the car door open.

She almost slides out on the ground and crab walks across the grass and down into a ditch, then up the other side and into the tree line. I wait until she disappears into the trees and put the car in gear. I hate doing this to her, but it's for her own good. And for mine.

I pull back onto the road and step on the gas. It will take her at least an hour to get to Port Angeles and call the sheriff. It will all be over by then.

I find the side road near Silent Ridge where the motor home is parked and drive slowly. I check right and left for any sign of movement. If there are cameras strapped to trees, I will never see them in the dark. I stop and put my body armor on. I don't think it will help if Rader slits my throat or shoots me in the head with a high-powered rifle, but it's better than nothing.

I get moving again. My headlights wash over the motor home. With its bark-and-cream color, it's almost invisible. Nothing is moving. While there are no lights on, the clouds part allowing a narrow beam of moonlight on the ground. I stop in the darkest spot I can find and roll the window down. The woods are alive with the deafening sounds you would expect this far from civilization. I tuck my .45 in the back of my waistband and get out.

If he's going to come at me, he will do it now.

CHAPTER FIFTY-EIGHT

I've waited long enough. As I approach the motor home, I hear something off in the trees to my left. My hand goes to my gun. The sound stops. I wait. Listen. The sound comes again. Like a small animal caught in a trap. My mind says Rader has set out bear traps in the darkness and is luring me into one.

My sense of survival says I should get the hell out of here. My heart says stay, Dan is here. Somewhere. Alive, I hope. Besides, I've come this far to get Rader and came alone because I didn't want Ronnie hearing all the things Rader will say.

I take a step forward and hear the sound again. I don't want to go there. Rader knows the area. I don't. The sound is louder now. A moan. Maybe it's Dan? The sound is coming from ten feet in front of me now.

My feet catch on something big as I rush forward and I nearly fall on top of the source of the noise. It's not Dan. It's a woman. I've tripped over her legs where she is sitting, propped against a tree. Her long, dark hair covers her face. Her arms are behind her and a rope seems to be wound around her. She looks dazed. Maybe drugged. She's smeared with something black. Dirt. Grease. Suet. It's dark and hard to tell but I can smell smoke. Rader wouldn't leave a conscious victim where he planned to kill me. I look around thinking this must be a distraction. The woman is bait. She starts moaning again and her frightened eyes open and fix on me. She panics and draws her legs back.

"I'm not going to hurt you," I say. "I'm here to help. Where is he?" I reach for my gun but too late.

"He's right here," the woman says, and I see one arm is freed of the ropes. She grabs me and I feel a sharp pinch in my calf and see the syringe in her hand.

My legs won't hold me and I collapse onto my side and I'm unable to move.

The woman slips the rope over her head and gets up. She brushes the dirt and grass from her jeans, shakes her hair out and pulls it back off her shoulders. She's my height, a little slimmer, but has at least fifteen years on me. I'm not good at guessing ages. She tosses the syringe into the woods.

"I have a little surprise for you, Rylee," she says, and even though I'm paralyzed I feel my skin crawl. I was stupid coming here alone. Michael has a partner. A psycho partner.

She stands over me, bends down and pats my clothing down and finds my .45. She pulls it out of my waistband and tosses it. I'm unable to see where she threw it but I hear it thud a good distance behind me. She finds the knife I keep in my boot and tosses it away.

I should be frightened at this point, but I'm too angry to be scared.

She gets down on one knee and looks into my eyes. "You won't be able to move for a while." She smiles. Her teeth are perfect. Bright white against her olive skin.

"You're probably wondering who I am. Sorry. You'll die without ever knowing who killed you. Just know that you killed people I cared about."

My mind is running a marathon. I've killed a few people. I don't know her. I've never seen her but she must be Michael's girlfriend. She must be talking about Alex or Marie. Or maybe there's a sister.

"What? Cat got your tongue? Well, you don't have to talk for me to read your eyes. You want to kill me as badly as I want to kill you."

She stands but keeps her eyes on mine. "My, my. You still think you can. I've been thinking of doing this for so long. Michael said you were surprisingly tough and relentless. Did you know Michael was afraid of you? He was. But I thought you'd be easy and I was right, Michael was wrong. How someone as reckless as you overcame Alex and Marie is a wonder. You would never have lasted five minutes with me, even without the drug."

I want so bad to tell her to shut the hell up. If she's going to kill me, she should do it and not talk me to death. When I get feeling back in my body, I won't talk. I'll just gut her like a fish.

"I want to show you something." She grabs my ankles and drags me across the rough ground. I can feel pressure in my hips and ribs and my head bounces over rocks and sticks but there is no real pain. Whatever she shot me up with has anesthetic properties as well as paralytic. If I live, I'll have to tell Marley.

She drags me around behind the motor home. I can see a window in it but there are no lights on inside. I wonder where Michael Rader is. Is she dragging me to a grave? My anger starts to lessen and fear seeps in. If I could only move. Just a little. Is Michael the one who is supposed to kill me? Or will they do it together?

She drops my legs and rolls me onto my side. My face lands in loose soil. There is a mound of red dirt, freshly dug up and piled a foot high. Some of it gets in my mouth, but I can't spit it out. I can feel it dissolve.

"Sorry, Rylee. I didn't mean for you to eat dirt just yet." She kicks the dirt away from my face and leaves me staring at a depression dug into the ground.

"Go ahead. Get a good look," she says, and I feel myself being shoved forward onto the mound of dirt. She turns my head until

I can see into the shallow pit. Michael Rader's severed head lies on his chest. His hands are placed on each side of the head as if he is holding it and preparing to put it on like a hat. His eyes are open, not really looking at anything.

I'm pulled onto my back again and I see her moving toward my feet. She picks up my legs and drags me toward the back side of the motor home. My head bounces against the ground, hard; I can see stars above me and behind my eyes. I stop moving and can see the back of the motor home. She leans down and I feel myself jostled, but don't know what she's doing until I see one of my arms held up with a noose slipped around the wrist. She pulls the other arm and slips a noose around it as well. My arms disappear over my head.

My toes and the tips of my fingers feel like they're being pricked with a thousand pins. The paralytic agent is beginning to dissipate. I have no idea how long it will take to do so, but I hope she takes her time with the preparations of my destruction. She likes to talk. I think of blinking to let her know I'm still alert, but it might make her give me a stronger dose of her poison.

She hoists me up with my back against the motor home, hanging by my arms. I think my feet aren't touching the ground. I try to make myself angry again. Adrenaline is my friend. I think of Monique when I first met her. How she took a chance on me and helped me get into college and continued to fund me and support me until Michael Rader came into her life. I think of how frightened she sounded when she told me that she couldn't help me anymore. And that she'd given copies of evidence I'd collected to Michael because he'd threatened to kill her daughter.

I wonder who this woman is. How does she know about me? "What the hell?" I say, and I surprise myself on hearing my voice. I hear her on the other side of the motor home.

"You should get your feeling back soon. Don't go anywhere. You'll miss the party."

I can feel my hands. They feel like balloons attached to my wrists. The rope is cutting off the blood supply. I try to stand and feel my toes touching the ground. I don't think I can stand to take the pressure from my wrists but I try.

I hear something go thud, thud, thud, and an *oompf* and the woman marches Dan around the side of the motor home. His arms are bound behind his back. A rope is stretched between his ankles, allowing him to walk very limited steps. She pushes him next to me and puts a hangman's noose around his throat. His face is bruised and swollen and bleeding.

"Dan." He knows I'm here but he doesn't look at me. I don't blame him. He's here because of me. He's here because I lied and didn't warn him.

The drug is wearing off fast, but I don't let on by trying to stand, although the pain in my hands makes me want to scream.

She steps in front of Dan with another syringe and is about to give him an injection. He doesn't look like he can take it.

"I want to ask you something," I say. My words are slurred.

She stops and looks at me.

"Come here. I want to look in your eyes so I can know if you're lying."

She pulls a second syringe from her pocket. "Don't worry. I have enough for you."

"You skanky insane bitch. I can't imagine what either of the Raders saw in you. Were you their maid? I mean, look at you. Alex preferred sweet young blonds like me."

She laughs but I can tell I've struck a nerve, so I go on.

"Michael probably couldn't get it up. Maybe that's why he killed men. Did you kill Michael because he liked men?"

She steps over to me and stares into my face. Her lips are a pencil line.

"Michael wasn't my lover. And he was never my partner. He was stupid."

"He was smart enough to kill those prisoners who might have become a complication for Alex."

She smiles. "You think so, huh? He wasn't protecting his brother. Michael and Marie were having an affair. He was protecting himself. And her."

I always wondered why Michael would take all the pictures of the dead girls from Monique. He wasn't protecting his brother's name. He was protecting himself. "Michael was helping Marie select the victims. He took some of the pictures, didn't he?"

She doesn't answer. She holds the syringe up and readies it.

"You're from Central America." It's a guess. I don't care where the hell she's from. I just want to stall. I can feel my feet and fingers now. I can imagine my fingers jamming a syringe in her eye.

She says, "Ecuador. I escaped and came here only to be a slave. Alex saved me. He gave me everything. Told me everything. He hated Marie. She was making him kill."

"How?" I already know she was using emotional blackmail to get Alex to do whatever she wanted.

She says, "Marie was paralyzed from the waist down from a car accident. Alex was driving. She used his guilt to make him kidnap and kill for her. She got off on it."

"Why are you doing this? Do you get off on it too?"

"I loved Alex. He was going to leave Marie and run away with me. But you killed him. I don't care that you killed Marie. If you hadn't, I would have. I tried telling him the accident wasn't his fault. But he had a big heart. He tried to make it up to her, but she was sick."

Yeah. She was sick. Not Alex. He was just following orders. He had such a big heart that he tortured the girls almost to death for seven days, raped them over and over, killed them and dumped their naked bodies to be found like roadkill. And this sick bitch knew all about it.

"How did you talk Michael into helping you?"

The corners of her mouth turn up in a smile. "I know you're stalling but it won't matter. No one knows you're here or they would have shown themselves by now. So I'll tell you. I've got time.

"Michael was in trouble at work. He killed a couple of prisoners and he was under investigation. He was paranoid. I convinced him that he needed to kill you. He tracked you down for me. Gave me the information I needed on Monique and her daughter."

I ask, "You killed Monique just to get my attention? You killed Michael because you didn't need him? Or are you going to blame all of this on him?"

"You're smart. Alex told me you were. That's part of the reason Michael was afraid of you."

"I'll take that as a yes. Michael is the killer. Okay. But how did you get Monique to come to Port Townsend? Was she looking for me?"

"I joined Monique's little group of do-gooders. We became friends. It wasn't hard. She was a very lonely woman. I convinced her you were in danger from Michael. I showed her the articles in the paper about the prisoners dying and told her I had sources inside the prison who said Michael was under suspicion. I was the one making hang-up calls to her phone. And to the other phones. Gabrielle's, the Blumes', Moriarty's. I knew you'd check."

She'd drawn me in like a moth to a flame. Made me think it was Michael I was after. I didn't know Alex had a mistress. Or that she would be crazy as bat shit and a killer like Marie.

Dan said nothing through all of this, but I could feel his eyes on me. If we live through this I will have to move. Change identities again. Start over. I'll probably lose any chance I have of making up with Hayden.

Right now all I can think of is protecting Dan.

"If it gives you any peace, after I kill you and your boyfriend, I'm done."

"I'll make you a deal," I say.

I'm in no position to deal. But she's curious.

"If you let Dan go, I won't find you and kill you."

She throws her head back and laughs so hard and long that tears run from her eyes. She catches her breath.

"You're not very smart, but you've got nerve. I'm going to give you just a little of my special concoction. Enough so you can hear your boyfriend scream while I flay his skin off. If you're a good girl, I'll give him a little near the end, but I think he'll pass out before he needs it."

"You're going to kill me," I say. "Why not tell me your name?"

"I'm no one. I'm everything you hate. I'm the one who got away. Everyone I killed is down to you."

She takes the plastic guard off the tip of one syringe and holds the other between her teeth. She lifts the front of my shirt and leans over to inject it into my stomach.

The drug has worn off enough that I knee her under the jaw as hard as I can. She stumbles back and falls hard on the ground. She looks at me and the hate in her eyes has turned to panic. I can see the dark serum run down her chin. I don't know how much of the serum she got in her mouth but it wasn't enough. She gets unsteadily to her feet and tries to spit the paralytic out. She pulls the long-bladed knife from her belt and moves toward me in jerking strides like she's drunk.

She isn't stopping and I know I'm as good as dead. She'll stab me and might have enough strength to kill Dan. I feel tears of rage build up in my eyes. I turn my head toward Dan and he's looking at me. There's no fear or panic in his eyes.

"I'm sorry, Megan," he says. "This isn't your fault."

I feel a lump in my throat and a tightness in my chest. I realize that I love him with all my heart. I've not felt this strong an emotion since I had to leave Hayden behind. I feel my heart breaking and wish I could say the words to him, but I can't.

She intends to kill me first. It's what I deserve, but I'm not giving up. If she gets close again I'm going to kick her in the groin. I'm going to get loose somehow and shove that knife down her throat and then slit her open to see if she has a heart. I'm going to—

She raises the knife over her head and runs toward me with the blade pointed at my chest. I hear a loud crack and then someone yells, "Drop the knife! Police!"

A hole appears in one side of her head and brains blow out the other side. She crumples like a marionette with its strings cut. My eyes won't leave her, expecting her to get up.

Dan says, "My god, Megan." His head has turned toward the sound.

Ronnie is standing twenty feet away, her gun thrust forward in both hands; her eyes are slits, as if she closed them. Sheriff Gray comes running up, out of breath.

"My god, Megan," he says, repeating what Dan said.

CHAPTER FIFTY-NINE

Dan is on a gurney in the back of an ambulance. I'm in another but refusing treatment until Sheriff Gray reminds me that I need evidence of my imminent demise to justify the shooting. For Ronnie's sake, I allow them to check me over and draw blood. I'm bruised and scraped with some small cuts on the back of my head and shoulders from being dragged. My wrists are bruised but the paramedic doesn't think I have nerve damage. He suggests I go to the hospital. I thank him for his concern and go over to see Dan.

Dan hasn't fared as well. He's been beaten severely. Some of the cuts will need stitches and he will be hospitalized to see if the poison he was injected with has caused permanent muscle and nerve damage. Where I only got a taste, Dan got a full dose when she surprised him in Snow Creek. I heard him telling the Clallam County Sheriff's Detective that he answered the door to a woman saying her car broke down. Next thing he knew, he was trussed up next to me. He was still pretty out of it.

He opens his eyes when I pull myself into the back of the ambulance and sit on the bench beside him.

"I'm so sorry, Dan."

He turns his head away. He won't look at me. I'm humiliated. He heard every poisonous word spoken. He knows more about me than anyone now. Even some things I just learned from her. He pretty well knows the whole story except for what I've done since ending Alex and Marie Rader.

My first "almost boyfriend," Caleb Hunter, couldn't look at me either after he witnessed what I was capable of.

My hand is on Dan's. "Can we talk?"

He doesn't respond.

The paramedic says, "We're taking him to the hospital. The other ambulance will take you."

I want to ride in the back with Dan, but I'm sure Dan doesn't want me there. Maybe when he feels better and has some time to digest all this, he will want to talk about it.

His creations are burnt to ashes. I lean over and kiss him on the temple. He doesn't pull away, but he doesn't turn toward me, either. I get out and walk over to Sheriff Gray and Ronnie.

The paramedics close the ambulance doors. The emergency lights come on and they pull away. I tell myself that I don't really love him. I tell myself that I was in an emotional state and didn't think I'd survive. I push everything in a box and push it in the back of my mind. I can feel it like a weight.

"This was reckless even for you, Megan," Sheriff Gray says.

Ronnie's expression is frozen. She's just killed someone and I can imagine the images and self-repugnance she is feeling.

"How did you know where to find me?"

"You can thank Ronnie for that," the sheriff says. "She figured it out."

"But how did you get here so fast?" I left Ronnie on foot and at least twenty or thirty minutes from anywhere. Cell reception was spotty at best. It would have taken Sheriff Gray an hour to get to her even if he was running a Code 3 response.

"She guessed where you were going and texted me while you were in the ladies' room at headquarters. She said to give you a twenty-minute head start and follow. I caught up with Ronnie walking down SR-101. When you ditched her, she used your phone to track you."

Ronnie held her phone up. "Track My Device" she says. "I linked my phone to yours a while back. Good thing I did too."

I can't argue with that, but I need to get a new cell phone number and burn mine. I don't like being tracked.

"So what did you hear?" I ask them.

Ronnie says nothing. Smart girl. Sheriff Gray gives me a guarded look. "We wouldn't let her give you or Dan another injection of that stuff."

That tells me what I need to know. They heard almost everything. My past is blown wide open and all they need to do is put the pieces together with police reports. I feel sick, but it's over.

Sheriff Gray hitches up his gun belt and looks away. "Looks to me like this Alex Rader killed his wife and went on the run. Did they ever find him?"

He's giving me an out, and so I shake my head.

Ronnie looks at the woman's body. "Any idea who she is?"

"No clue."

Tony points and says, "We found the body of a man in a grave over there. His head was cut off. Was that Michael Rader?"

"Yes."

"Did she kill him?" Tony asks.

"She must have. She had some kind of grudge against him. Maybe she's a family member or girlfriend of one of his prison victims."

"And that's all you know?" he asks.

"Yes, Sheriff." *It's all I'm going to tell you.*

Ronnie asks, "Do you want to go to the hospital and check on Dan? I'll take you."

I feel a spike driven into my chest. I want to go, but I know I'd better not. This problem between us is like a popped pimple. Best not to touch it. Let it heal so it doesn't get infected.

"No. I want to go back to the office. I have a lot of paperwork. I guess we all do." Mine will be creative writing.

The coroner for Clallam County shows up and is trundled off by one of the deputies in the direction of Michael Rader's body.

A detective finishes asking questions of the first arriving deputies and turns his attention to me and Ronnie.

Sheriff Gray sees him and says, "I guess we'll be here a while."

The detective comes up to us.

"Howdy, Sheriff Gray."

"Hi, Mike. This is Detective Carpenter and Detective Marsh."

"Detective Mike Felson. I'd ask how you're doing, but if you'll excuse me saying so, you don't look too good."

Sheriff Gray says, "If you can make your questions short, I'm sure we can all come to your office or you can come to mine in the morning and we'll give complete statements."

Mike says, "Tony, I know where to find you. The deputies here have told me enough to piece this together for now, but I'll come to your office around nine a.m. tomorrow if that's doable. We haven't found Detective Carpenter's duty weapon yet, but if my guys find it I'll bring it tomorrow. You can secure Detective Marsh's weapon. For now you can go back home." He looks at me. "Anything you need to tell me before you cut out?"

"I had a knife in my boot. She threw it out there in the trees somewhere."

"We'll look."

Sheriff Gray smiles and shakes his hand. Mike gives us a parting shot. "Don't leave the country."

He's a joker. Two dead bodies, two almost victims, and he's making a joke.

I like him.

CHAPTER SIXTY

I ride back to the office with Tony and Ronnie. He will send a deputy to pick up my car and leave it at the office. We're mostly silent the entire trip for different reasons but all pertain to the same incident. I'm in no shape to even go into the office. Ronnie offers to let me sleep on her couch and I take her up on it.

"Do you feel up to driving?" I ask her while Sheriff Gray goes into the office.

"I'm fine, Megan," she says. She doesn't look fine. But I can drive if I have to.

Sheriff Gray comes out. "You know the routine," he says to Ronnie. "I have to send your weapon to Crime Scene for ballistics tests. But in the meantime, you both need to have something." He has two .45 semiautomatics tucked into the back of his waistband. He hands one to me and one to Ronnie.

"Don't get into trouble with these," he says. "Don't go anywhere but straight home. Go to sleep. Be back here at nine o'clock to give your statements to Detective Felson. Then you're off for a couple of days."

"What about the reports?" I ask.

"You'll do them tomorrow before you take some time off. Like last time."

I want to argue. I need to get the report done while this is fresh, but I can barely keep my eyes open.

"Go home," he says.

"She's staying with me tonight," Ronnie says.

"Okay. And, Ronnie?"

"Yes, Sheriff."

"We'll have that swearing-in ceremony in a few days. You did good out there. I'm proud of you."

How about me? I didn't get killed. I think he should be proud of me. But he heard a lot of stuff the crazy woman said and I don't think I'm his favorite person right now.

Ronnie thanks him and we go to her place. The Big Red Barn is a B&B that Ronnie has on long-term lease. It's fitting since it was the scene of last month's drama. Neither of us want to go for a drink. I'm afraid of mixing alcohol with poison. Ronnie shouldn't start drowning her stress with the stuff. We go straight to her place like the sheriff ordered.

Once there, I plop down on the big leather comfortable couch. I may never move again.

"Do you want the bedroom, Megan? It might be more comfortable."

"I'm fine here."

"Do you want to shower?" she asks.

"Go to bed," I say.

She turns to go and comes back to the couch. "Megan."

"Yeah," I say. I'm just about asleep. I'm safe-ish. I'm hungry but it'll wait.

"What's it like?" she asks.

"What's what like?"

She comes and sits at the end of the couch. There's still enough room for a marching band.

"What's it like? I killed her. I…"

"You saved me." I feel a knot forming in my throat. "You did a good thing, Ronnie. Don't ever think any differently. You didn't hesitate."

"Yeah," she says in a small voice. "I didn't hesitate."

I sit up and slide up next to her and put my arm around her shoulders. It's uncomfortable for me but I do it anyway. "It's hard. You'll think about it a lot. *A lot.* But you have to remind yourself why you did it. She was a killer. She was going to kill me and Dan. She almost did. She wouldn't have hesitated to kill you."

I can see Ronnie's face is pale. She faced death not long ago. That's something you always remember. She lived. Because of me. Now I was alive because of her. That's what friends are for. Or partners.

"You've been a good partner," I say, and I mean it this time. How can I not mean it?

We sit like that for a few minutes. Neither of us talking. Not needing to. Then Ronnie sits up straight. "What's next?"

I remember all too well.

"We are on paid leave. Me for almost getting killed. You for the shooting. We will both have to talk to the department shrink. She'll ask a lot of questions about how you feel. Be honest with her." *I'm going to lie again and pretend like it bothers me.* "Then she'll file a report that you can go back to work and then the big day." I force a smile.

"Big day?" she asks.

"You get sworn in. You'll be a real cop. Now, go to bed and let me get to sleep."

Ronnie says good night and goes to her bedroom. I need to pee, but I'm too exhausted to get up. I close my eyes and a series of events runs through my mind. Alex Rader. Dead. Marie Rader. Dead. Monique Delmont. Dead. Michael Rader. Dead. Unknown killer bitch with a knife. Dead. Ronnie's expression after the killer's head exploded. Lifeless. She wasn't shocked. She wasn't angry. She was in the moment. She didn't hesitate. She was more like me than I was comfortable with.

No one should be like me.

I think she'll be okay. She bounced back from being kidnapped and beaten. She'll get through this. I hear her crying softly in the other room and I feel relief. She's not so much like me after all. I feel bad for Ronnie, but I feel great that that psychotic bitch is dead.

I slide my blazer and boots off but leave the shoulder holster on. I use the blazer like a cover. I have to get some rest before I talk to the Clallam County Sheriff's Detective tomorrow. And write my reports. I don't want to think about any of this. I remember I've got to call Gabrielle and Clay to let them know it's over.

Ronnie is softly snoring. I try to quiet my mind and go to sleep, but I call the new cell number Gabrielle has given me to let her know it's safe to go home. She deserves that much.

A man's voice answers. "Who is this?"

The voice sounds familiar. I ask, "Detective Megan Carpenter. Who is this?"

"Hi, Megan."

It's Clay. But Gabrielle is in Maine with her son. I don't say hello. "What are you doing answering Gabrielle's new phone?"

"Gabby's sleeping."

Gabby? "You're in Maine?"

"No. She didn't feel safe there and called me. She's back here."

I hear Gabrielle's voice in the background. "Who is it, Clay?" He says to her, "It's Detective Carpenter. She wants to talk to you."

I don't know why I feel hurt. Clay acted like he was interested in me but I remind myself I don't do relationships. Never works out. The last person I got close to was almost killed because of me and will never have anything to do with me. Ever.

Gabrielle comes on the line.

"Megan. What is it?" She sounds sleepy. And concerned. "I talked to Sebastian a few hours ago. He was fine then."

I force myself to call her Gabby since she called me Megan. "Hi, Gabby. It's nothing about Sebastian. I thought you should know the danger is over. We've got the killer." *But maybe you should worry about Clay ditching you. Cops make for horrible relationships.*

"Clay already told me. I've been staying at his place for a while. Sheriff Gray called him to give us the news."

"I'm so, so happy for you."

She asks, "Excuse me?"

I didn't realize I said that out loud. "I mean I'm glad you aren't in danger and can get on with your life. I'm sure Detective Osborne's taken good care of you."

She thanks me and disconnects.

CHAPTER SIXTY-ONE

I ride to the office with Ronnie. She's in a quiet mood. That means she only talks when she has something to say or to ask a question and not her incessant stream-of-consciousness blabbering.

"Did you sleep last night?" she asks me.

"Just fine," I say. Every time I was about to nod off last night my mind would conjure up an image of Dan being skinned alive and screaming. I'm surprised that I feel as good as I do—physically—with the little sleep I got.

"Marley called this morning while you were in the shower," she says.

Of course he did.

"He's coming in early to do the DNA from… you know."

I know but I want her to say it. Confronting your fear, your monster, is the best way to get past it.

"What DNA?" I ask.

"From last night. The two bodies. The one is probably Michael Rader. I wonder if they did any good identifying the woman."

She stops at a McDonald's drive-through and we order six coffees, six apple pies. I pay.

We get to the office and my eyes cut toward the place where I found the cigarette butt. I don't know why I do that. I doubt that she even smoked. The cigarette butt could have been left there by anyone. The fact that she was stalking me made me think of my other stalker: Wallace. Maybe I'm being pessimistic. Maybe she was

Wallace. Or Michael Rader was. They're both dead and that's an end to that. I only know it's not Hayden. He doesn't hate me that much.

Ronnie and I carry our cache of McDonald's treasure into the office.

"Coffee and pie for everyone," Ronnie says. I grab a coffee before it's all gone. Ronnie apparently has returned to drinking water.

Minus one point.

Sheriff Gray pours three creamers and three packs of sugar into his paper coffee cup and stirs with one of those toothpick-thin stirrers. He seems to be in a good mood. That's good for me and for Ronnie.

"I have the crime scene reports," he says. "Photos, fingerprints, the woman's knife, a list of things found inside the motor home."

And? I want to ask. But I wait for him. It's his story.

"I got Michael Rader's personnel file from Monroe Correctional Complex. The fingerprints match the body we found. We can't find any next of kin. His brother, Alex Rader, is still in the wind. Kitsap County is looking for him as a murder suspect. The Monroe superintendent wasn't broken up over Michael's death.

"Crime scene found some rope behind the motor home and matched it to the rope you said the woman used to bind herself to the tree. As far as the woman goes, we couldn't find anything on her. No fingerprints or DNA on file. It will be difficult to identify her because of"—he pauses and looks at Ronnie—"because of the damage to her face. We got one clean profile shot and the lab thinks they can create the other side using that to give us a photo we can circulate."

"Anything connecting her to the murders?" I ask.

"Yang is working on it. He told me this morning that two blood types were found on Rader's body. He'll run DNA on both."

She apparently cut herself while hacking Rader's head off. Poor her.

"Clallam County Sheriff's Deputies found a stolen rental car," Sheriff Gray says. "Rader's truck was found parked behind the Wendy's in Port Angeles. We were able to lift latent prints from both her body and Rader's. Her fingerprints were in both vehicles. The rental company said it was stolen off of their lot and wasn't rented to anyone. There was nothing in the car to help us identify her. Rader had a moped registered to him as well. It was found hidden in the woods near the crime scene covered with brush. Her fingerprints were on it."

It looks like the only way I'm going to get her identified is by putting her picture out to every law enforcement agency in the US plus the news media. The crime lab techs might put a good photo together with a face and profile shot, but I've seen her. Something is off in the photo.

Maybe if the picture had a knife raised overhead it would be more like her.

"I'll take care of sending the photos off, Sheriff," I say. Ronnie will be busy with paperwork.

Detective Mike Felson shows up early and takes us, one at a time, into the interrogation room to get our statements. He takes Sheriff Gray's first and they're in there with the door closed for half an hour. I can't help but wonder what they had to talk about all that time. All Sheriff Gray knows about the shooting is that he saw Ronnie shoot the crazy bitch.

The door opens, Tony comes out and Felson motions me inside. I go in and sit in a chair across from him. I try not to show how nervous I am. I know I shouldn't be nervous. The questions will be about the two killings. If he were here to arrest me, he would be reading me my Miranda warning.

Felson's first question is: "How are you feeling this morning? Are you up for this?"

I relax. I answer his questions and don't add anything. The trick is to answer the questions fully enough but not too elaborately.

I'm good at that. He taped my statement and we were done in fifteen minutes.

"Detective Carpenter, I know this is stressful for you. I've been in the same spot as you before and I can tell you, it's not easy. The only criticism I have, and you can tell me to go to hell if you want, is that you should never have gone there alone. Sheriff Gray swears by you and that's good enough for me. And that's why I don't want to see you get yourself killed. I'm honored to meet you."

He says this and stands to shake my hand. I don't want to tell him to go to hell. He didn't say anything that I don't already know.

"I'm ready for Detective Marsh, if you want to send her my way," Felson says.

I meet Ronnie at the door. She looks composed and confident. She should be. It was a righteous shooting. I hope she sticks to simple answers and doesn't get into what the killer was saying to me before she fired the shot.

Ronnie goes in and shuts the door.

CHAPTER SIXTY-TWO

I know there will be a press conference this morning. I'm hoping Sheriff Gray will take care of that. I don't talk to reporters. Sheriff Gray suggested holding off on showing any photos to the press until I send them to other law enforcement agencies. That's what I was going to do, but it makes him feel in charge to make the decisions.

I settle for giving the profile shot of the unknown killer to law enforcement for the time being, since one side of her face had been blown off.

Good shooting, Ronnie.

I also have her prints and DNA sent to the FBI and Interpol. She was a stone cold killer and I find it hard to believe she hasn't done this before. I also gave them Marley's information about the drug she was using. How the Raders hooked up with her I'll probably never know, but she was definitely in love with Alex.

It's no use wondering what she might have told me if she hadn't lost her mind—literally. To do that, I might have had to take her into custody. That wasn't going to happen. She was dead the moment she stuck the needle in my leg.

We finish off our coffees and the McDonald's apple pies. Ronnie takes frequent breaks to make coffee or refill some mugs. She doesn't complain about doing it, and her coffee is extra-strong, the way most of us like it.

She still opts for bottled water.

Finally, we're done with what paperwork we can do. I'm so spent from yesterday's drugging and this morning's activities that I want to sleep on my desk. Sheriff Gray comes in carrying a double-layer chocolate cake with one birthday candle on top. Nan finds paper plates, napkins, plastic plates and a cooler of bottled water. All I want is black coffee. Lots of it. Just to get me through another half hour.

Nan lights the candle and Tony gathers everyone around for his announcement. He is holding a document and reads it out loud. It's the oath that Ronnie will take to uphold the Constitution and the laws of the state of Washington. I have it memorized. I take these things seriously.

She raises her hand, repeats the oath and signs the paper, then Tony digs in his shirt pocket. He takes out a six-pointed silver deputy sheriff's star with a picture of George Washington on the seal. Instead of pinning it to her shirt, he hands it to me.

"Megan, I thought you'd like to do the honors."

I agree. She saved my life. I take the badge and pin it to Ronnie's shirt over her heart. Before I realize what I'm doing, I hug her and say in her ear, "Congratulations, Red."

Ronnie squeezes me until I can't breathe and I can feel her vibrating with excitement. She *should* be excited. She's made deputy a heck of a lot faster than most reserve deputies. Plus I think she's on the fast track for detective. Worse things could happen.

Sheriff Gray invites everyone for a drink after work but I beg off. I'm going to check on Dan at the hospital. He is being kept at the hospital for observation because of breathing difficulty. I call the hospital and hear that he's going to be hospitalized for another night. He's a lightweight. I ask Sheriff Gray if I can take off. He reminds me I have an appointment with the shrink tomorrow. He's made the appointments for me and for Ronnie. It's okay. I want to get back to work as soon as possible.

*

I go to the hospital and enter through the ER. The security guard gives me directions to the floor. I get to the door of Dan's room and hear laughing and a female voice. I peek around the door, thinking I'll see a nurse, but it's Jess Moonbeam. His perky little high schooler from work. She's bent over the bed, hugging him. Her face is against his. I'm not jealous but I feel my face go red. I turn to leave but I don't. I have to at least apologize for getting him into this. Also, I want to know what he's going to do about what he heard last night. What he might say and who he might say it to. Ronnie and Sheriff Gray may not grill me with questions now, but my future is still on the line. I may have to leave town. The country. I don't want to go. But I know how to disappear at the drop of a hat.

I step into the room and Jess straightens up guiltily. A light of recognition comes on behind her dark eyes and she points at me.

"She's the one that pointed a gun at me."

I want to point a gun at her now.

"Dan, I apologized to her. I was looking for you."

I'm not going to apologize again. She's lucky I don't tell him how unhelpful she was and how she doesn't answer the phones. I think he should fire her and get some grumpy old hag to watch the place.

He looks much better now that he's gotten some of the poison out of his system. His color is back and he's sitting up. His eyes look focused.

"Thanks for coming by," he says to Jess. "Would you mind checking on the store before you go home? If there are any important messages, let me know."

Jess looks from him to me and back at him. She smiles sweetly at him.

"Okay, Dan," she says. "I've got your number." She gives me a death star look as she carefully goes around me and out of the door.

"How are you doing?" I ask. It's a stupid question. He's in the hospital, for God's sake. He's been poisoned by some crazy woman who was getting ready to skin him because he's my friend.

He doesn't answer. Instead, he reaches a hand out for me. I cross the room and he takes my hand in his. I start to say something else stupid, like "I'm sorry" or "is there anything I can get you?" The usual hospital visit crap.

He squeezes my hand tightly. "Megan, I appreciate what you did out there. She was going to kill me. You offered yourself as a trade. I don't know what to say. Really. You saved me."

Now I know he heard all the other stuff that spilled out of the bitch's mouth.

"Dan, she was after *me*. I shouldn't have involved you."

"What do you mean, Megan? You didn't involve me. She was crazy. She's probably been watching you for a long time. Otherwise, she wouldn't have left the pictures in my mailbox. I think she wanted to see how close we were. I gave her exactly what she wanted."

"It's my fault. I feel horrible, Dan."

He doesn't let go of my hand. "No. It's her fault. I care about you a great deal and it must show."

"She burnt your things up."

"I can make new ones. I hear I owe you for saving my house as well."

"It isn't livable, Dan. You lost everything."

"I haven't lost *you*. Have I?"

CHAPTER SIXTY-THREE

I leave the hospital after Dan is ordered to go to sleep. I want to stay but I don't want to start crying. He doesn't hate me. In fact, I think he's falling in love with me. That's a good thing. I think.

I'm suddenly not tired and go to meet the crew for a drink, but everyone has already left. I go home. I left a light on in the office but it's totally dark inside. I draw my .45 and go down the side of the house to the back. I look to see if there are any lights on or if a window is broken. It looks okay. I go back to the front and try the doorknob. It's unlocked and turns easily in my hand.

The smart thing to do is call the police. I don't do the smart thing all the time. I turn the handle and push the door open. There's a dim light coming from the kitchen. I put my purse down by the door and step inside. I leave the door open in case I have to run. I move quietly down the hall and peek into my office. Nothing has been moved. The bear is still on my desk where I left it. That seems like days ago.

I move back down the hallway to the kitchen. I can hear something. It sounds like chewing. It confuses me. Wild animals don't open doors and then shut them. They don't pick locks. I know I locked the door.

I move closer and hear the sound of someone smacking their lips. I look around the corner. The refrigerator door is open and it blocks my view of the table. I can see under the door that a pair of size eleven shoes are planted on the floor. I see who it is and re-holster my .45.

"Hayden," I say. I push the refrigerator door shut.

He says, "I let myself in," and goes back to munching on his sad sack sandwich. I see an empty packet of tuna, a jar of peanut butter, and a jar of jam on the table. Only Hayden would eat a PB&J and tuna on stale bread. I want to vomit.

"I can see that," I say. "I thought I had a burglar."

"No. Just me," he says, as if his sudden appearance after ducking out on me is normal. "Where were you last night?"

I don't answer. I'm still protecting him from the bad things. "Can I get you something to drink with that?"

"You're out of Scotch. I looked in your cabinets but the bottle was empty. Well, it is now."

I pull out an empty chair and sit. "Do you want to talk?"

He gets up and goes to the doorway. "No. I just wanted something to eat. I was here last night and you weren't home. I've gotta go."

He says this in an accusatory tone, like he expects me to never be around. I want to explain.

"Hayden," I say, but he's gone. I hear the front door shut.

I sit for a minute or two. I don't know what's going on here. I don't know if he's trying to punish me. I know he picked the lock. I didn't know he could do that. I never taught him. Maybe Mom did. Or maybe it's something he learned in the service. It doesn't matter. I'll have to put a better lock on the door. I want him to come back, but not like that.

I get up and pull a kitchen chair to the front door. I lock the door and wedge the chair back under the doorknob. I go to my office and open the desk drawer. Hayden's right. The bottle is empty. He left the cap on top of my desk. I flick it into the trash can.

There's part of a box of wine in the refrigerator. I get it and an empty jelly jar that I use for a cup and bring it back into the office. I twist the knob on the wine box and fill the jar with Zinfandel.

"Zinfandel" rhymes with "Infidel," sort of. And that's how Hayden, fresh back from Afghanistan, makes me feel.

One minute I'm walking on air, realizing that Dan cares about me. The next I'm treated like I have an infectious disease by my brother.

I open the drawer where I keep the tape player and box of tapes. It doesn't look disturbed, but I'll have to buy a safe that I can bolt to the floor. Too many people know too much about me as it is.

I take the tape player out, slide a cassette into the slot, and hit "play." While the tape reel catches up, I lean back and sip the wine.

Dr. A: You felt betrayed by Monique?

Me: Yes. Monique was the only real connection I had to a normal world. I'd lied to Hayden when I promised I'd be back for him and left him with my aunt Ginger. I was still on the run. The police in Port Orchard were still looking for me to ask about my stepfather's murder. When I called Monique for help, it was because she was the only person I could turn to. When she told me she couldn't help me anymore, I took it to mean she didn't want to. And when I found out she gave away all the evidence we needed to prove Alex Rader was a serial killer, I think I hated her. She told me Michael Rader had threatened her and her children, but I was in a pinch myself. I wasn't thinking about her safety.

Dr. A: But now you are?

Me: Yeah. I know she was scared. I don't know what I would have done if someone threatened to hurt or kill Hayden. I guess I would have done the same thing. But at the time I couldn't believe she was letting me down. To me it felt like a betrayal. My whole life was like that. Everyone I looked up to betrayed me in some way or other.

Dr. A: How are you dealing with it?

Me: I'm not. I'm just eating it like every other bad thing. Monique is a good woman. I can't hate her. I can't be mad at her. I can only be mad at myself for putting faith in her. In anyone.

I turn the tape off. I remember that session with Dr. Albright. I was still a little miffed at Monique back then for giving Michael Rader the evidence. I knew Dr. Albright expected me to be a grown-up about it, but I resented Monique offering to help me and then abandoning me. What I resented even more was that I could never talk to her again. Maybe I was fooling myself, but I thought we had become friends. I didn't have any friends back then. Losing one was a slap in the face. Now I've lost her for good. Monique was a casualty of war. Collateral damage in the war that I have started with killers, evil people, monsters.

On the positive side, Ronnie is showing some promise. She took the psycho woman out without hesitation. I just hope she won't start enjoying it.

And I think "Wallace," my stalker, has been put to rest. I put my gun in the safe in my closet. I don't feel the need to keep it next to me anymore. I put the tape player in the desk drawer and flop down on my bed. I'm drifting off to sleep when I hear my computer ding, indicating I have email. I ignore it. Tomorrow is another day. It'll wait.

I'll go see Rowena Perkins in the morning. I promised to tell her what happened. Maybe I'll have some of her "special tea" and work on the fireman puzzle with her. And then I'll spend the day with Dan. He's given me a second chance and I have a feeling he's better than a fireman puzzle.

A LETTER FROM GREGG

Dear reader,

I want to say a ginormous thank you for choosing to read *Silent Ridge*, the third book in the Detective Megan Carpenter series. If you did enjoy it and want to keep up to date with all my latest releases, take a moment to sign up at the following link. Here's a promise: Your email address will never be shared and you can unsubscribe at any time.

www.bookouture.com/gregg-olsen

Detective Megan Carpenter is a rule breaker and a woman with a past. That combination propels her forward, while keeping a wary eye over her shoulder. She's smart. She's broken. She's awesome. I'm thrilled to let you know that Megan will back for three more books. And with each one, the layers of this complex woman will be revealed. So hang on. Keep reading.

Keep rooting for Det. Carpenter.

I am.

I hope you loved *Silent Ridge*, and if you did I would be very grateful if you could write a review. I'd love to hear what you think, and it makes such a difference helping new readers to discover one of my books for the first time.

I love hearing from my readers—you can get in touch on my Facebook page, through Twitter, Goodreads or my website.

Thanks,
Gregg

 GreggOlsenAuthor

 @Gregg_Olsen

 @GreggOlsen

Printed in Great Britain
by Amazon